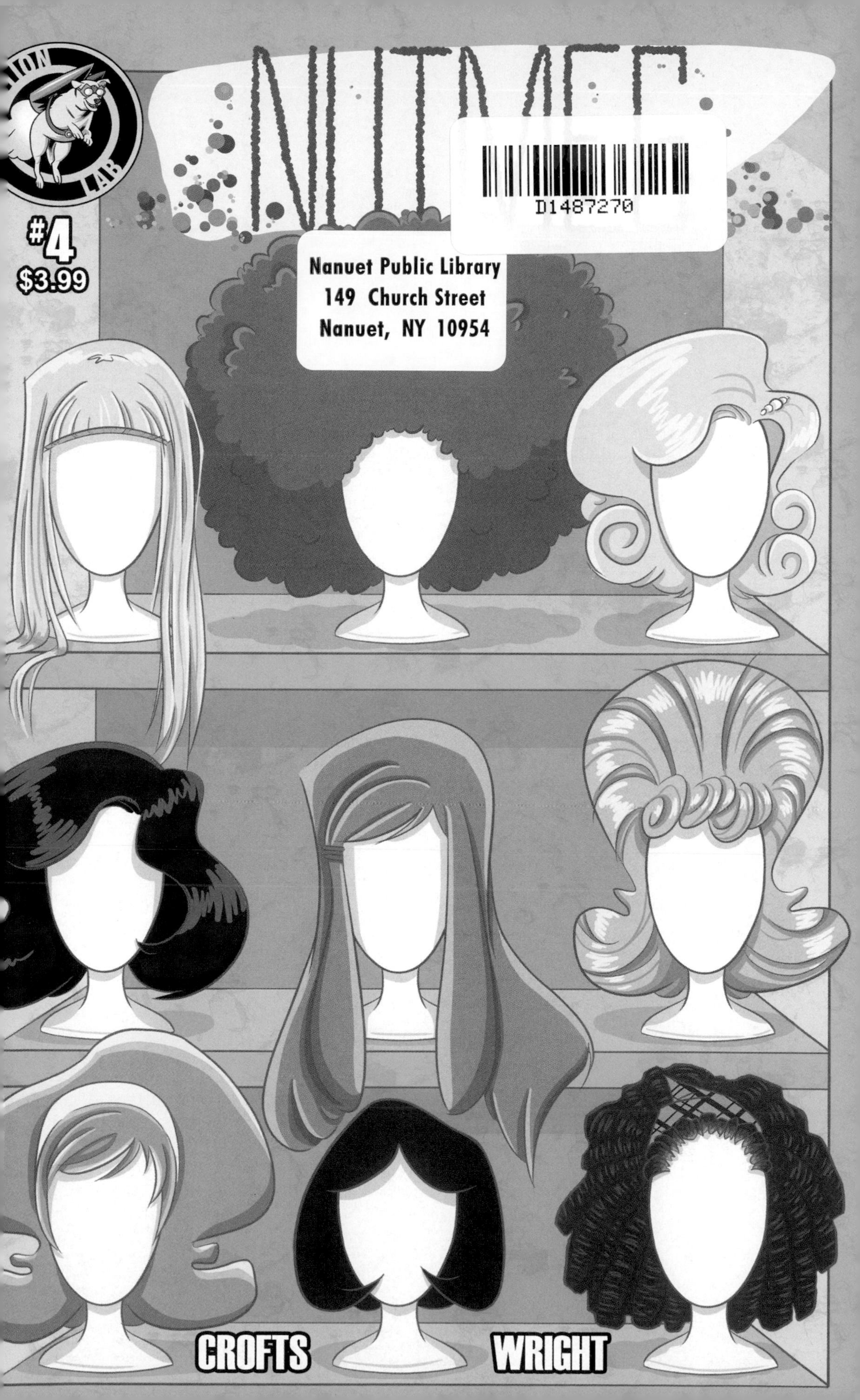
NUTMEG
#4
$3.99
CROFTS
WRIGHT

FROM ALEX KAIN & RACHEL BENN

BEYOND THE
WESTERN
DEEP

AVAILABLE IN FINER STORES EVERYWHE

For over 100 years, the animal races of the Four Kingdoms have lived side-by-side in uneasy truce. But when conflict ignites in the north, old alliances threaten to send the world into chaos. Experience the beginnings of an epic all-ages fantasy in this first collected volume!

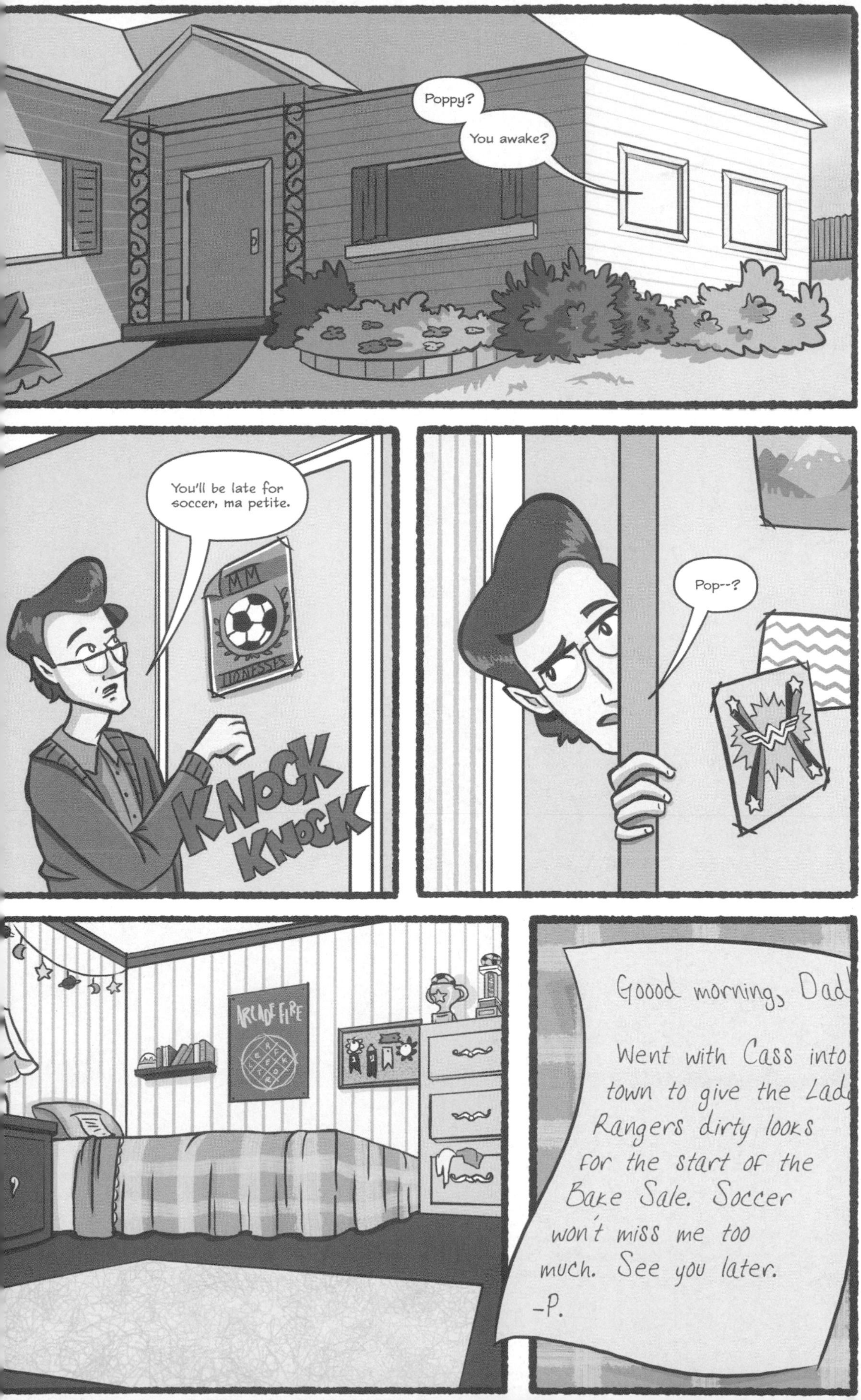
Poppy?
You awake?
You'll be late for soccer, ma petite.
KNOCK KNOCK
Pop--?
ARCADE FIRE
Goood morning, Dad
Went with Cass into town to give the Lad
Rangers dirty looks for the start of the Bake Sale. Soccer won't miss me too much. See you later.
-P.

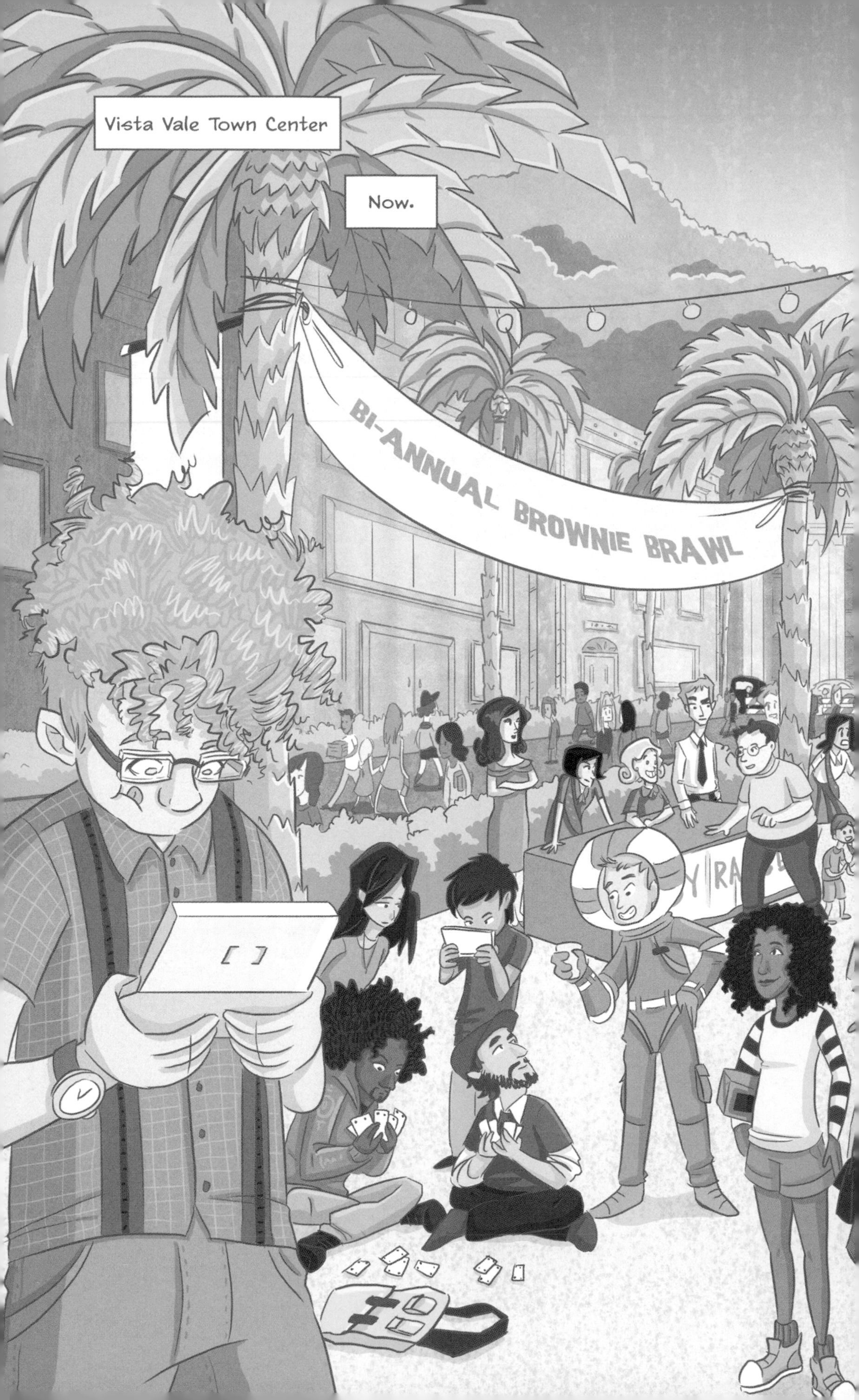
Vista Vale Town Center
Now.
BI-ANNUAL BROWNIE BRAWL

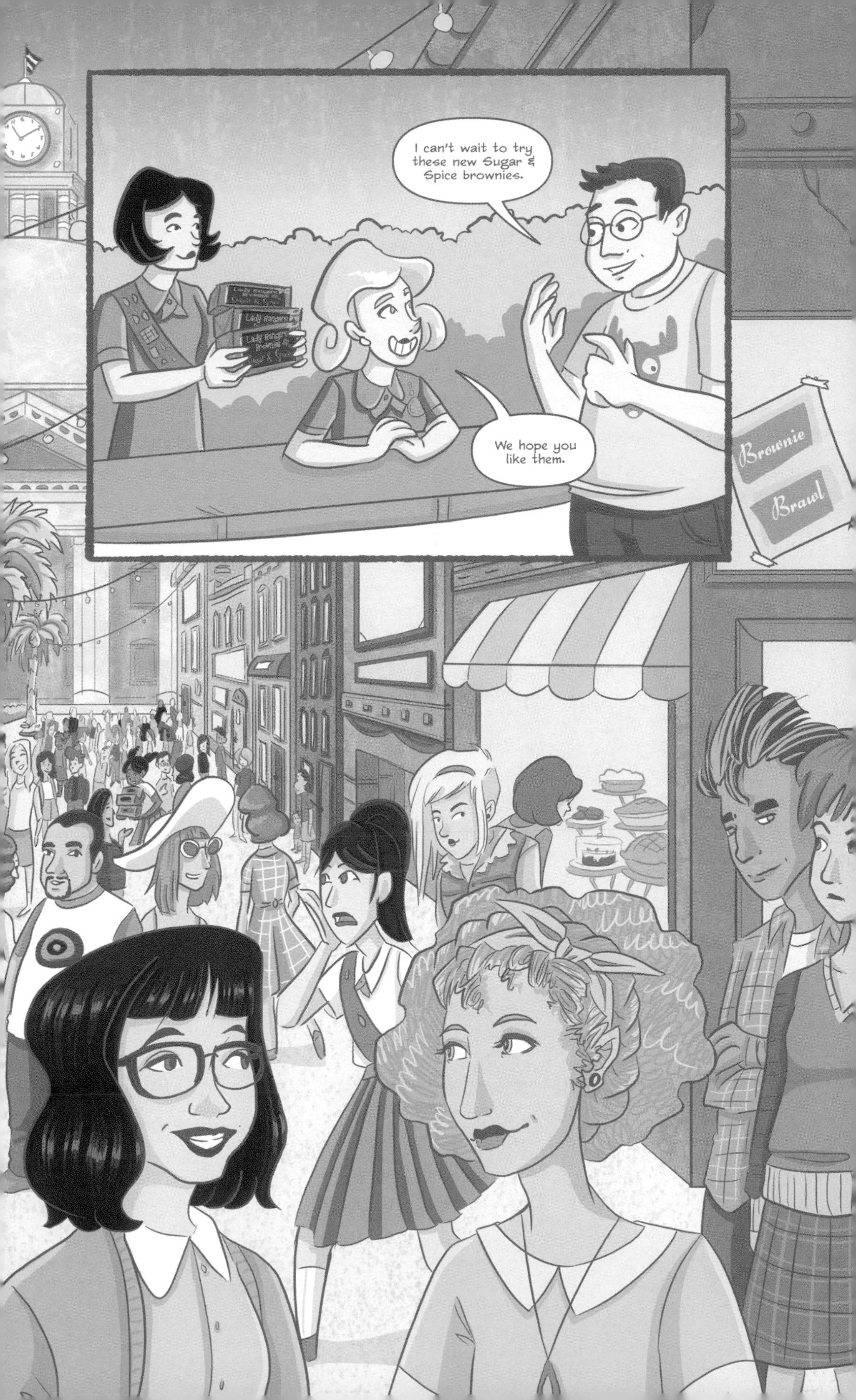
I can't wait to try these new Sugar & Spice brownies.
We hope you like them.
Brownie Brawl

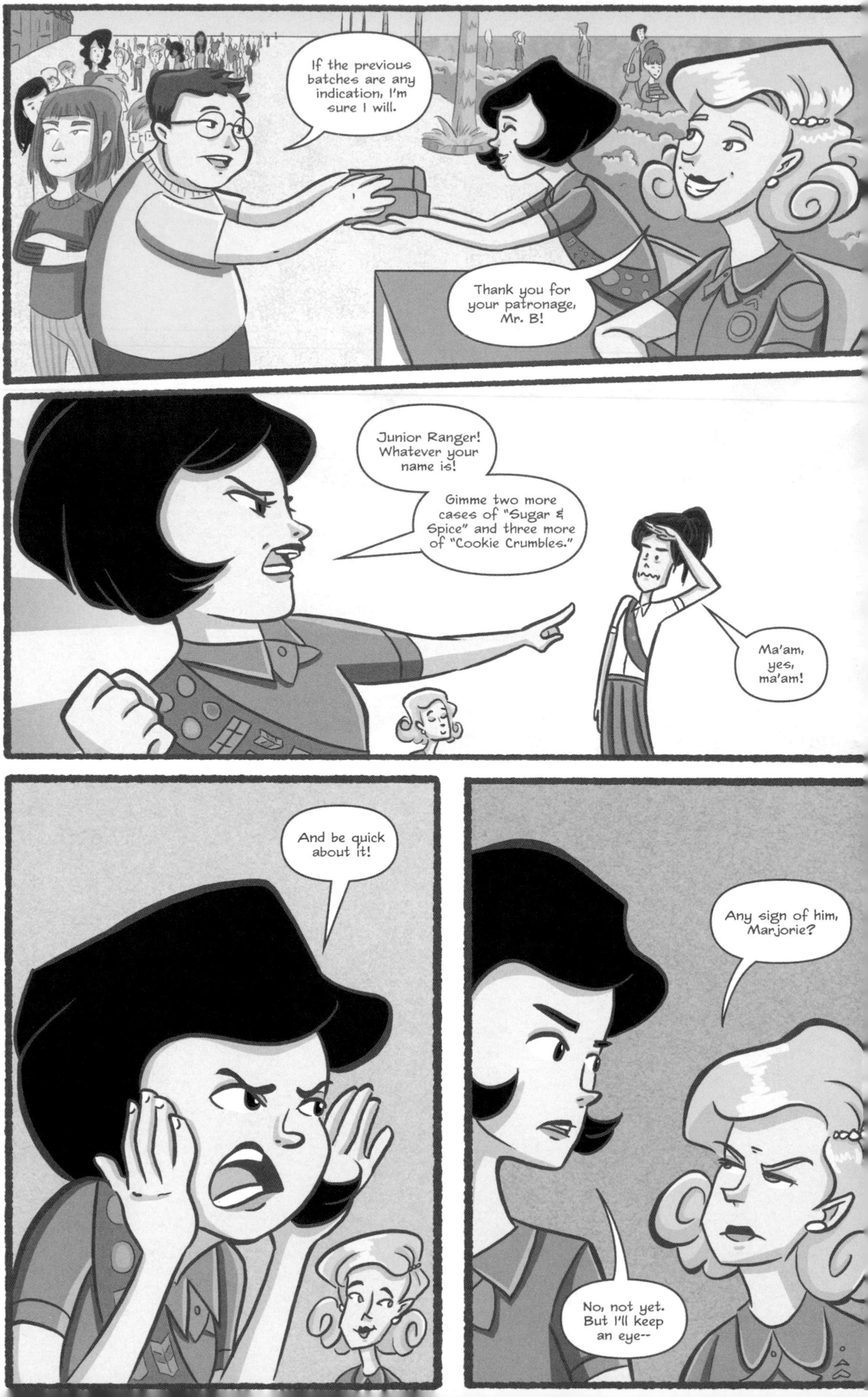
If the previous batches are any indication, I'm sure I will.
Thank you for your patronage, Mr. B!
Junior Ranger! Whatever your name is!
Gimme two more cases of "Sugar & Spice" and three more of "Cookie Crumbles."
Ma'am, yes, ma'am!
And be quick about it!
Any sign of him, Marjorie?
No, not yet. But I'll keep an eye--

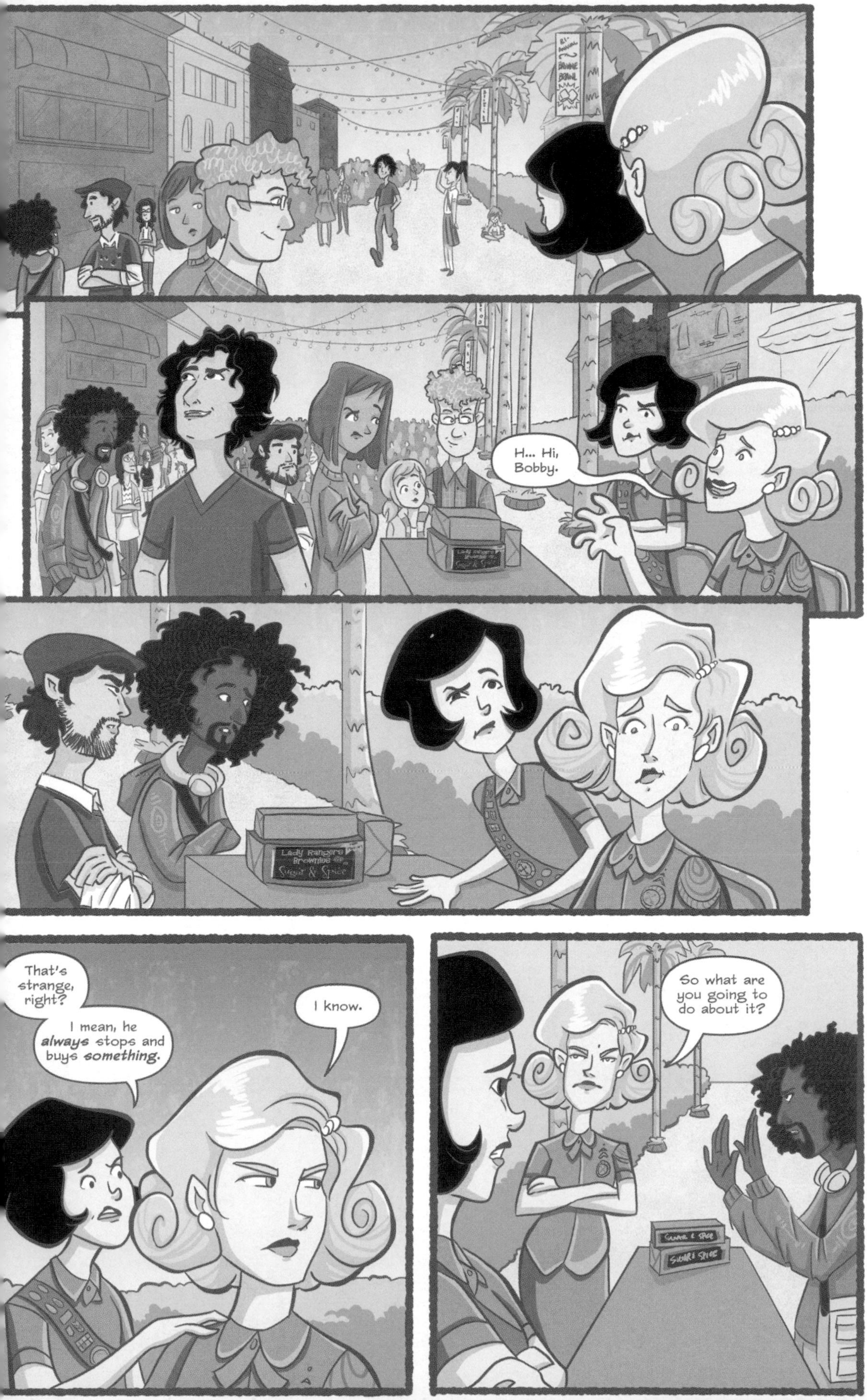
H... Hi, Bobby.
That's strange, right?
I mean, he *always* stops and buys *something.*
I know.
So what are you going to do about it?

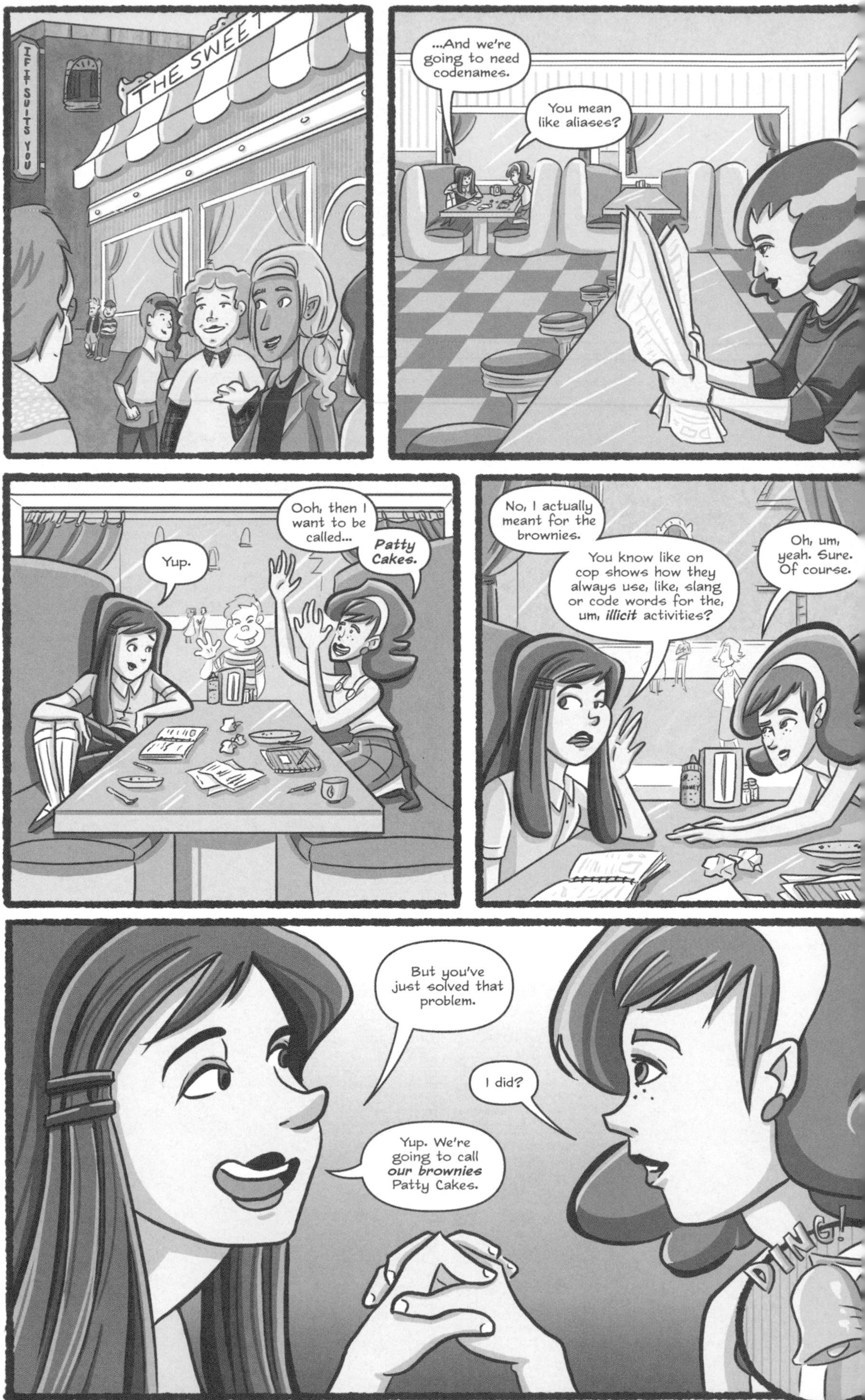
THE SWEET
IF IT SUITS YOU
...And we're going to need codenames.
You mean like aliases?
Yup.
Ooh, then I want to be called... **Patty Cakes.**
No, I actually meant for the brownies.
You know like on cop shows how they always use, like, slang or code words for the, um, ***illicit*** activities?
Oh, um, yeah. Sure. Of course.
But you've just solved that problem.
I did?
Yup. We're going to call ***our brownies*** Patty Cakes.
DING!

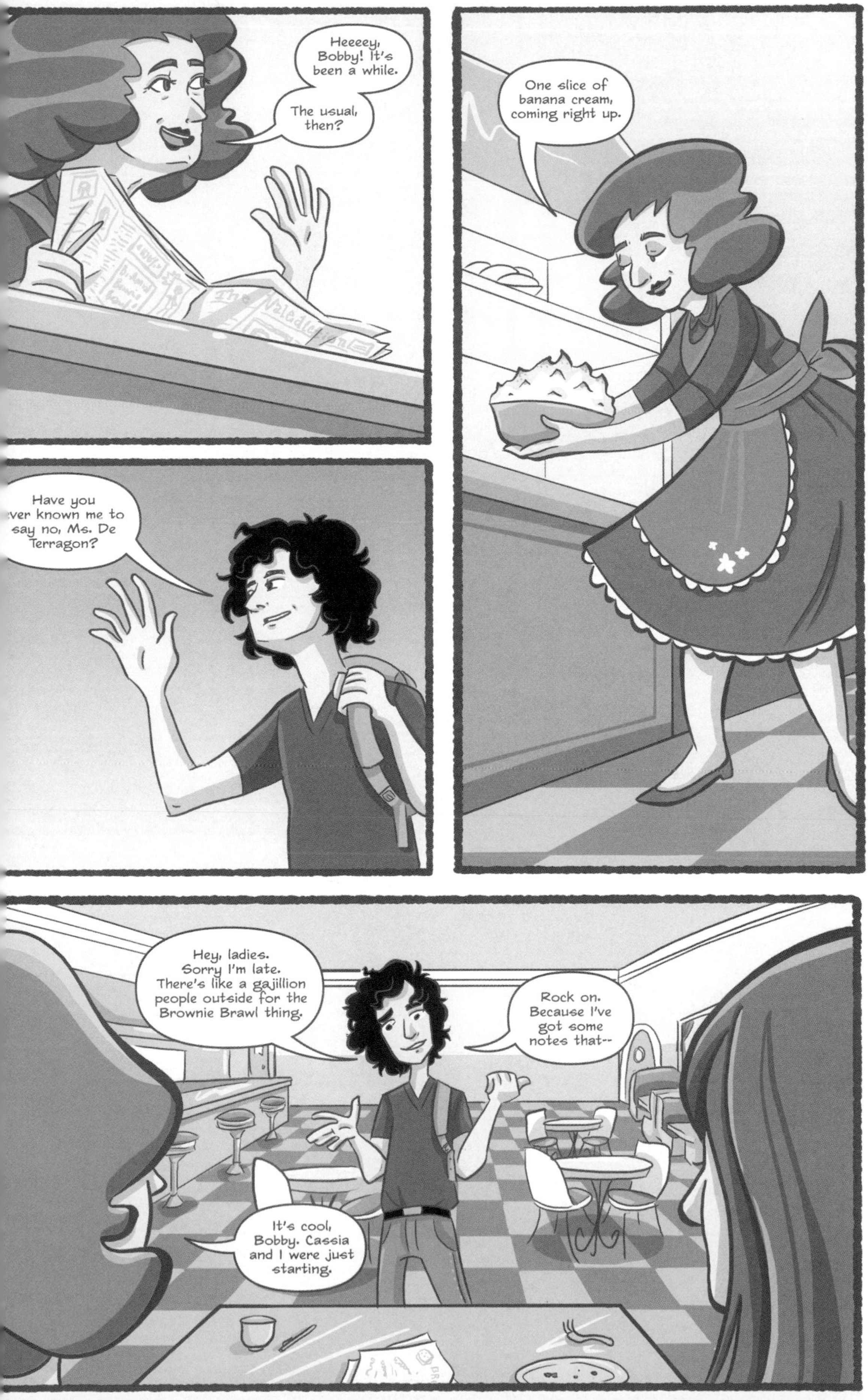

Heeeey, Bobby! It's been a while.
The usual, then?
One slice of banana cream, coming right up.
Have you ver known me to say no, Ms. De Terragon?
Hey, ladies. Sorry I'm late. There's like a gajillion people outside for the Brownie Brawl thing.
Rock on. Because I've got some notes that--
It's cool, Bobby. Cassia and I were just starting.

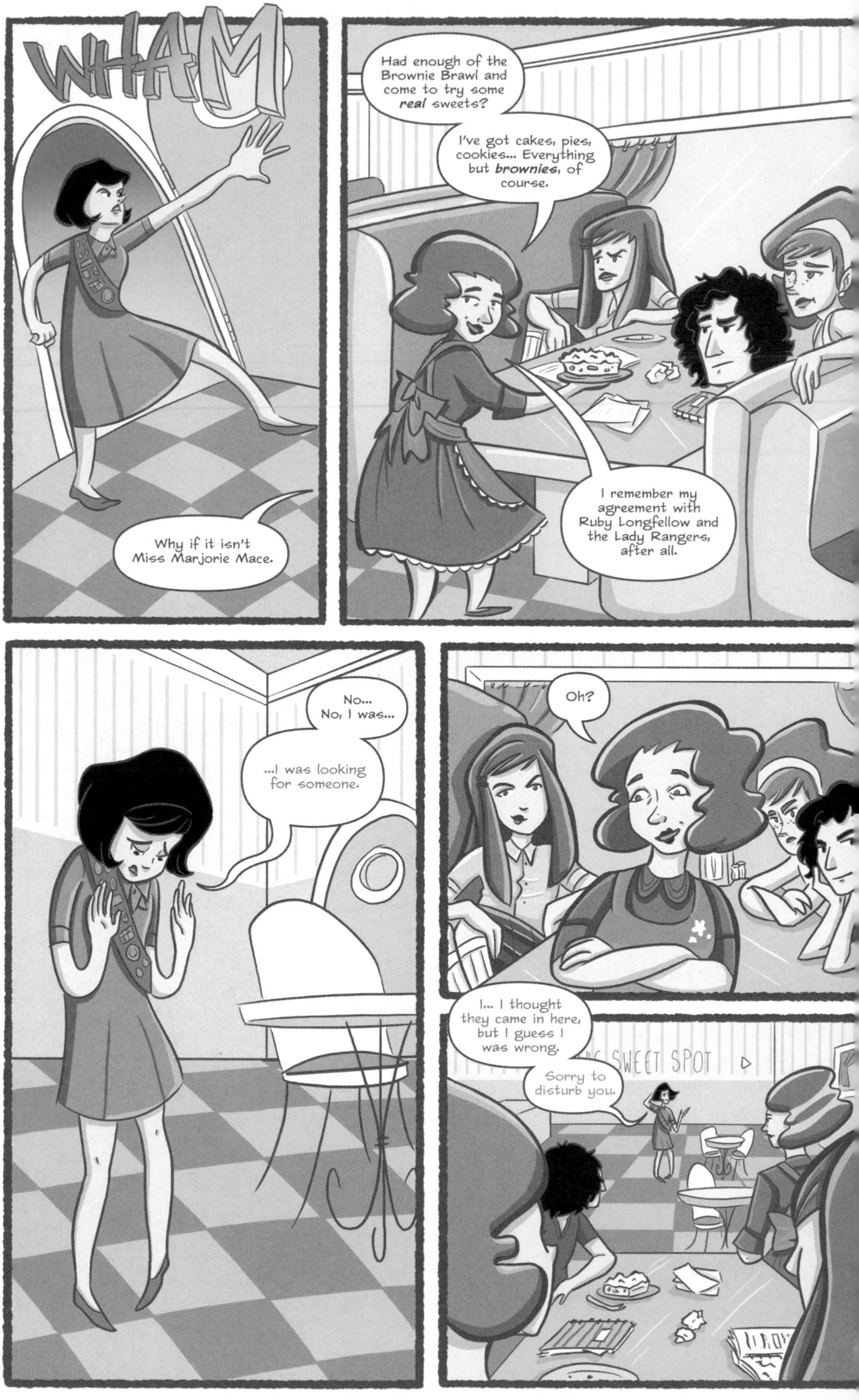
WHAM
Why if it isn't Miss Marjorie Mace.
Had enough of the Brownie Brawl and come to try some *real* sweets?
I've got cakes, pies, cookies... Everything but *brownies*, of course.
I remember my agreement with Ruby Longfellow and the Lady Rangers, after all.
No... No, I was...
...I was looking for someone.
Oh?
I... I thought they came in here, but I guess I was wrong.
Sorry to disturb you.
SWEET SPOT

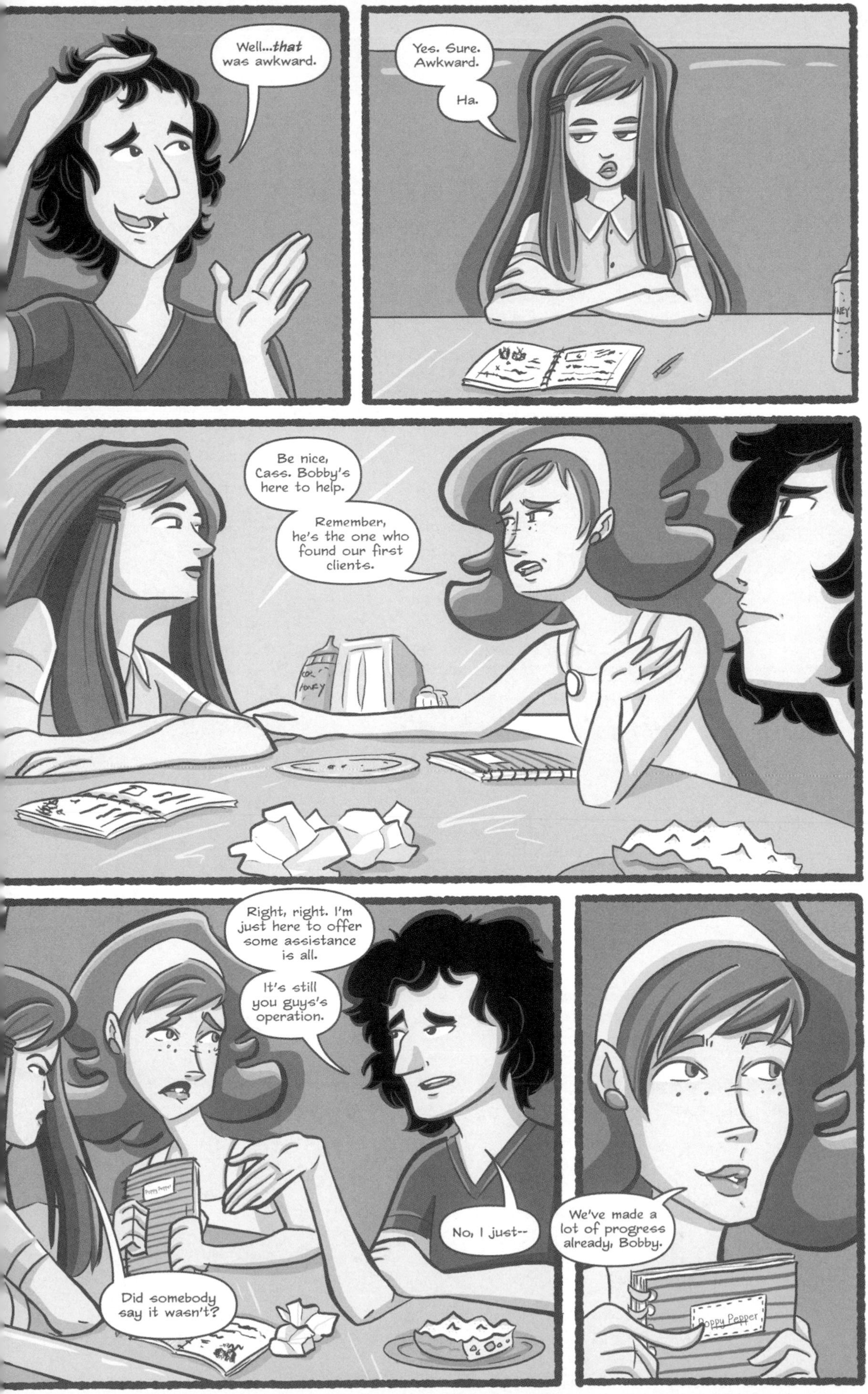
Well...*that* was awkward.
Yes. Sure. Awkward.
Ha.
Be nice, Cass. Bobby's here to help.
Remember, he's the one who found our first clients.
Right, right. I'm just here to offer some assistance is all.
It's still you guys's operation.
Did somebody say it wasn't?
No, I just--
We've made a lot of progress already, Bobby.
Poppy Pepper

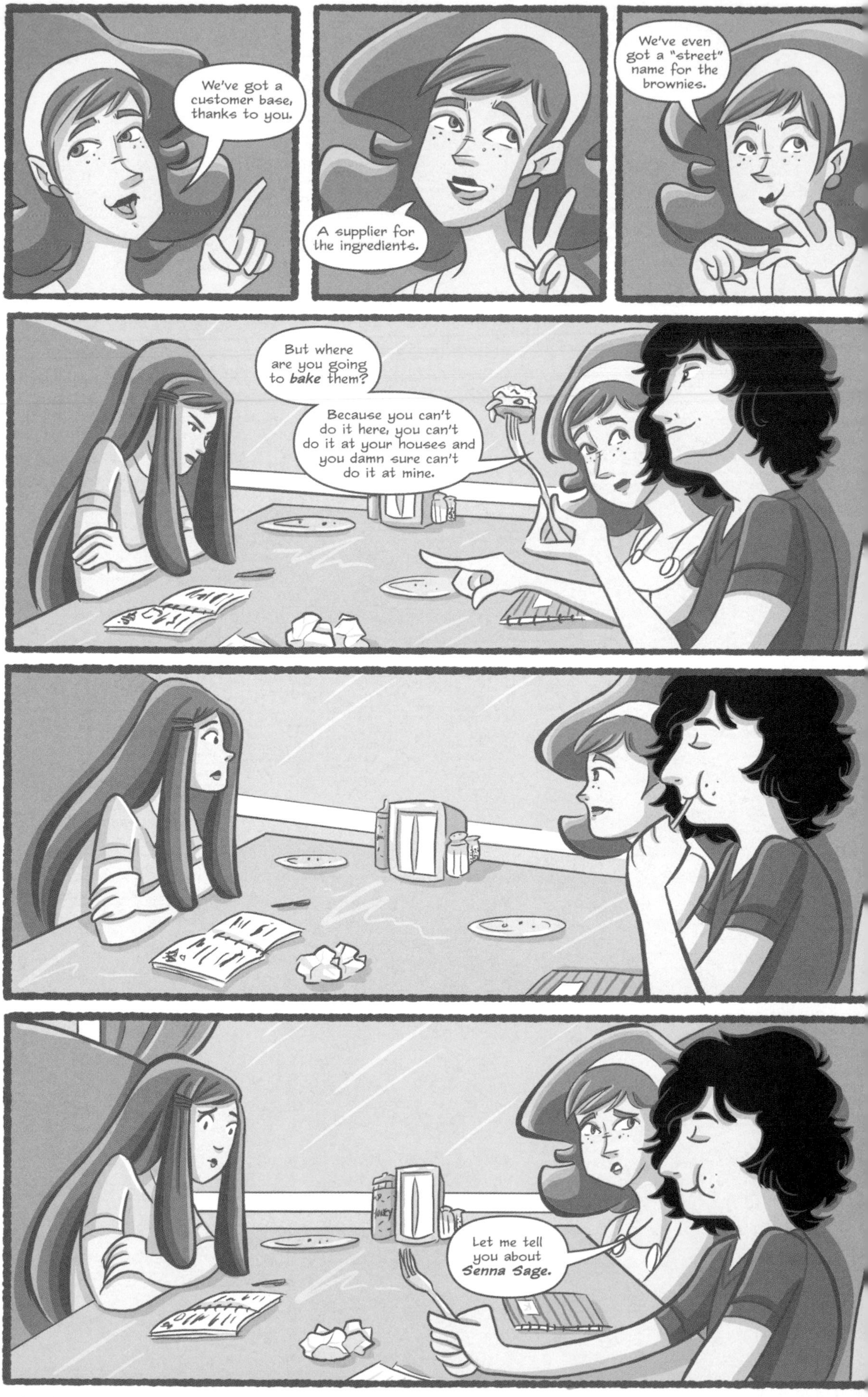
We've got a customer base, thanks to you.
A supplier for the ingredients.
We've even got a "street" name for the brownies.
But where are you going to *bake* them?
Because you can't do it here, you can't do it at your houses and you damn sure can't do it at mine.
Let me tell you about **Senna Sage.**

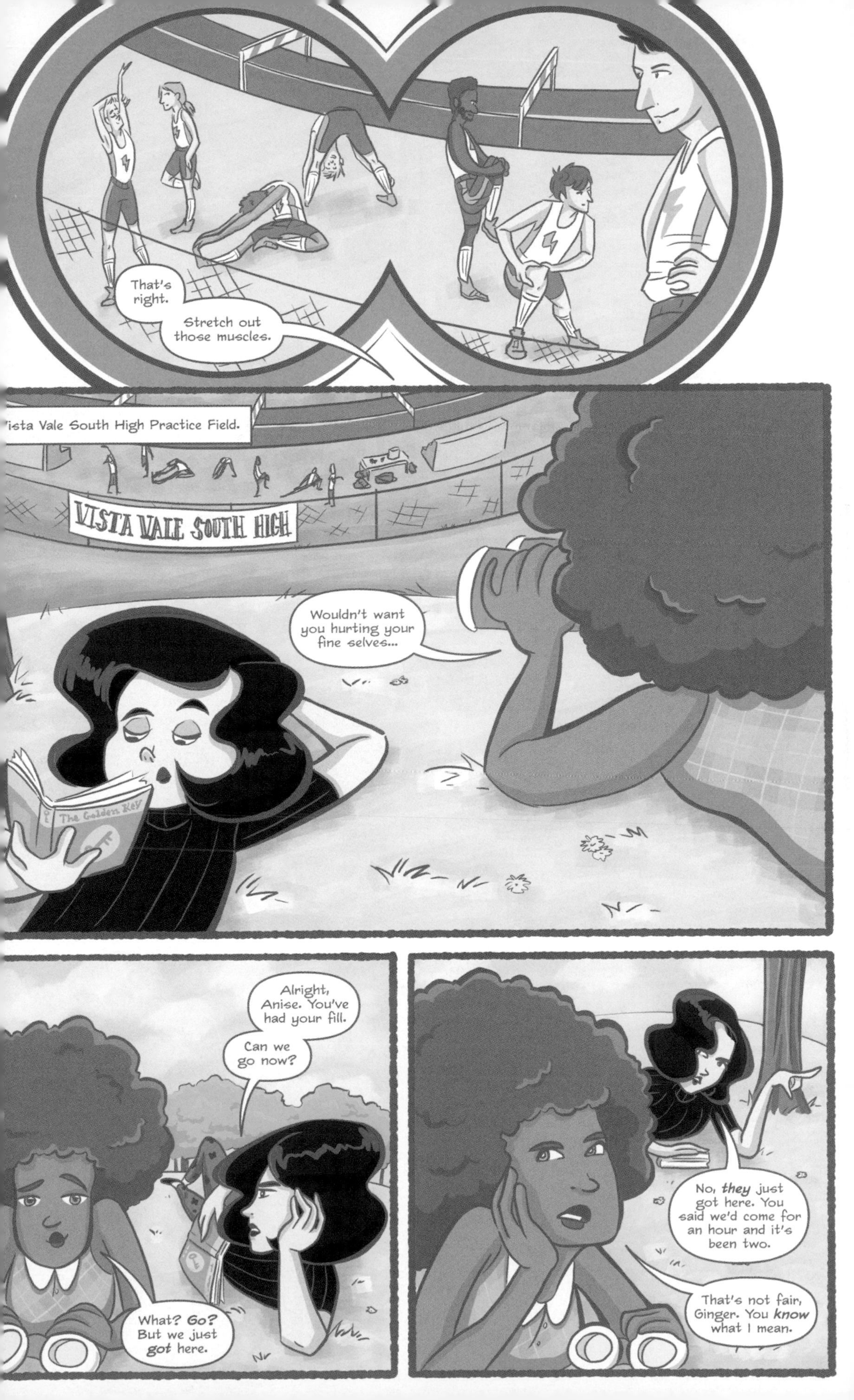
That's right.
Stretch out those muscles.
Vista Vale South High Practice Field.
VISTA VALE SOUTH HIGH
Wouldn't want you hurting your fine selves...
The Golden Key
Alright, Anise. You've had your fill.
Can we go now?
What? *Go?* But we just *got* here.
No, *they* just got here. You said we'd come for an hour and it's been two.
That's not fair, Ginger. You *know* what I mean.

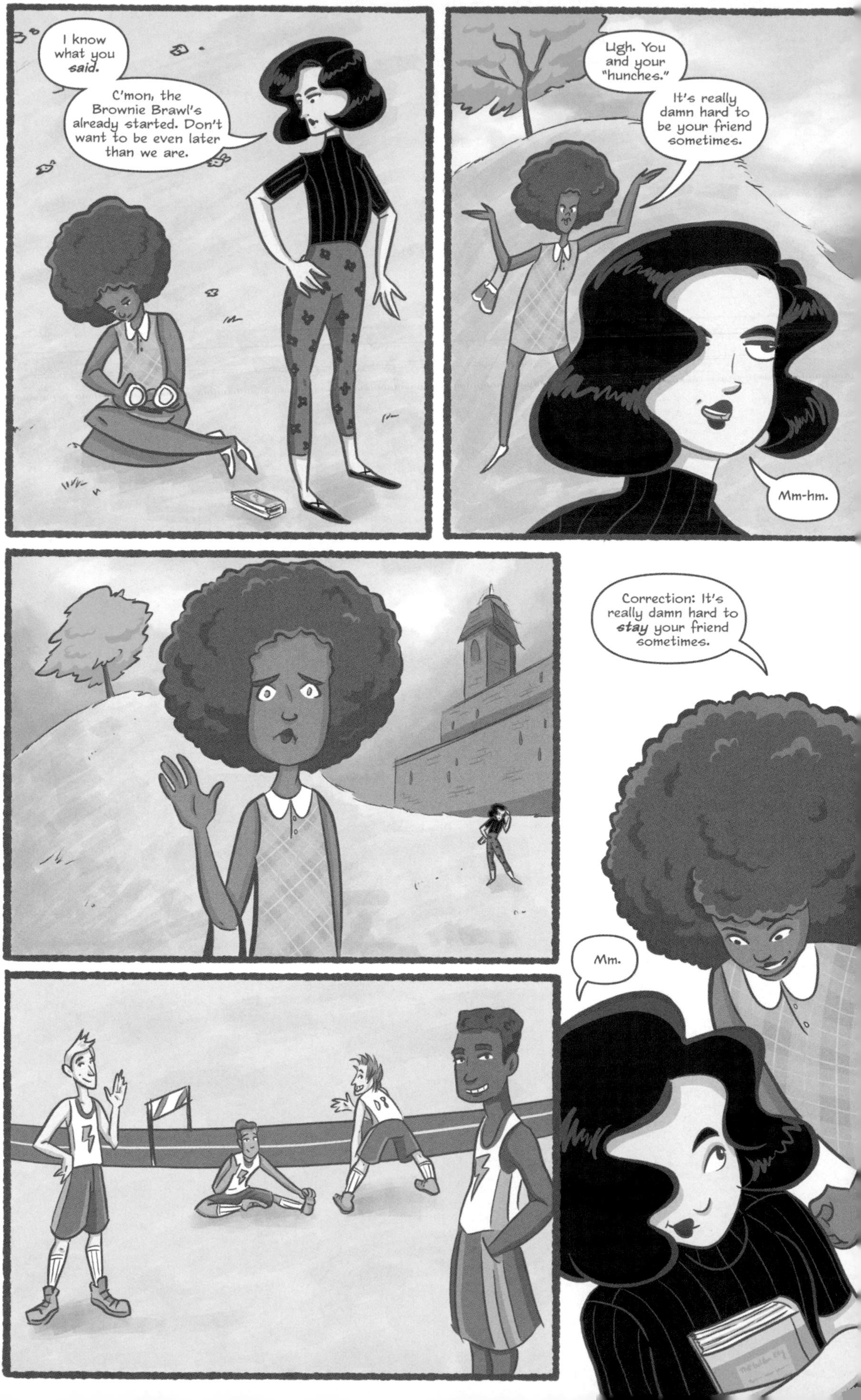
I know what you *said.*
C'mon, the Brownie Brawl's already started. Don't want to be even later than we are.
Ugh. You and your "hunches."
It's really damn hard to be your friend sometimes.
Mm-hm.
Correction: It's really damn hard to *stay* your friend sometimes.
Mm.

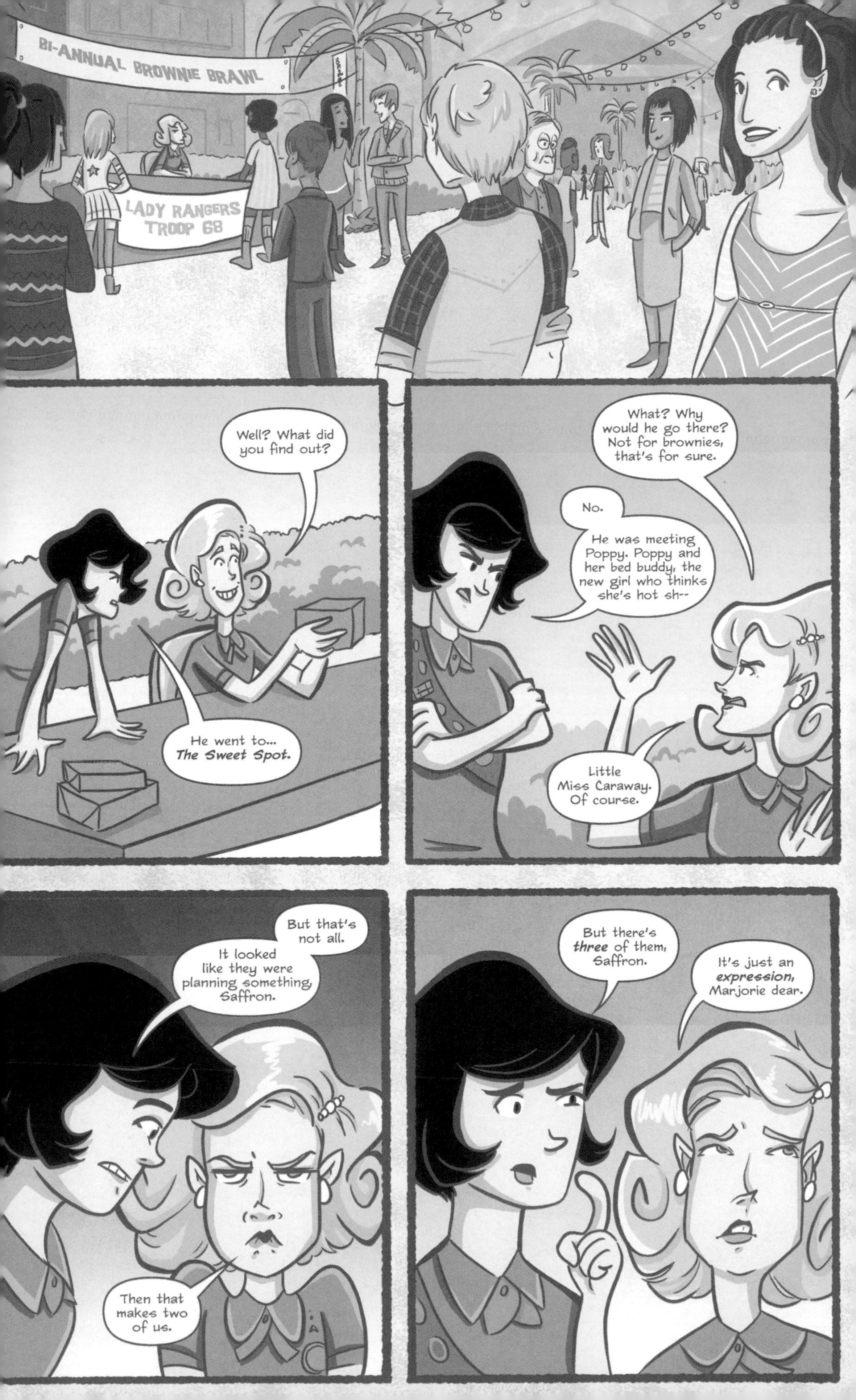
BI-ANNUAL BROWNIE BRAWL
LADY RANGERS TROOP 68
Well? What did you find out?
He went to... *The Sweet Spot.*
What? Why would he go there? Not for brownies, that's for sure.
No.
He was meeting Poppy. Poppy and her bed buddy, the new girl who thinks she's hot sh--
Little Miss Caraway. Of course.
But that's not all.
It looked like they were planning something, Saffron.
Then that makes two of us.
But there's *three* of them, Saffron.
It's just an *expression,* Marjorie dear.

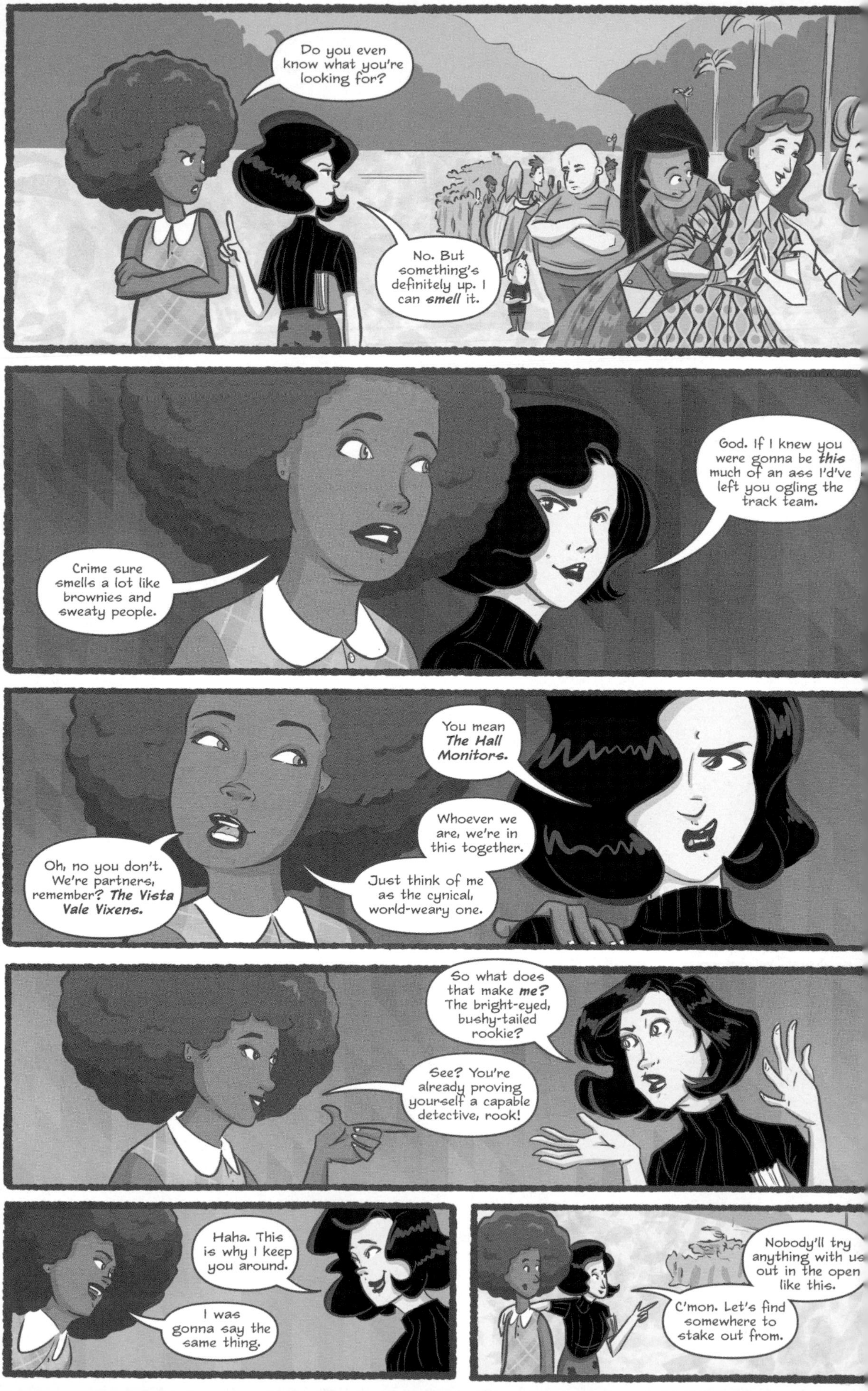
Do you even know what you're looking for?
No. But something's definitely up. I can *smell* it.
Crime sure smells a lot like brownies and sweaty people.
God. If I knew you were gonna be *this* much of an ass I'd've left you ogling the track team.
Oh, no you don't. We're partners, remember? *The Vista Vale Vixens.*
You mean *The Hall Monitors.*
Whoever we are, we're in this together.
Just think of me as the cynical, world-weary one.
So what does that make *me*? The bright-eyed, bushy-tailed rookie?
See? You're already proving yourself a capable detective, rook!
Haha. This is why I keep you around.
I was gonna say the same thing.
Nobody'll try anything with us out in the open like this.
C'mon. Let's find somewhere to stake out from.

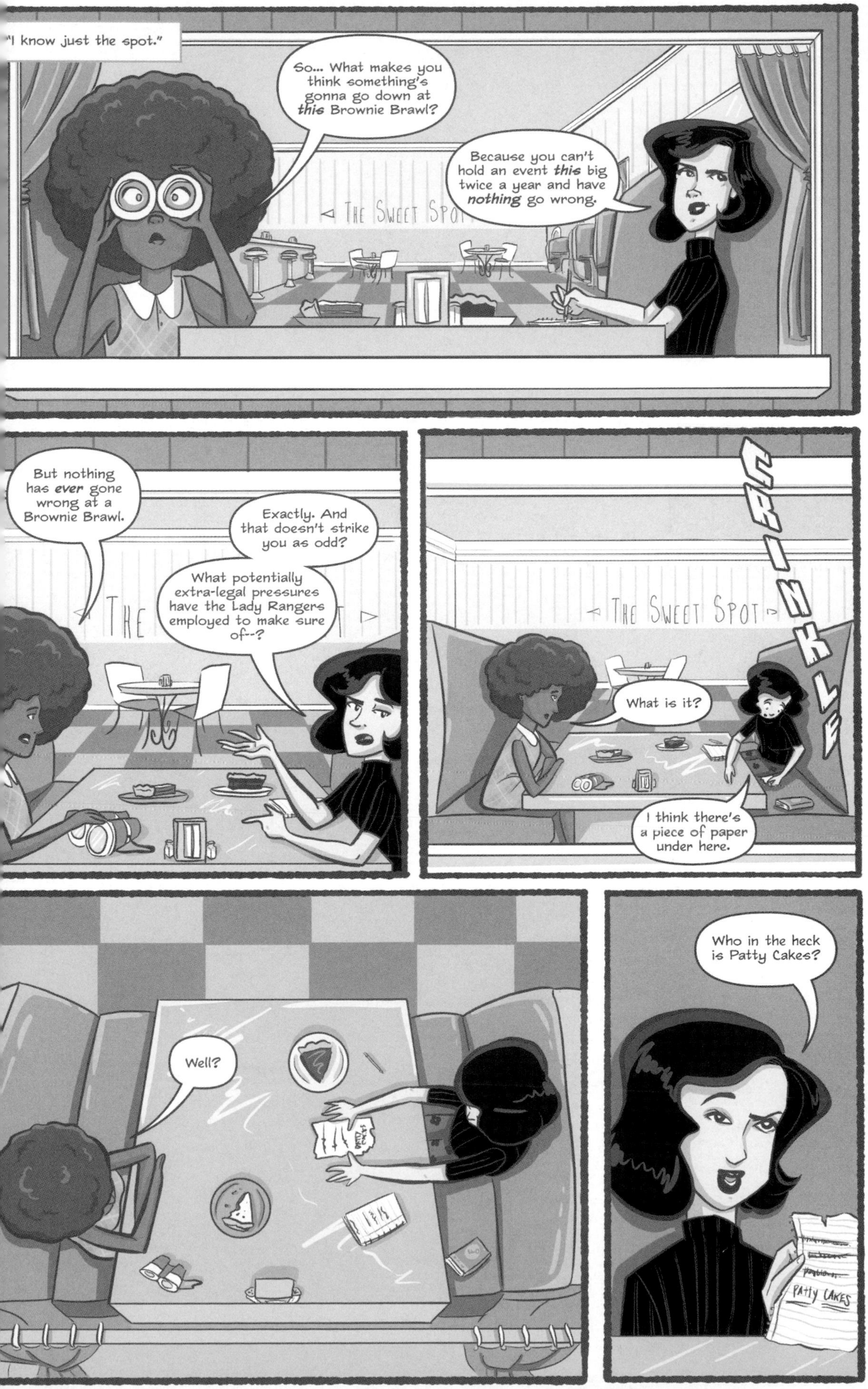
"I know just the spot."
So... What makes you think something's gonna go down at *this* Brownie Brawl?
Because you can't hold an event *this* big twice a year and have *nothing* go wrong.
THE SWEET SPOT
But nothing has *ever* gone wrong at a Brownie Brawl.
Exactly. And that doesn't strike you as odd?
What potentially extra-legal pressures have the Lady Rangers employed to make sure of--?
CRINKLE
THE SWEET SPOT
What is it?
I think there's a piece of paper under here.
Well?
Who in the heck is Patty Cakes?
PATTY CAKES

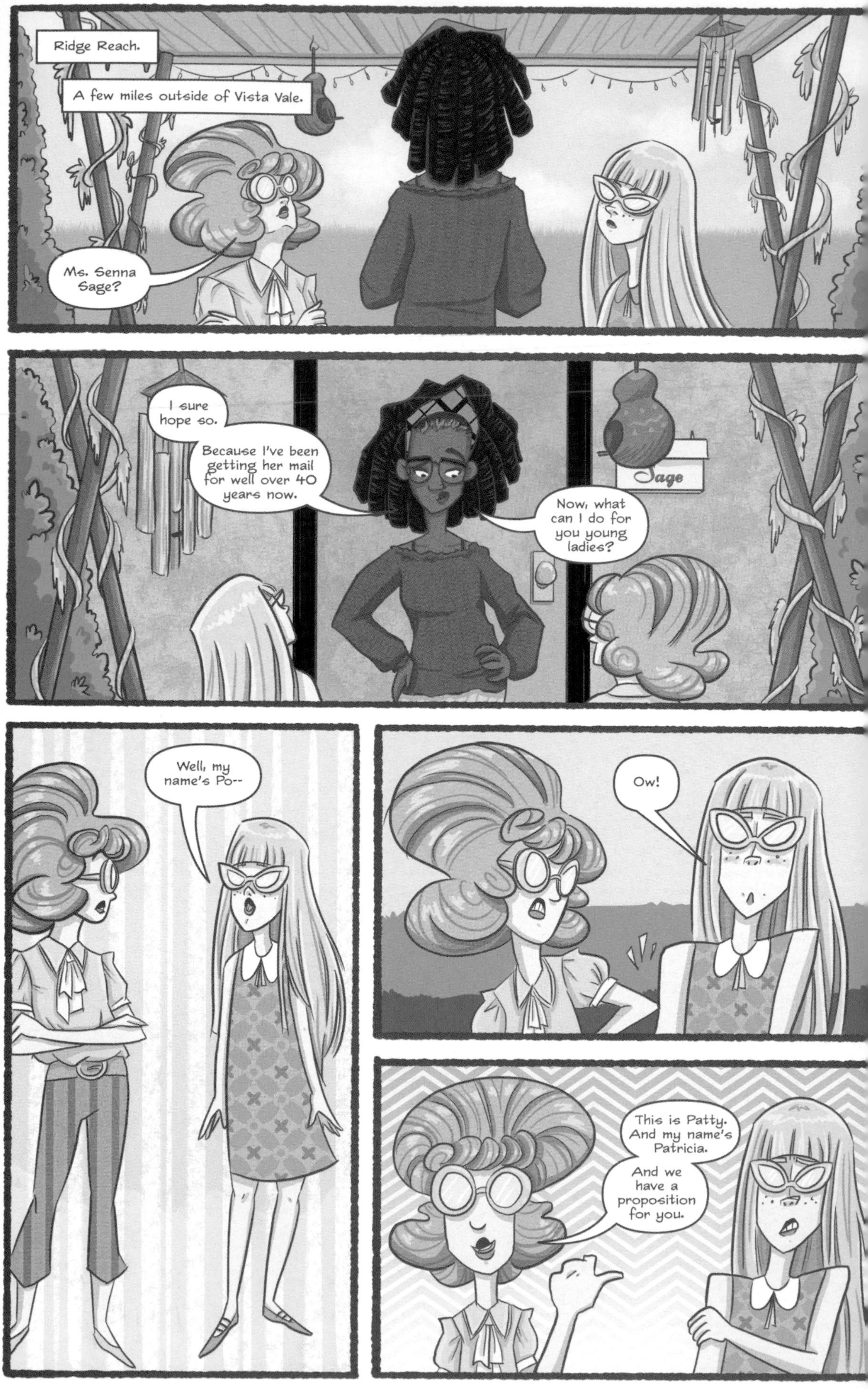
Ridge Reach.
A few miles outside of Vista Vale.
Ms. Senna Sage?
I sure hope so.
Because I've been getting her mail for well over 40 years now.
Sage
Now, what can I do for you young ladies?
Well, my name's Po--
Ow!
This is Patty. And my name's Patricia.
And we have a proposition for you.

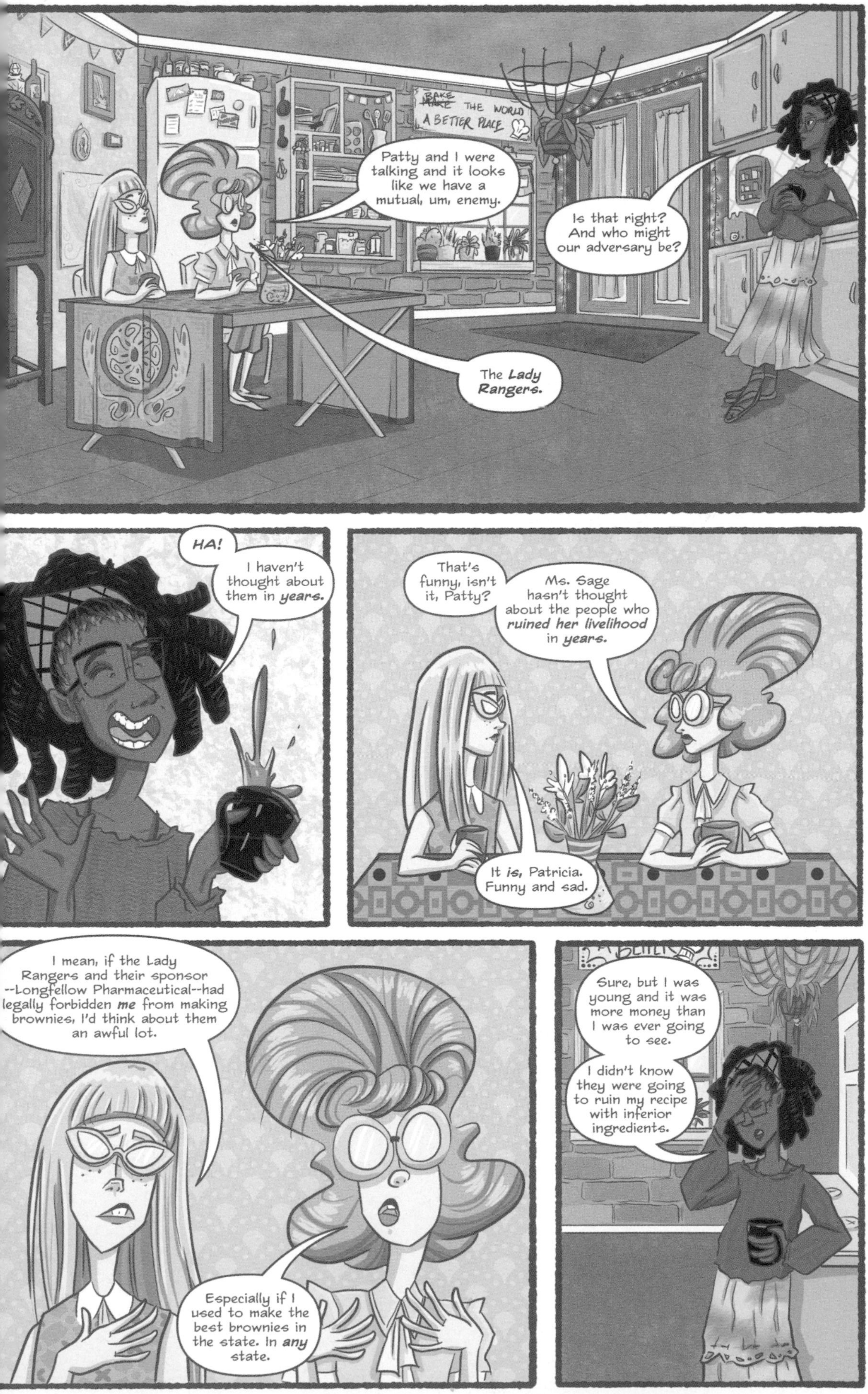

BAKE MAKE THE WORLD A BETTER PLACE
Patty and I were talking and it looks like we have a mutual, um, enemy.
Is that right? And who might our adversary be?
The **Lady Rangers.**
**HA!**
I haven't thought about them in ***years.***
That's funny, isn't it, Patty?
Ms. Sage hasn't thought about the people who ***ruined her livelihood*** in ***years.***
It *is,* Patricia. Funny and sad.
I mean, if the Lady Rangers and their sponsor --Longfellow Pharmaceutical--had legally forbidden ***me*** from making brownies, I'd think about them an awful lot.
Especially if I used to make the best brownies in the state. In ***any*** state.
Sure, but I was young and it was more money than I was ever going to see.
I didn't know they were going to ruin my recipe with inferior ingredients.

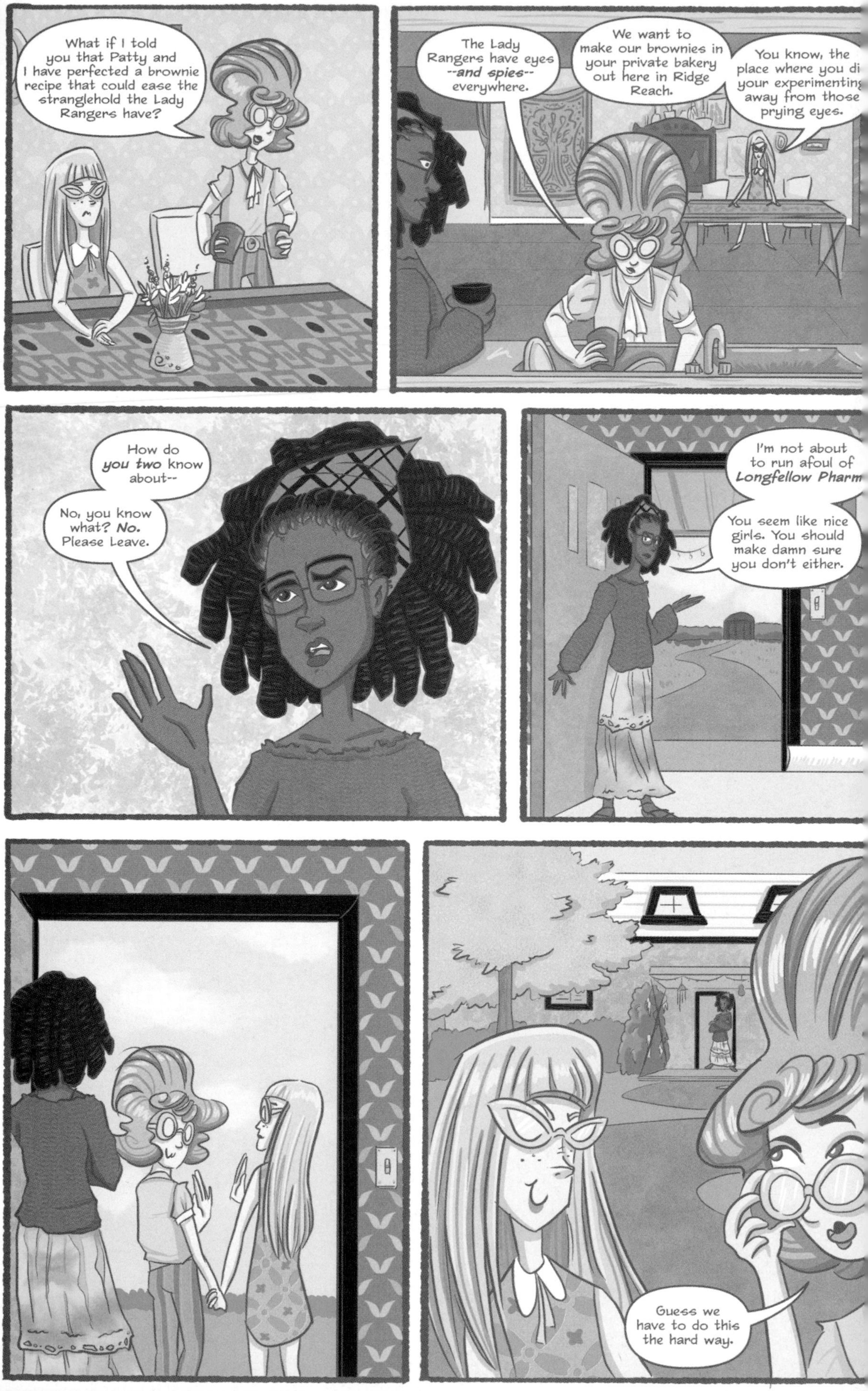

What if I told you that Patty and I have perfected a brownie recipe that could ease the stranglehold the Lady Rangers have?
The Lady Rangers have eyes *--and spies--* everywhere.
We want to make our brownies in your private bakery out here in Ridge Reach.
You know, the place where you di your experimenting away from those prying eyes.
How do *you two* know about--
No, you know what? ***No.*** Please Leave.
I'm not about to run afoul of ***Longfellow Pharm***
You seem like nice girls. You should make damn sure you don't either.
Guess we have to do this the hard way.

Later.

What are we even *doing,* Cass?

Shhh!

I just want to go on record as saying I was against "the hard way" from the start.

Noted.

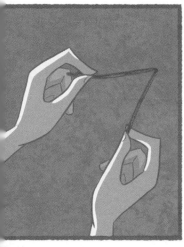

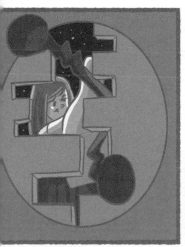

What do they teach you at those Connecticut Prep Schools?

KA-CHACK

Nothing...

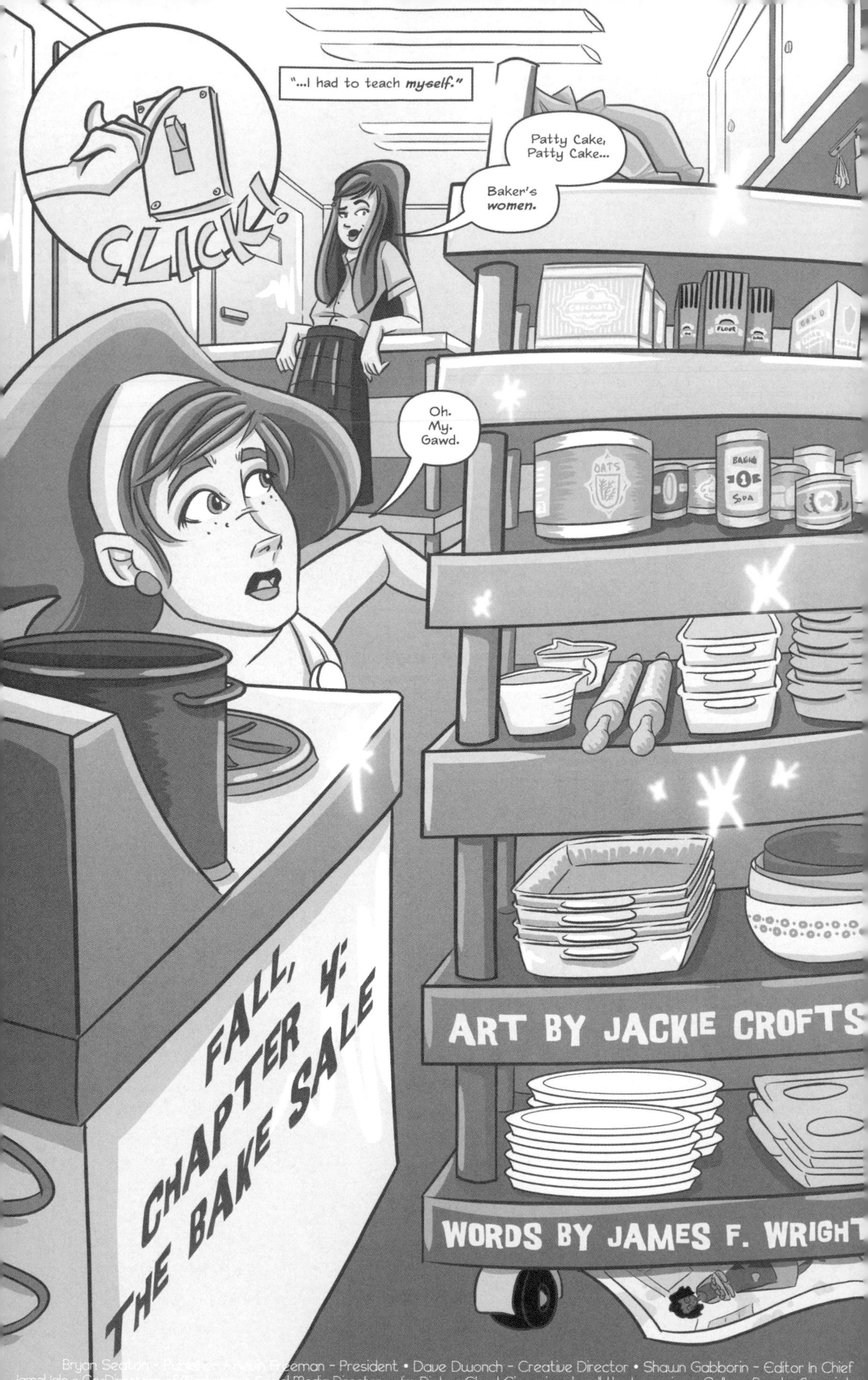
CLICK!
"...I had to teach myself."
Patty Cake, Patty Cake...
Baker's women.
Oh. My. Gawd.
ART BY JACKIE CROFTS
WORDS BY JAMES F. WRIGHT
FALL, CHAPTER 4: THE BAKE SALE

Bryan Seaton - Publisher • Kevin Freeman - President • Dave Dwonch - Creative Director • Shawn Gabborin - Editor In Chief
Jamal Igle - Co-Directors of Marketing • Social Media Director - Jim Dietz • Chad Cicconi - ate all the brownies • Colleen Boyd - Associate

# THE COOLING RACK

CONTACT: @NUTMEGCOMIC · NUTMEGCOMICS@GMAIL.COM

is month in The Cooling Rack we're doing something a little different. We've had a huge outpouring of pport in the creation of this book, from friends and family, co-workers and complete strangers, so we wanted take a moment to share with you some of the incredible things we've received. We say it often, but it means the world to us that people are enjoying our book and characters as much as we enjoy making them.

## My Review On Your Comic #1

My first comment on the comic is that it was cool and I can not wait for the second edition to come out. I also like how you put that highschool theme in the story like two best friends against the "Mean Girls". It was like watching a mini movie in my head. I loved Cassia's attitude. It seemed as if she is not going to put up with anyones shenanigans. I hope at the end of the comic Cassia falls in love with Bobby. Also you should put some type of twist in the story. Like maybe the "mean girls" sabotage Cassia and Poppy's brownies to try and make them lose. I do not know I'm just shooting ideas. But your comic was awesome so far. Keep it up!

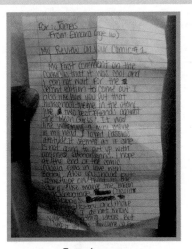

For: James
From: Emara (age 16)
My Review On Your Comic #1

For: James
From: Emara (age 16)

Art by: Jules Rivera - julesrivera.com - **Misfortune High** and **Valkyrie Squadron** writer/artist.

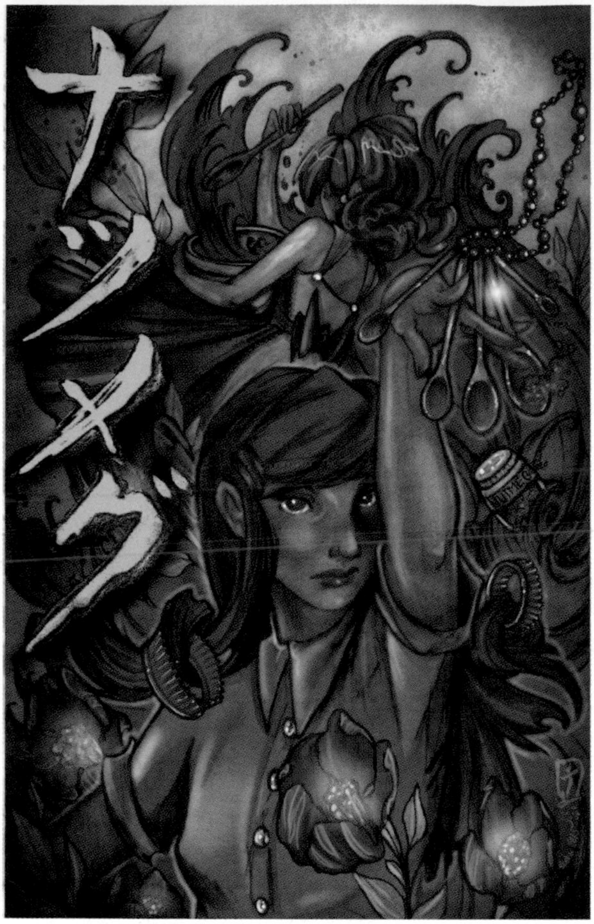
ナツメグ

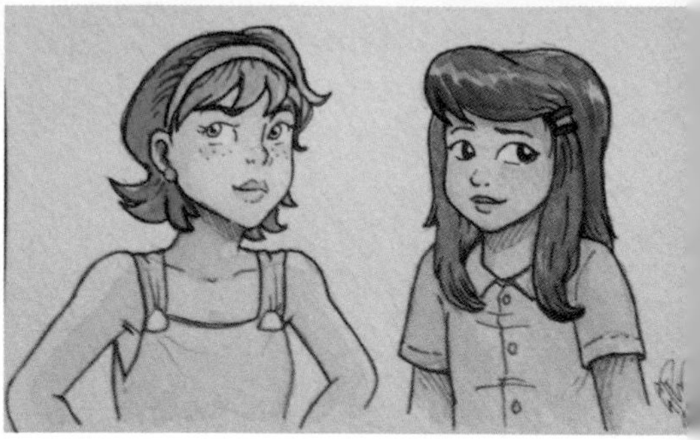

(Above)

Art by: G Pike
titleunrelated.com

Webcomic artist/writer for **Title Unrelated.**

(Left)

Art by: Teika Hudson
teikahudson.com

A highly successful and sought-after tattoo artist in Calgary, Alberta. She's easily one of the 5 nicest people you will ever meet.

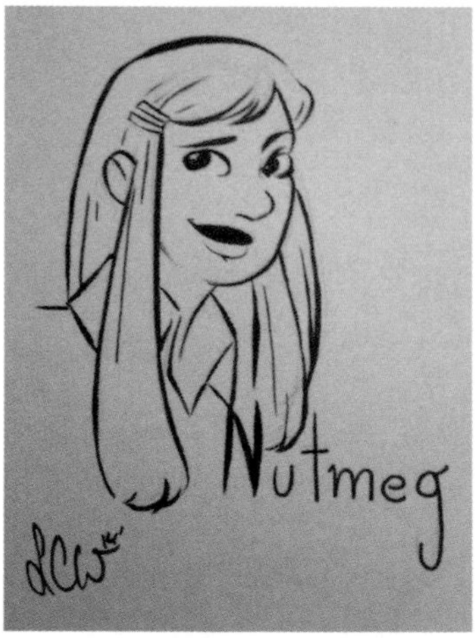
Nutmeg

(Above)

Art by: Leia Weathington
ahappygoluckyscamp.com

Creator of epic fantasy series **The Legend of Bold Riley.**

(Right)

Art by: Brian Reyes

Writer/artist of **Dark Horizon**, an edgy, tongue-in-cheek parody of junior high English textbooks in Japan.

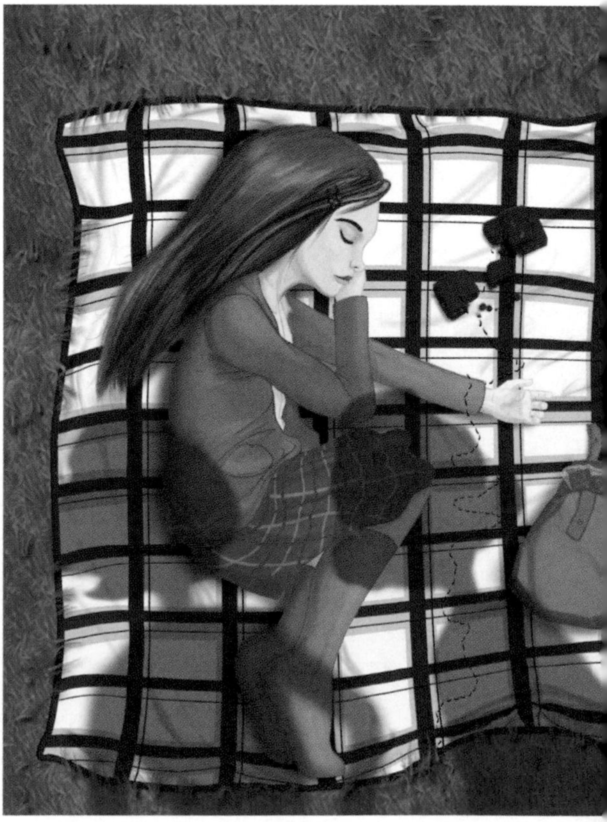

# SOURCREAM SOFTIES

Nicole is a friend of James's and every once in a while she will show up with some new confectionery concoction, more often than not a delicious batch of cookies. Among those, the most striking and eminently edible are the **Sour Cream Softies** from her grandmother's recipe. We all just call them pillow cookies, because if you make them right that's exactly what they look and feel like. So, enough rambling from us. We'll let Nicole take it away from here.

Ingredients:

3 Cups of flour (add last)
1 tsp. of salt
½ tsp. of baking powder
½ tsp. of baking soda
½ Cup of butter (softened)
1½ Cups of sugar
2 eggs
1 tsp. of vanilla
1 Cup of sour cream
3 Tbsp. of cinnamon-sugar

400-12min. SourCream Softies
3 cups flour— ADD last
1 tsp. salt
1/2 tsp. bak. pd.
1/2 tsp. bak. soda
1/2 cup butter
11/2 cups sugar
2 eggs
1 tsp. vanilla
1 cup sour crea
cinn-sugar
greased pan
sprinkle on
just before bake

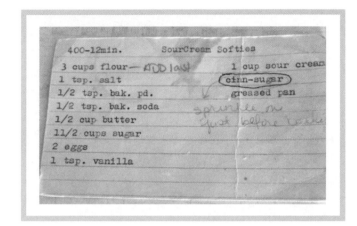

Steps:

Preheat oven to 400°F.

In a large bowl, mix together salt, baking powder, baking soda, butter, sugar, eggs, vanilla, and sour cream.

Once blended, add the flour—one cup at a time—while continuing to stir to make sure everything is incorporated into the batter.

When the batter is formed, scoop it into balls and place on a greased baking sheet.

Sprinkle with cinnamon-sugar.

Bake for 12 minutes.

Enjoy!

Hotel

## PAGE 11

[*Note:* Panel Two *should ideally be the biggest panel on the page since there's a lot to see there.*]

### ONE:
P.O.V. Binoculars. And in their sights? BOYS. A buffet of CUTE HIGH SCHOOL BOYS in their TRACK & FIELD UNIFORMS, stretching before practice.

| 1 ANISE/off: | That's right. |
| 2 ANISE/linked/off: | Stretch out those muscles. |

### TWO (big panel):
ANISE and GINGER sit in the shade beneath a large tree, on a HILL overlooking the VISTA VALE SOUTH HIGH BOYS' TRACK & FIELD TEAM on the PRACTICE FIELD down below. Anise holds a pair of BINOCULARS to her eyes—they're practically glued there. Ginger couldn't be bothered. She's lying on her back, lazily thumbing through the pages of a NOVEL.

| 3 CAPTION: | Vista Vale South High Practice Field. |
| 4 ANISE: | Wouldn't want you hurting your fine selves... |

### THREE:
GINGER turns from her BOOK to speak to ANISE, who lowers the BINOCULARS but keeps her eyes off-panel toward where the boys are practicing.

| 5 GINGER: | Alright, Anise. You've had your fill. |
| 6 GINGER/linked: | Can we go now? |
| 7 ANISE: | What? **Go?** But we just **got** here. |

### FOUR:
GINGER points off-panel toward the boys' practice. ANISE rolls her eyes.

| 8 GINGER: | No, **they** just got here. You said we'd come for an hour and it's been two. |
| 9 ANISE: | That's not fair, Ginger. You **know** what I meant. |

We want to show you a bit of our process when writing and illustrating Nutmeg. Up on the top, we have James' script from page 11 of this issue.

Once I've got the words in front of me, I get to work sketching thumbnails. My workflow with Nutmeg has moved to all digital now using the Cintiq Companion. After sketching, I move onto lines, flats, highlights, and finally lettering.

I do one task on all pages before moving to the next. So if I'm inking I will ink all 20 pages in a row before moving onto coloring. It helps me concentrate on one thing at a time so I'm not constantly shifting gears. Everything is done in Photoshop aside from the lettering, which I do in Illustrator. Easy as pie, right?

As Aero-Girl, Jacqueline Mackenzie is the protector of Foxbay. As the sidekick to Battle J[...] her father, her life couldn't be any better; but tragedy is just around the corner! Will she [...] ready to defend her city against the evil of Dr. Chimera and his army of AniMen? Ca[...] Aero-Girl be the hero she (and her father) always dreamed of being?

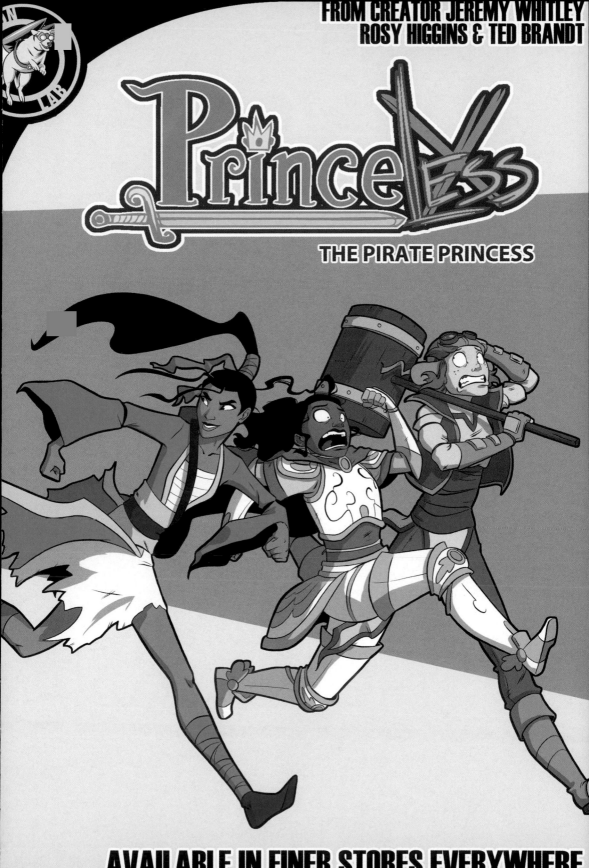

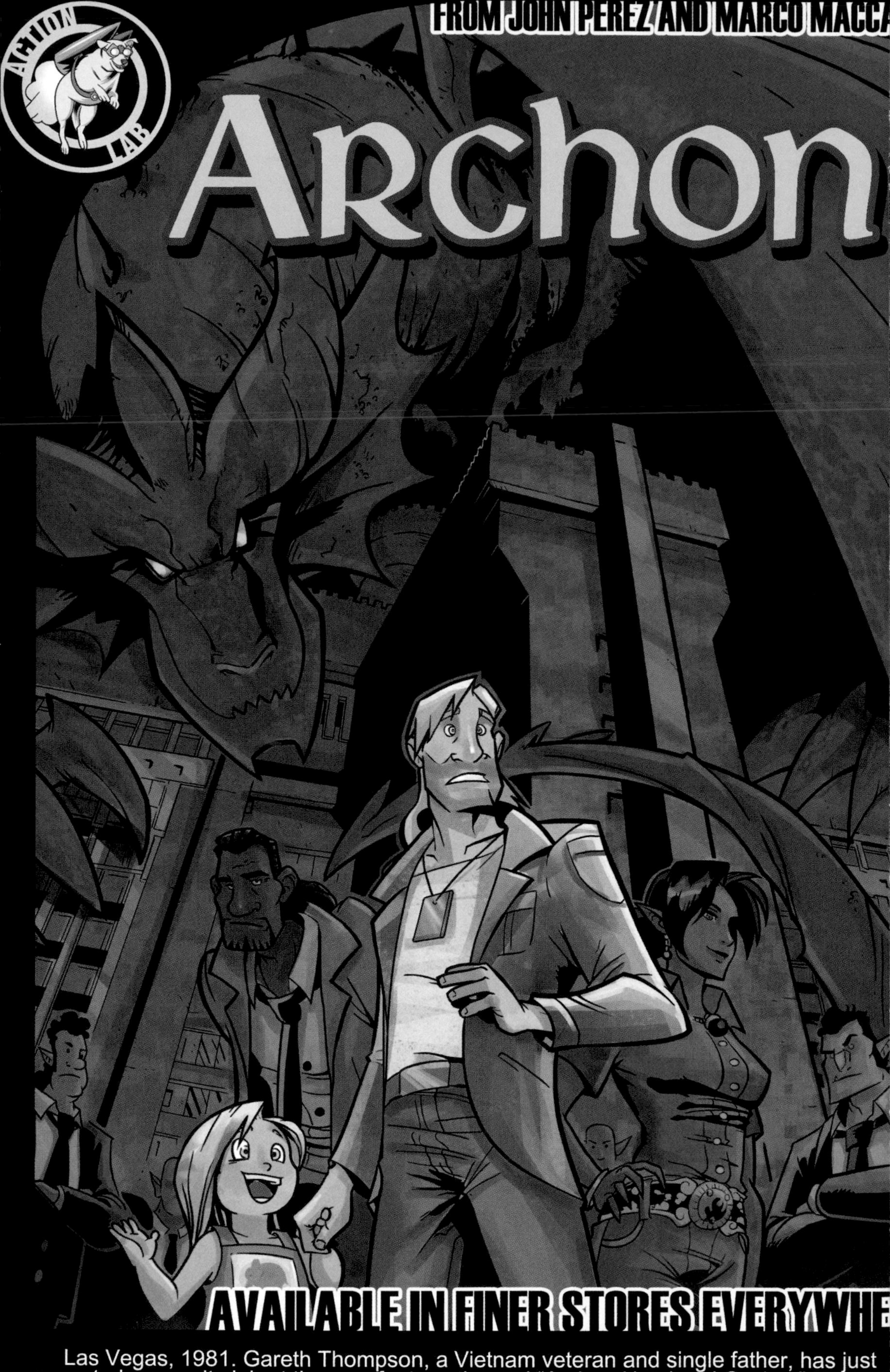
FROM JOHN PEREZ AND MARCO MACCA
Archon
AVAILABLE IN FINER STORES EVERYWHE

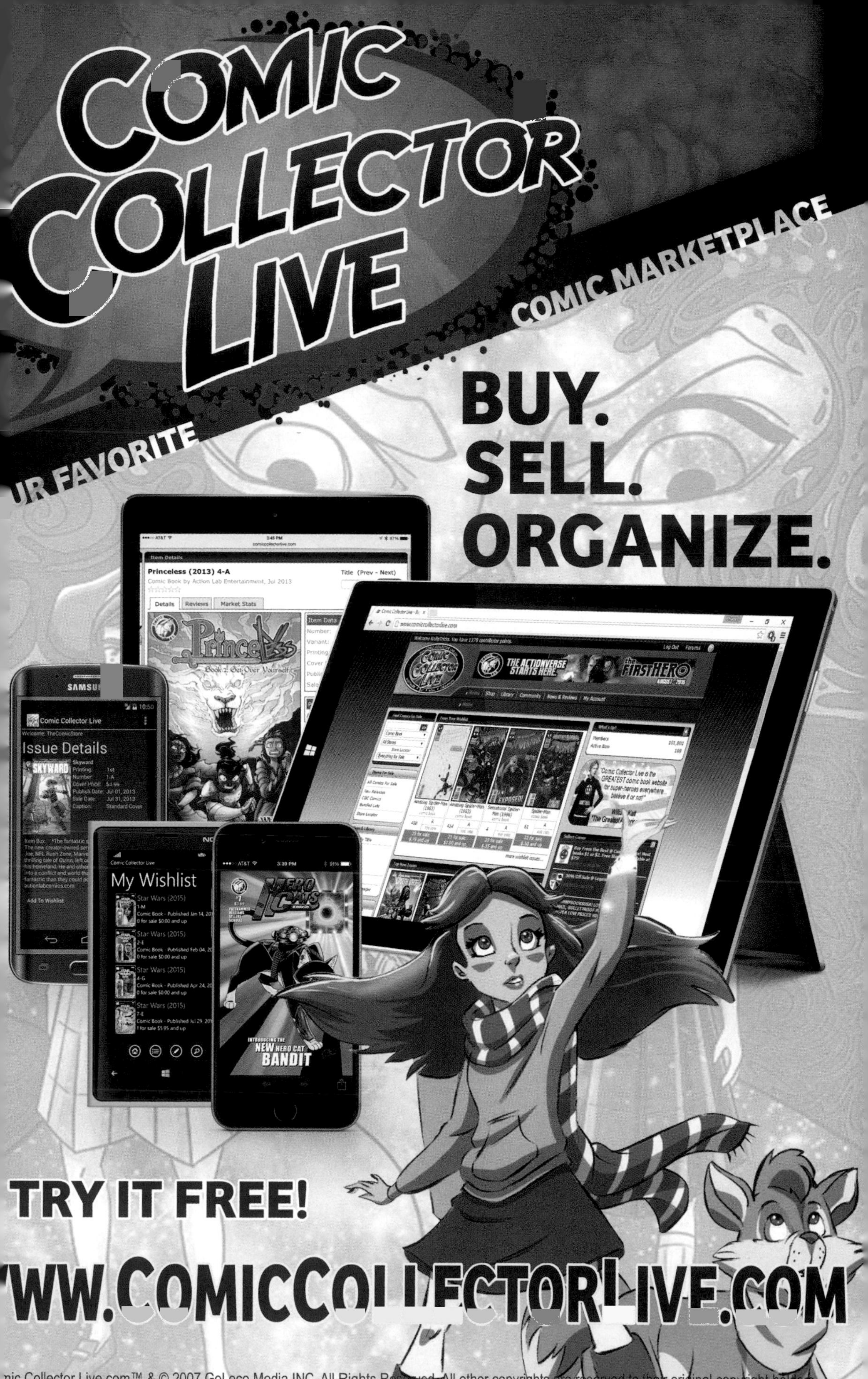
COMIC COLLECTOR LIVE
UR FAVORITE COMIC MARKETPLACE
BUY. SELL. ORGANIZE.
TRY IT FREE!
WW.COMICCOLLECTORLIVE.COM

READ MORE NOW

**ACTIONLABCOMICS.COM**

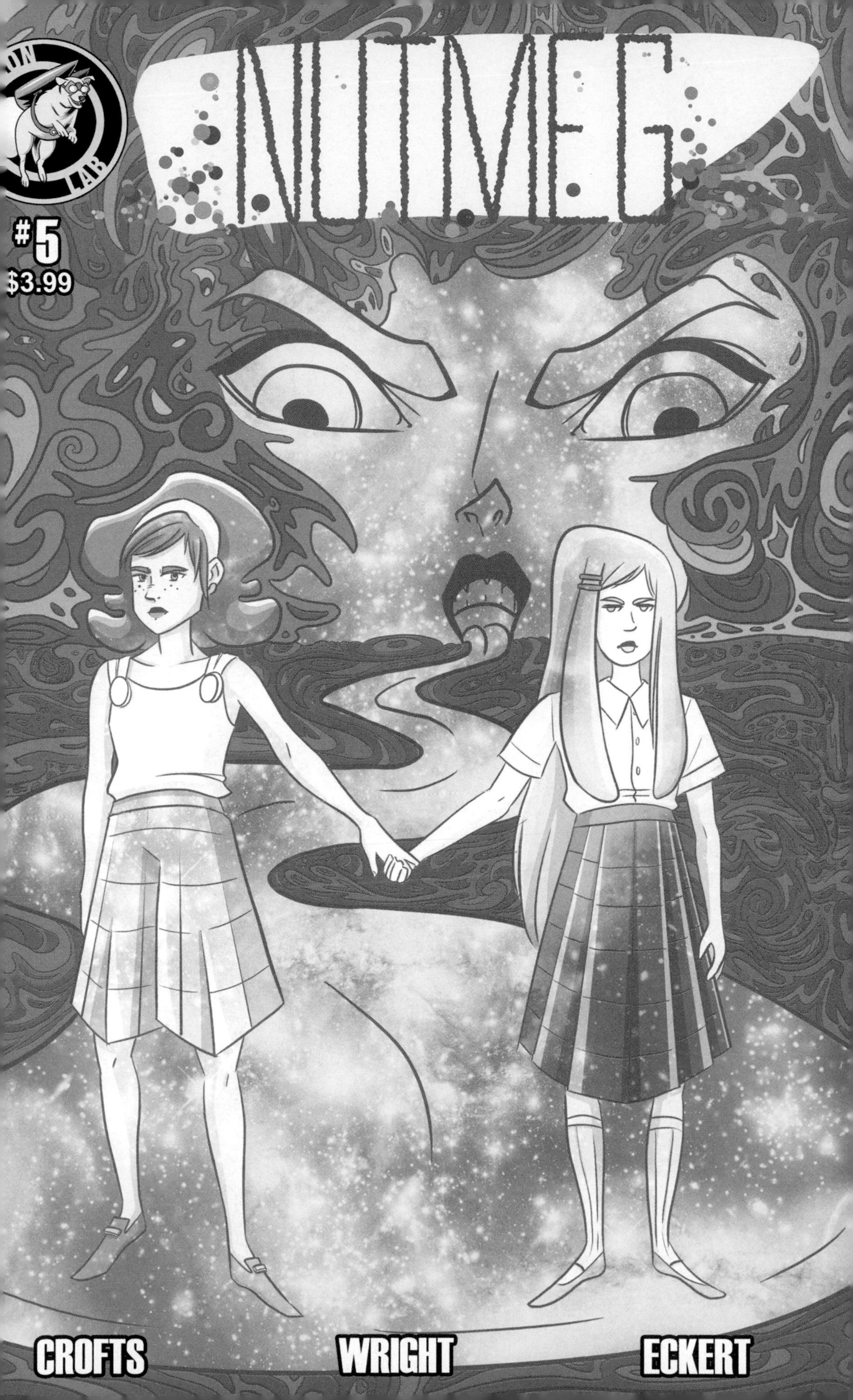

NUTMEG
#5
$3.99
CROFTS
WRIGHT
ECKERT

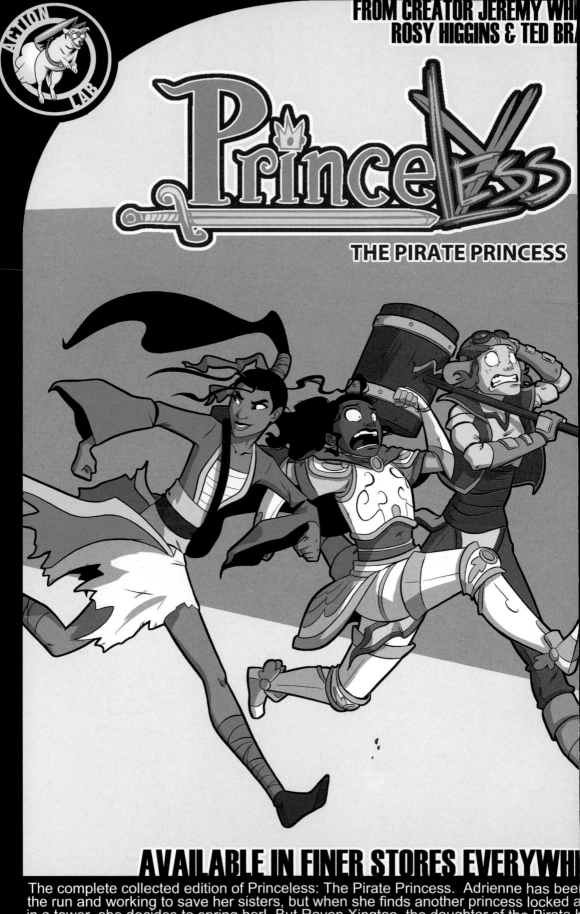

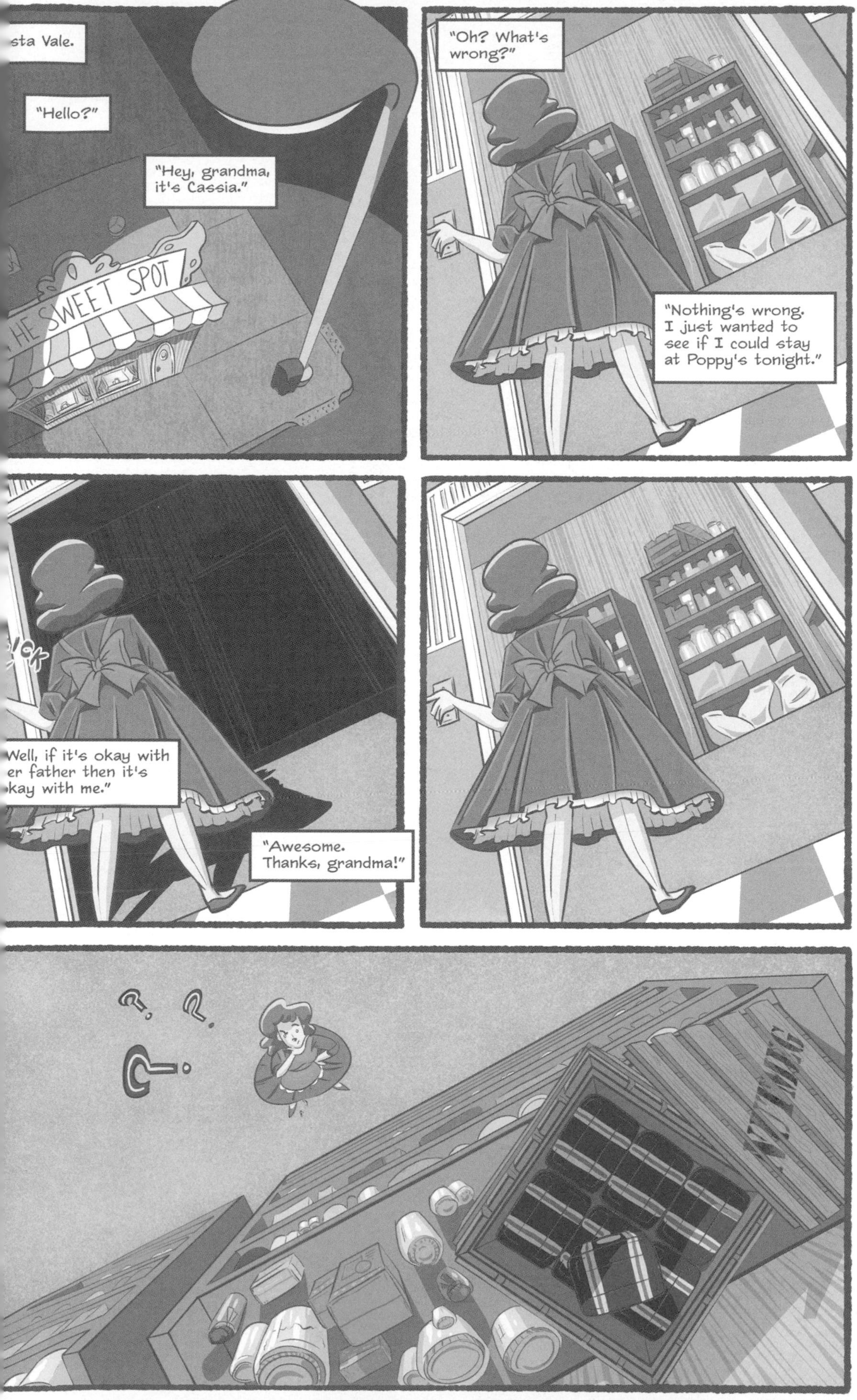
sta Vale.
"Hello?"
"Hey, grandma, it's Cassia."
HE SWEET SPOT
"Oh? What's wrong?"
"Nothing's wrong. I just wanted to see if I could stay at Poppy's tonight."
Well, if it's okay with er father then it's kay with me."
"Awesome. Thanks, grandma!"

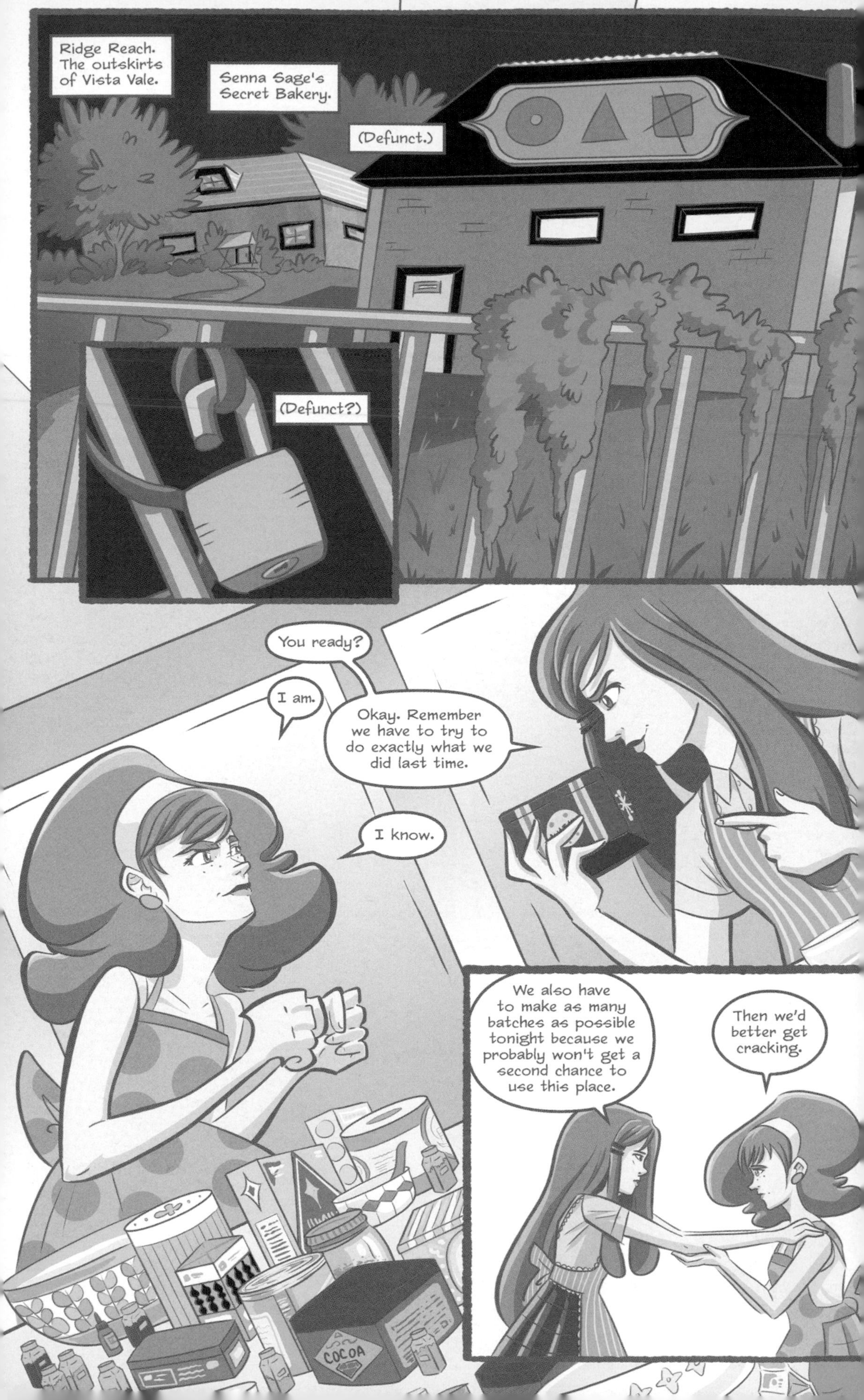
Ridge Reach. The outskirts of Vista Vale.
Senna Sage's Secret Bakery.
(Defunct.)
(Defunct?)
You ready?
I am.
Okay. Remember we have to try to do exactly what we did last time.
I know.
We also have to make as many batches as possible tonight because we probably won't get a second chance to use this place.
Then we'd better get cracking.
COCOA

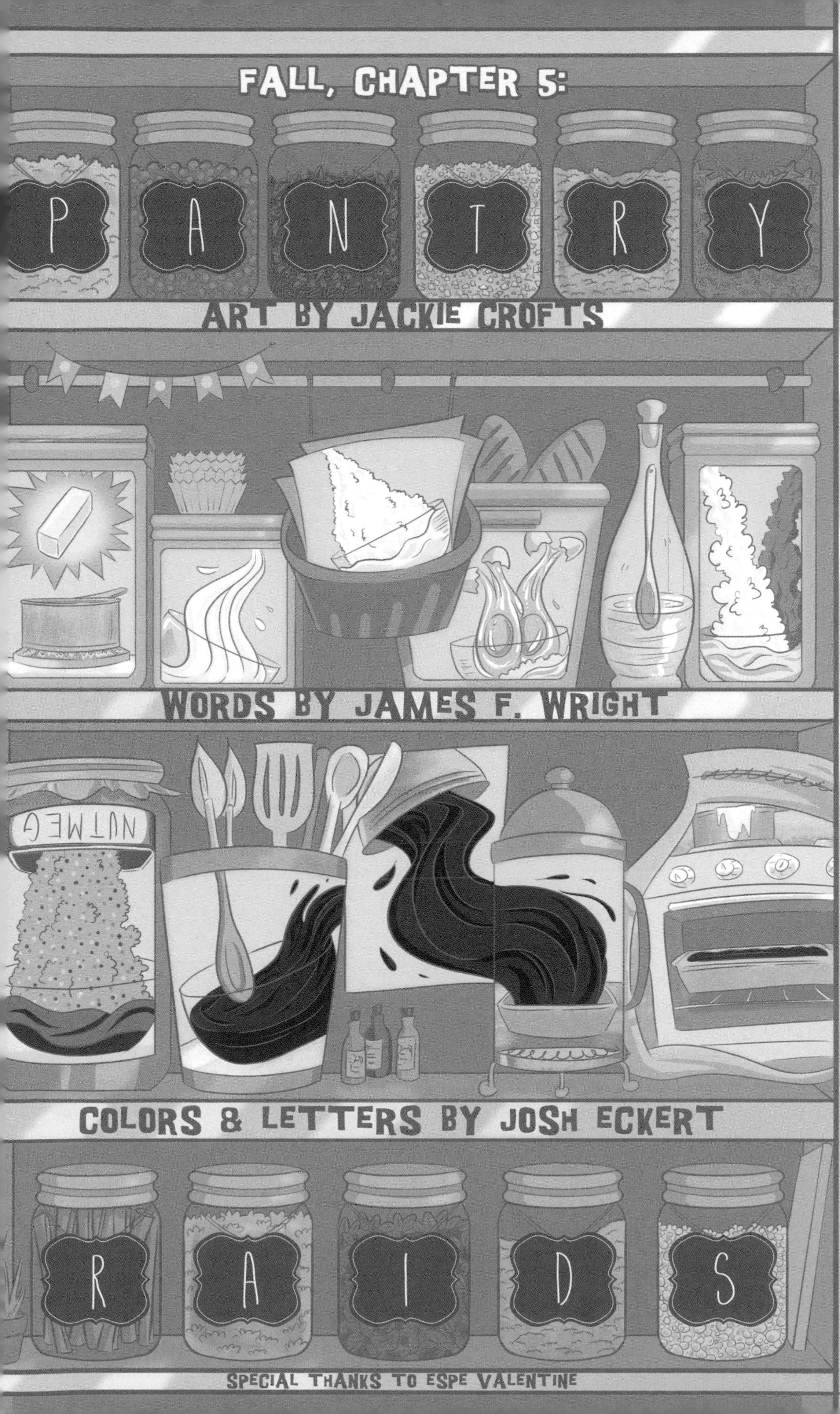
FALL, CHAPTER 5:
PANTRY
ART BY JACKIE CROFTS
WORDS BY JAMES F. WRIGHT
NUTMEG
COLORS & LETTERS BY JOSH ECKERT
RAIDS
SPECIAL THANKS TO ESPE VALENTINE

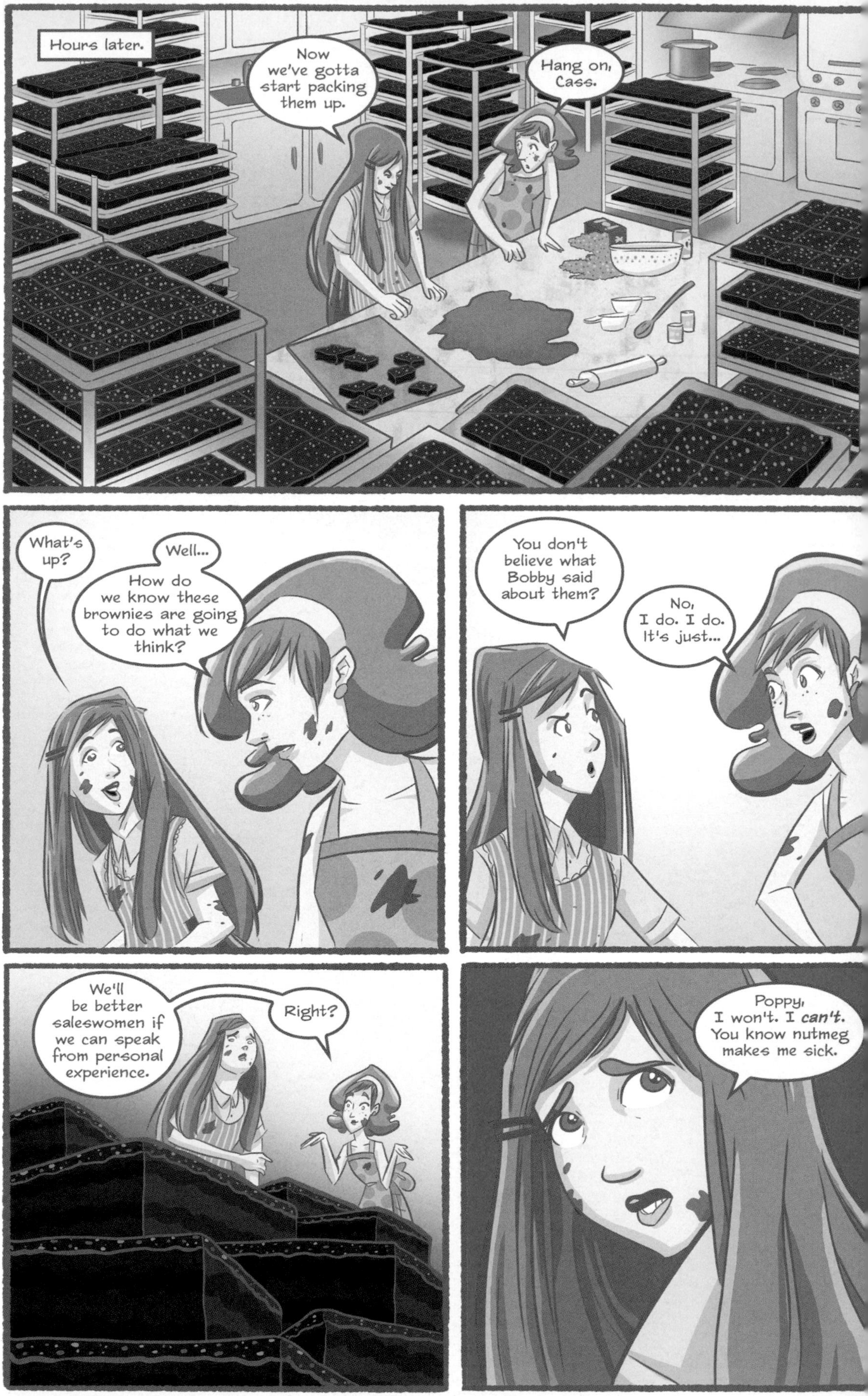
Hours later.
Now we've gotta start packing them up.
Hang on, Cass.
What's up?
Well...
How do we know these brownies are going to do what we think?
You don't believe what Bobby said about them?
No, I do. I do. It's just...
We'll be better saleswomen if we can speak from personal experience.
Right?
Poppy, I won't. I *can't*. You know nutmeg makes me sick.

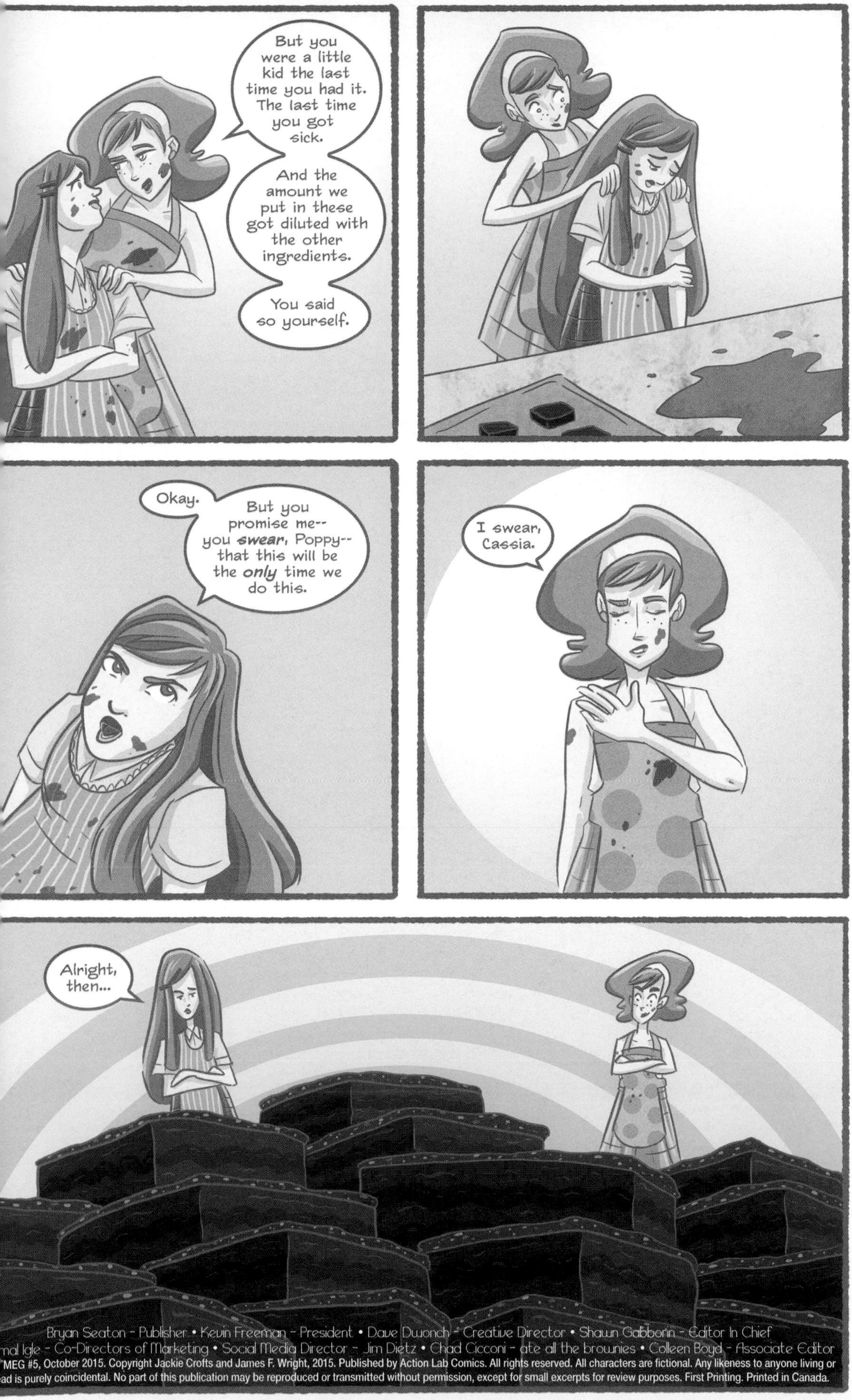

But you were a little kid the last time you had it. The last time you got sick.
And the amount we put in these got diluted with the other ingredients.
You said so yourself.
Okay.
But you promise me--you *swear*, Poppy--that this will be the *only* time we do this.
I swear, Cassia.
Alright, then...



Bryan Seaton - Publisher • Kevin Freeman - President • Dave Dwonch - Creative Director • Shawn Gabborin - Editor In Chief
nal Igle - Co-Directors of Marketing • Social Media Director - Jim Dietz • Chad Cicconi - ate all the brownies • Colleen Boyd - Associate Editor

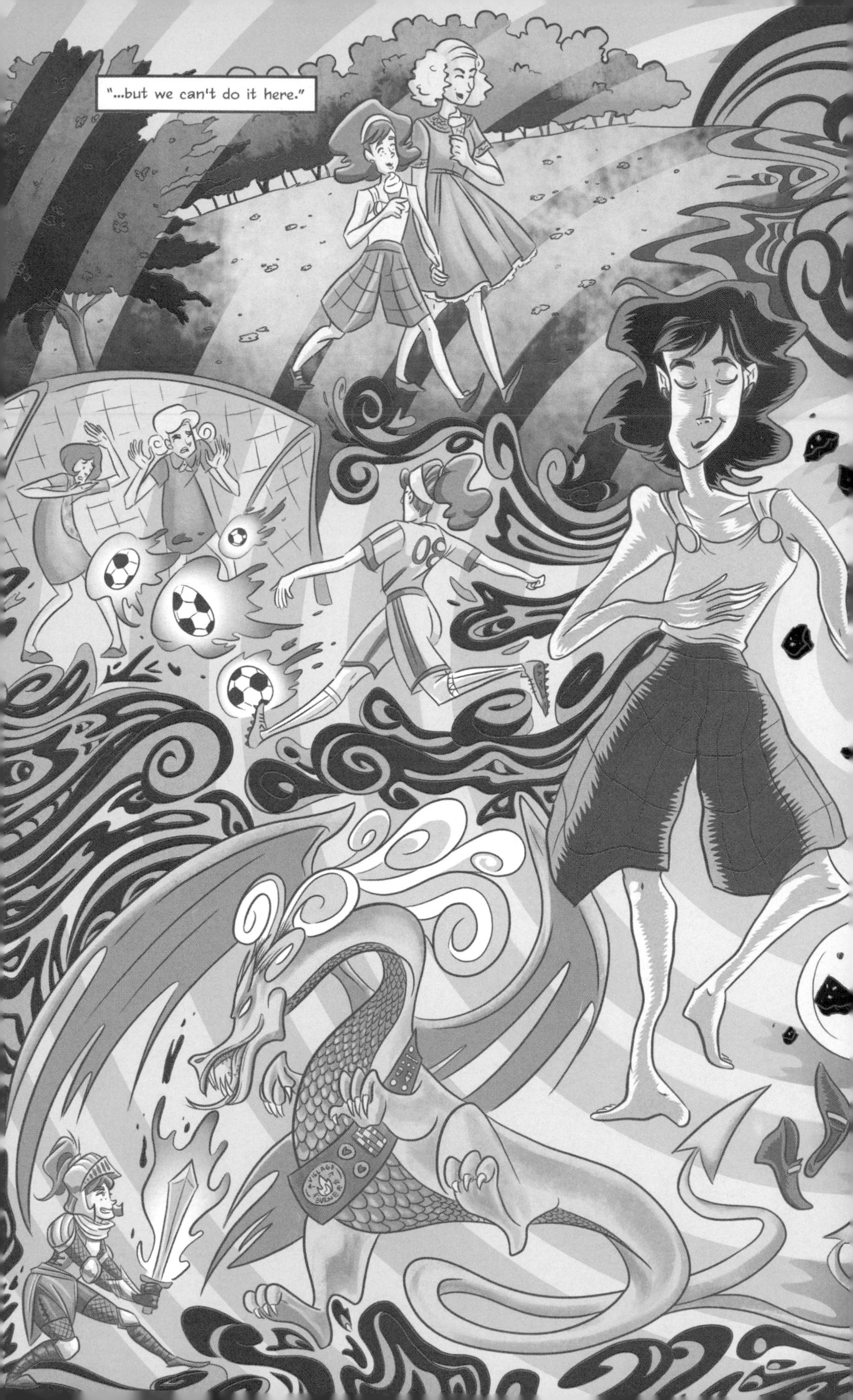
"...but we can't do it here."

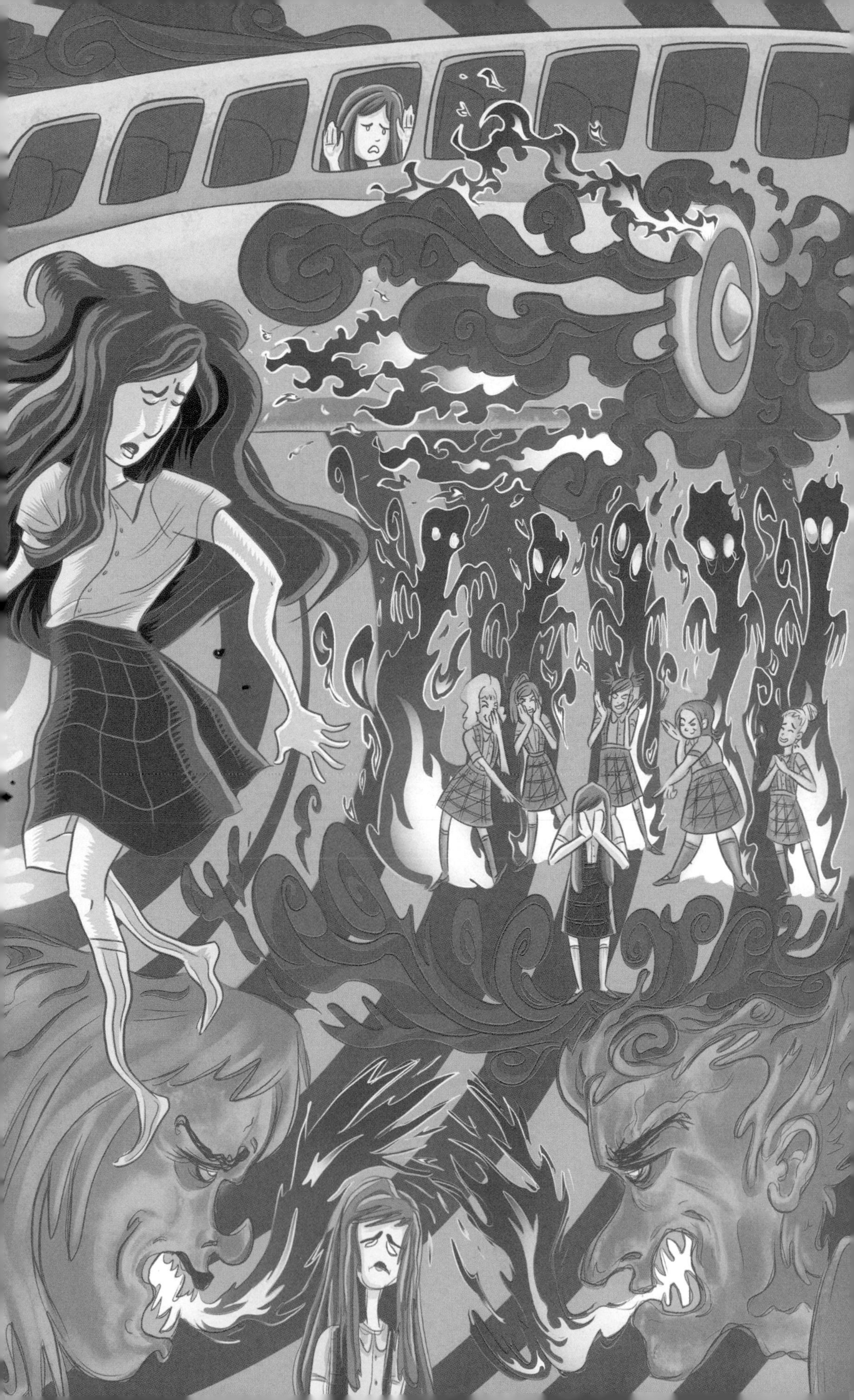

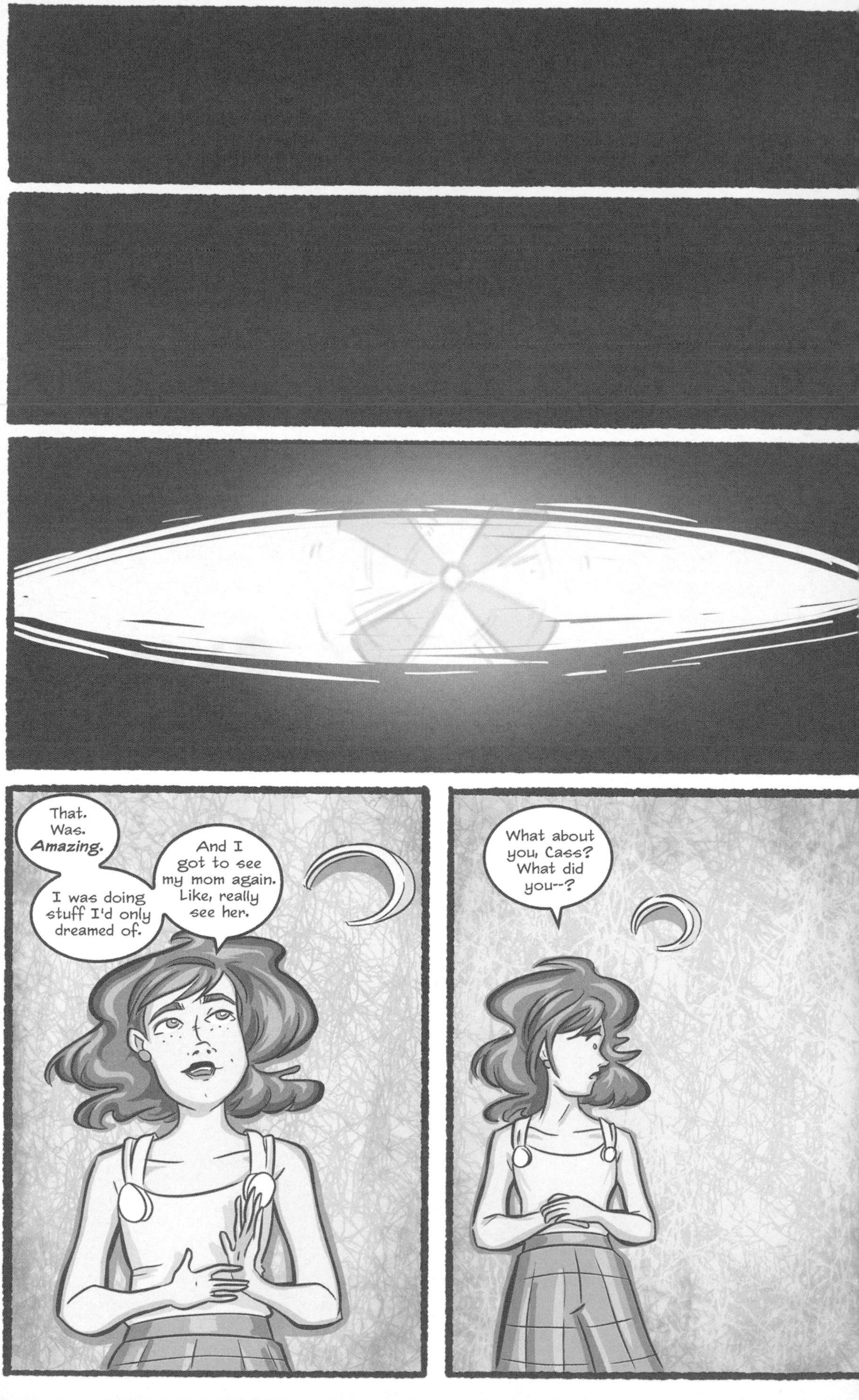
That. Was. *Amazing.*
I was doing stuff I'd only dreamed of.
And I got to see my mom again. Like, really see her.
What about you, Cass? What did you--?

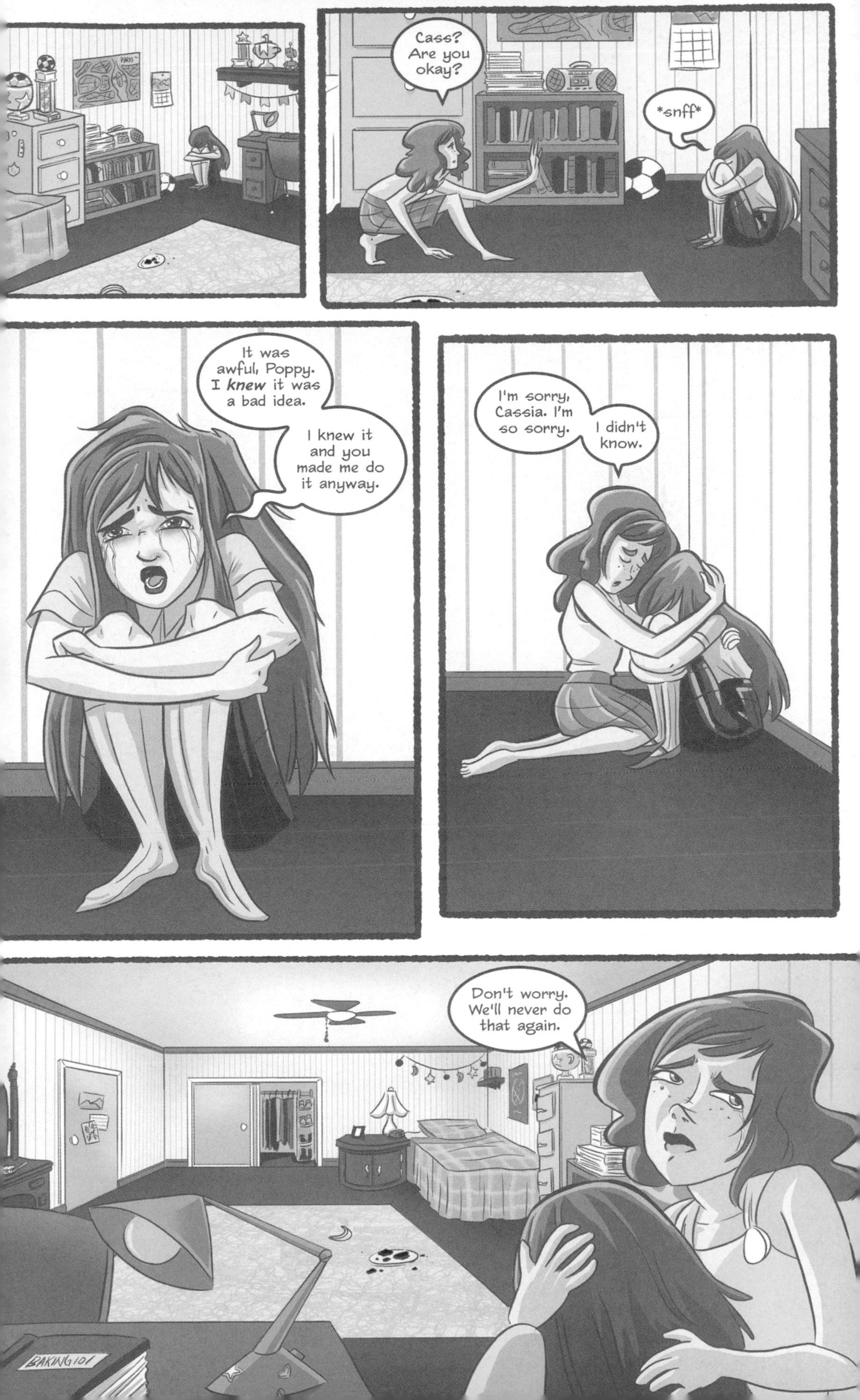
Cass? Are you okay?
*snff*
It was awful, Poppy. I **knew** it was a bad idea.
I knew it and you made me do it anyway.
I'm sorry, Cassia. I'm so sorry.
I didn't know.
Don't worry. We'll never do that again.
BAKING 101

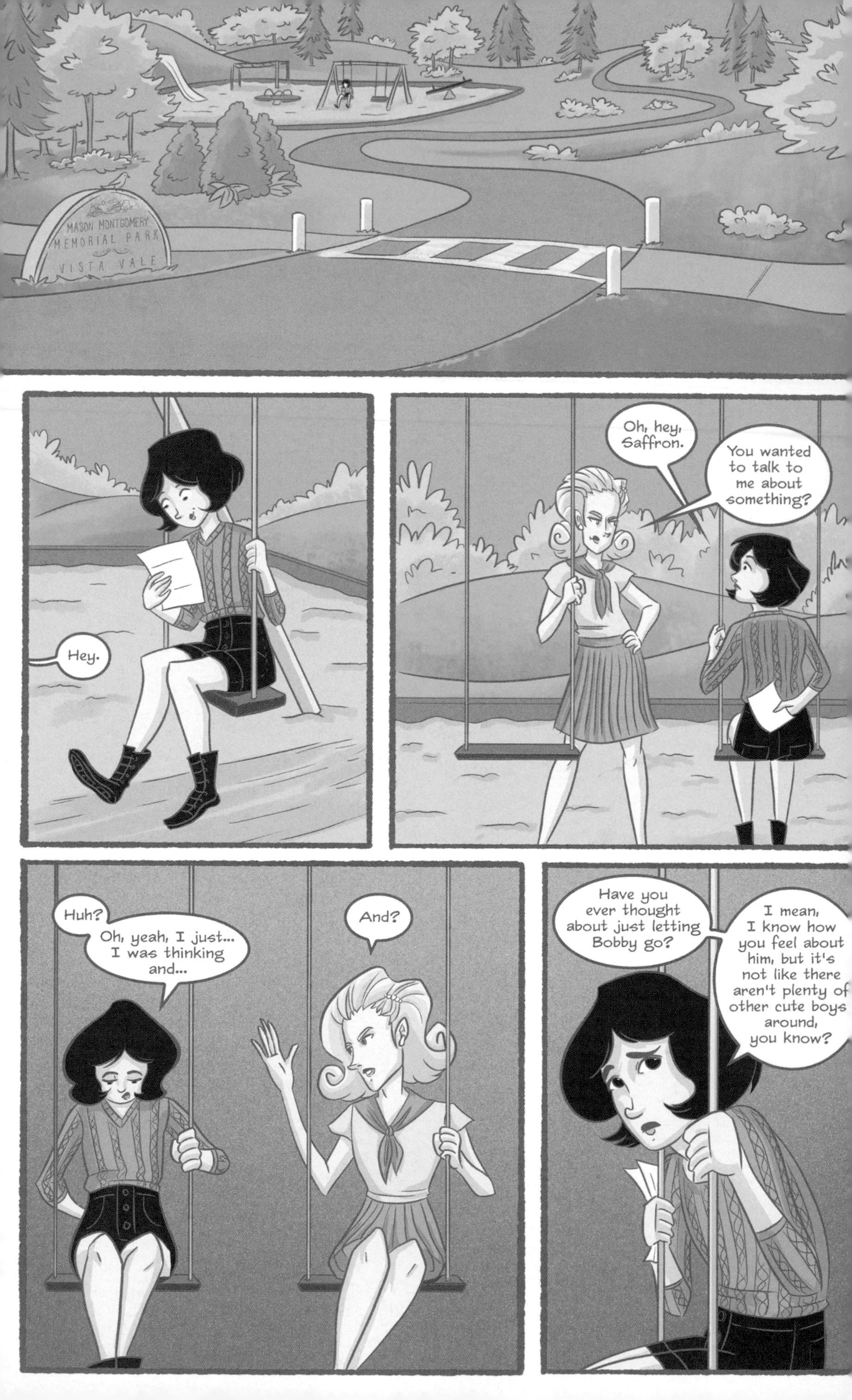
MASON MONTGOMERY
MEMORIAL PARK
VISTA VALE
Hey.
Oh, hey, Saffron.
You wanted to talk to me about something?
Huh?
Oh, yeah, I just... I was thinking and...
And?
Have you ever thought about just letting Bobby go?
I mean, I know how you feel about him, but it's not like there aren't plenty of other cute boys around, you know?

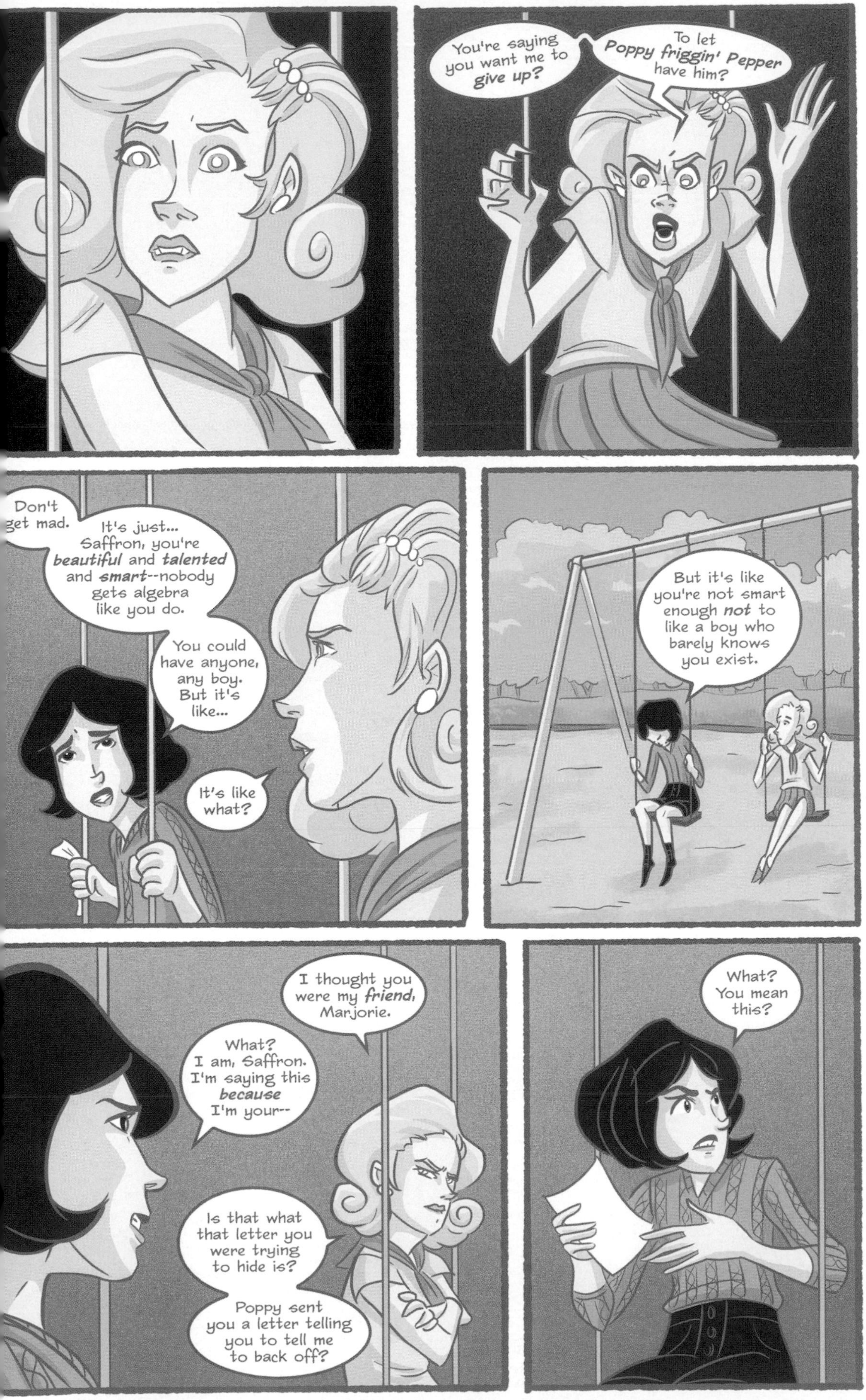

You're saying you want me to give up?
To let Poppy friggin' Pepper have him?
Don't get mad.
It's just... Saffron, you're beautiful and talented and smart--nobody gets algebra like you do.
You could have anyone, any boy. But it's like...
It's like what?
But it's like you're not smart enough not to like a boy who barely knows you exist.
I thought you were my friend, Marjorie.
What? I am, Saffron. I'm saying this because I'm your--
Is that what that letter you were trying to hide is?
Poppy sent you a letter telling you to tell me to back off?
What? You mean this?

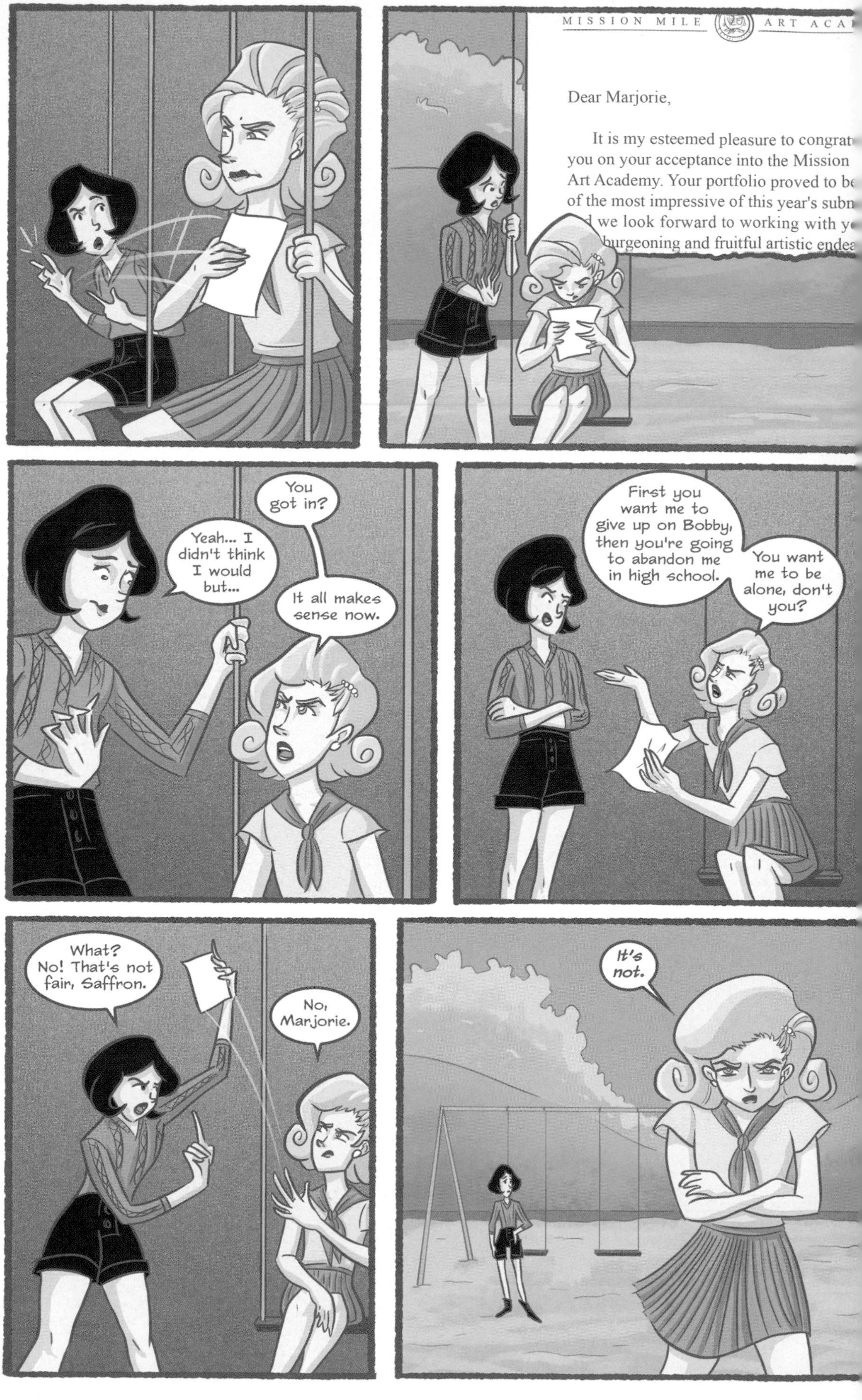
MISSION MILE ART ACA
Dear Marjorie,
It is my esteemed pleasure to congrat
you on your acceptance into the Mission
Art Academy. Your portfolio proved to be
of the most impressive of this year's subm
d we look forward to working with y
burgeoning and fruitful artistic endea
You got in?
Yeah... I didn't think I would but...
It all makes sense now.
First you want me to give up on Bobby, then you're going to abandon me in high school.
You want me to be alone, don't you?
What? No! That's not fair, Saffron.
No, Marjorie.
It's not.

Vista Vale.

The Stark Household.

What are you two doing, anyway?

It's a recap, Mom.

It's been a week since the Brownie Brawl kicked off, Mrs. Stark, so we're reviewing the work we've done in the meantime.

Your cases, you mean?

Yup. There was Cody McClanahan who was caught jaywalking.

Twice.

McCLANAHAN, COD
JAYWALKIN
092514

Then there was serial litterer Richard Jacobs.

He wanted the streets as dirty as his conscious.

JACOBS, RIC
TTERER

Last, but not least? Ms. Riley.

White shoes. *After* Labor Day.

MRS. RILEY
HITE SHOE

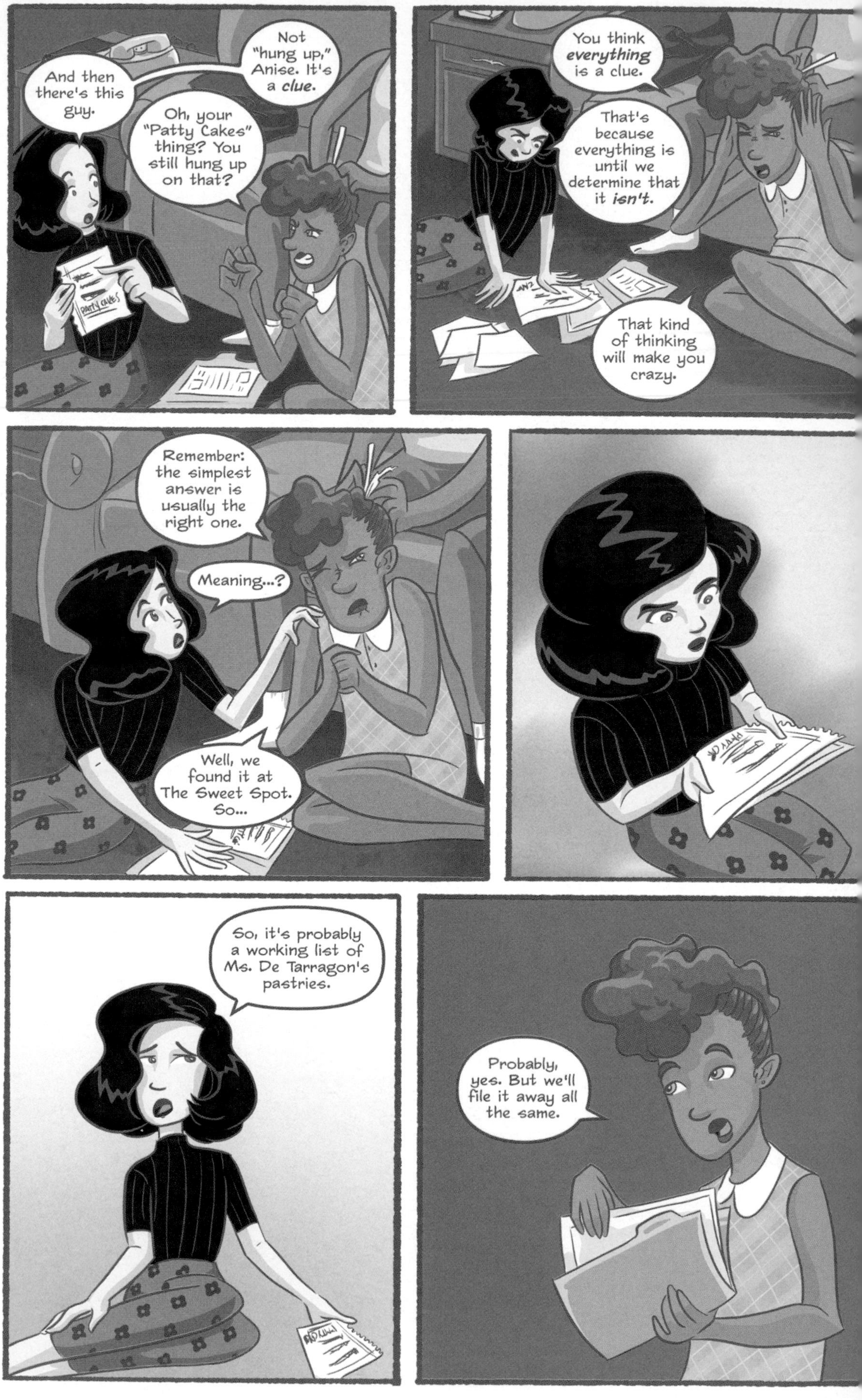
And then there's this guy.
Oh, your "Patty Cakes" thing? You still hung up on that?
Not "hung up," Anise. It's a *clue.*
You think *everything* is a clue.
That's because everything is until we determine that it *isn't.*
That kind of thinking will make you crazy.
Remember: the simplest answer is usually the right one.
Meaning...?
Well, we found it at The Sweet Spot. So...
So, it's probably a working list of Ms. De Tarragon's pastries.
Probably, yes. But we'll file it away all the same.

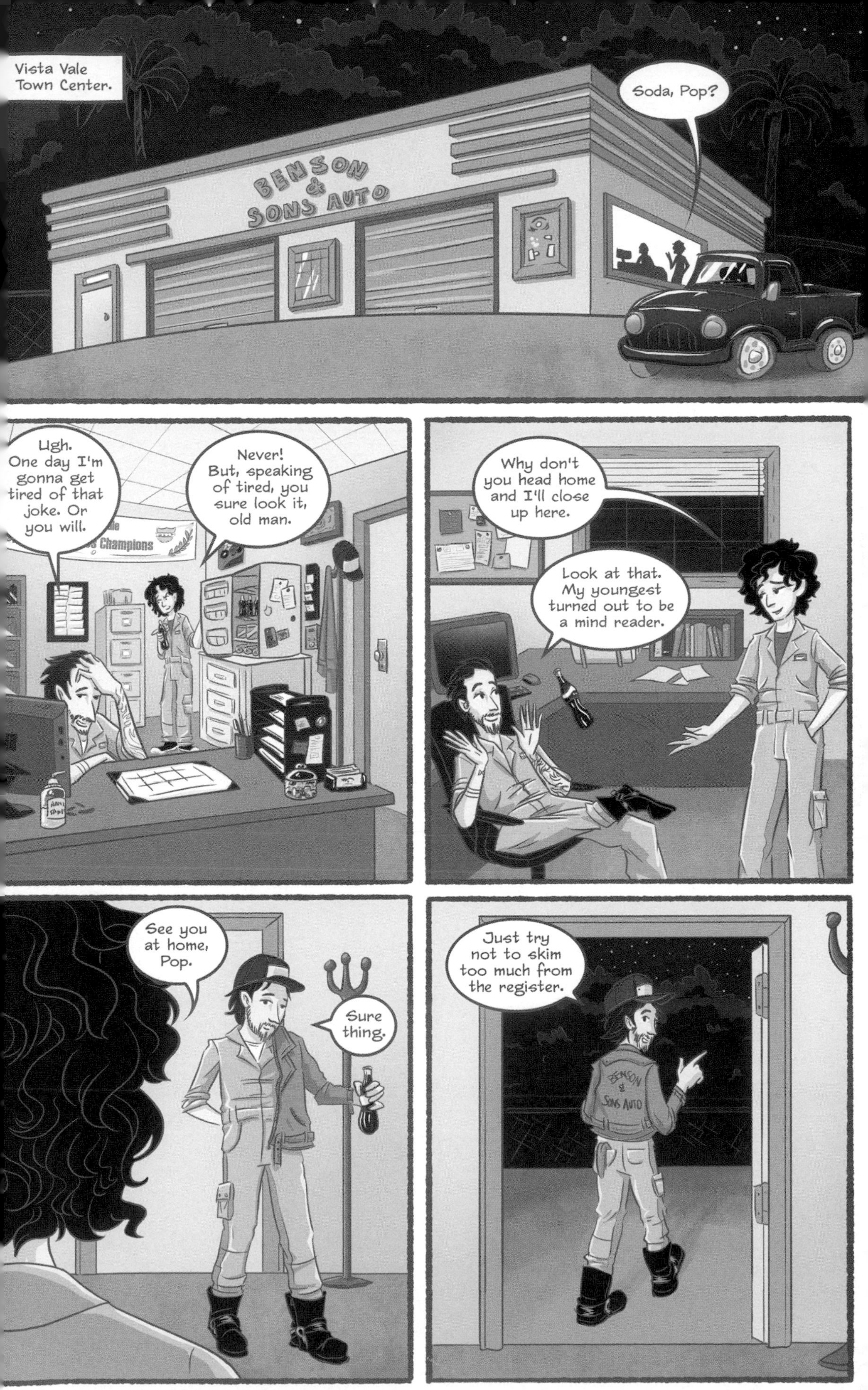
Vista Vale Town Center.
BENSON & SONS AUTO
Soda, Pop?
Ugh. One day I'm gonna get tired of that joke. Or you will.
Never! But, speaking of tired, you sure look it, old man.
Why don't you head home and I'll close up here.
Look at that. My youngest turned out to be a mind reader.
See you at home, Pop.
Sure thing.
Just try not to skim too much from the register.
BENSON & SONS AUTO

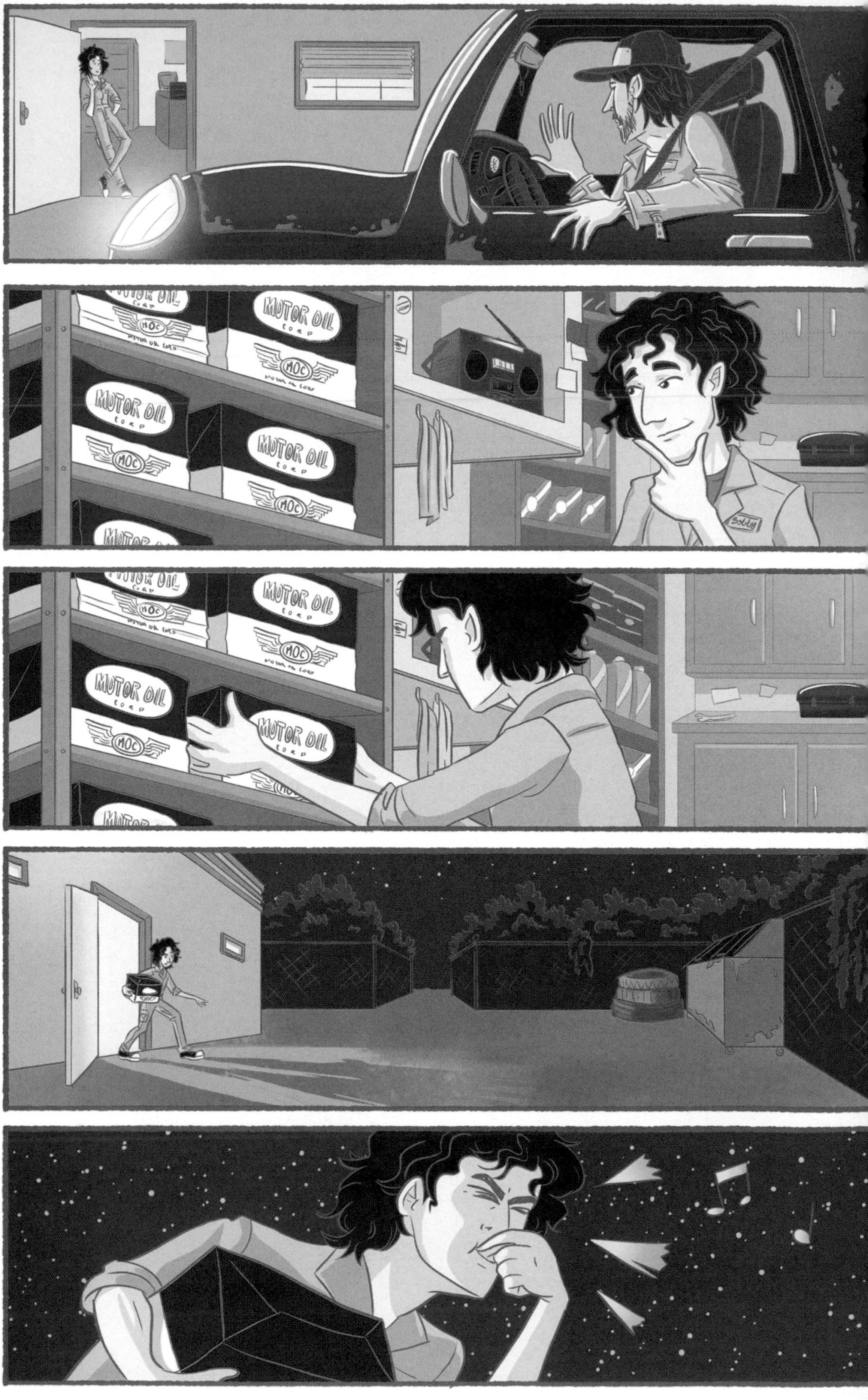
MOTOR OIL
CORP
MOC

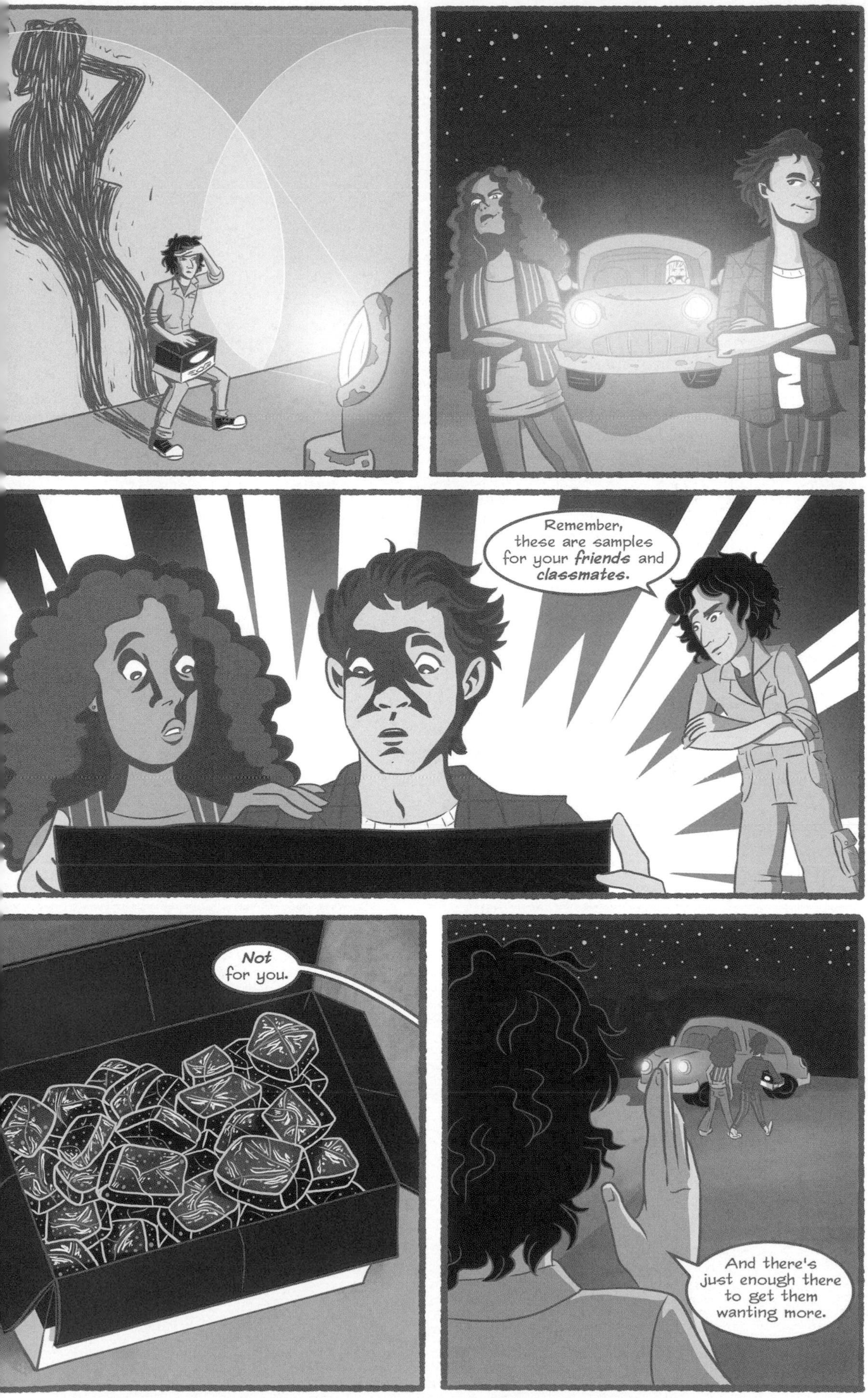
Remember, these are samples for your *friends* and *classmates.*
*Not* for you.
And there's just enough there to get them wanting more.

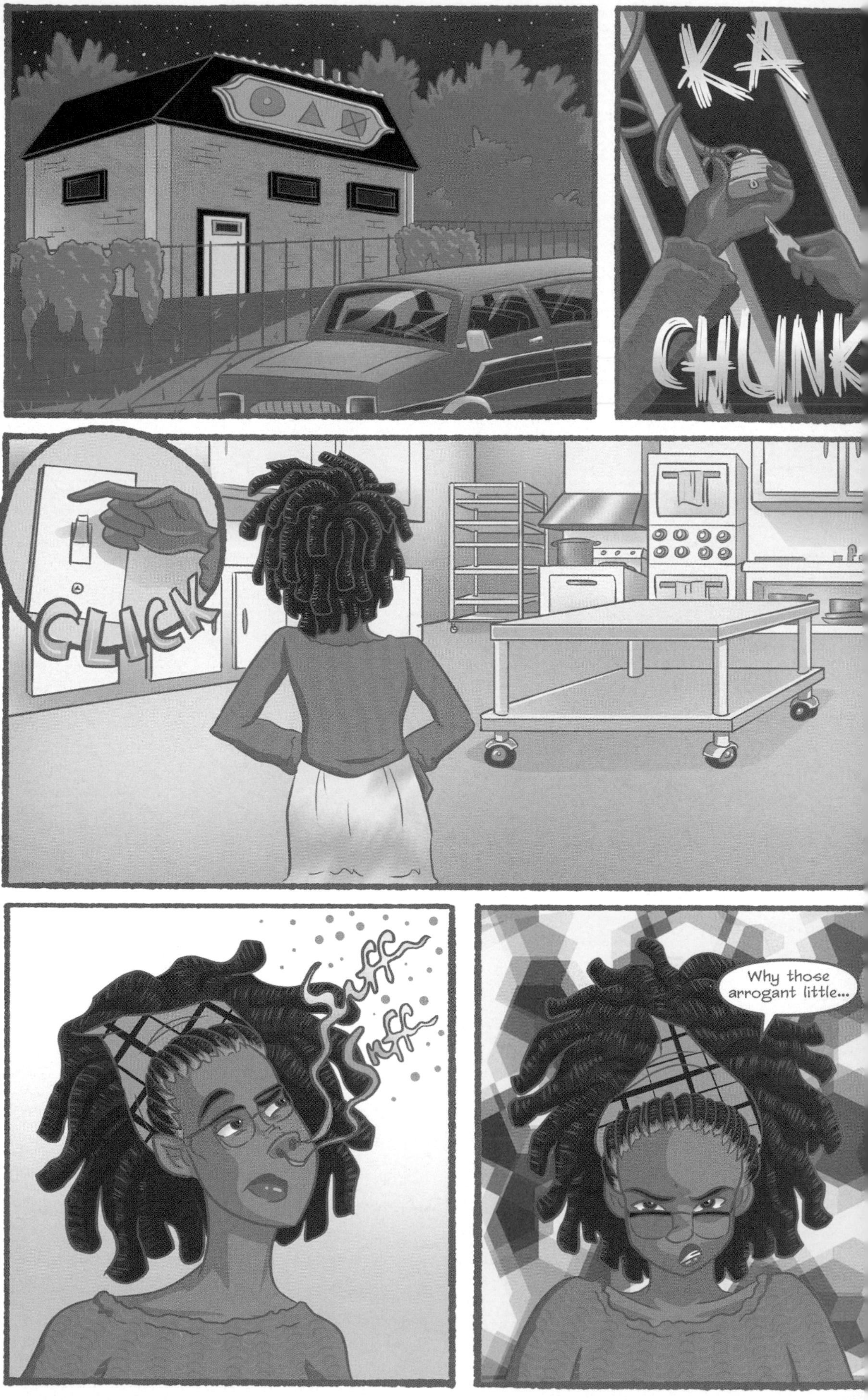
KA
CHUNK
CLICK
Snff
Snff
Why those arrogant little...

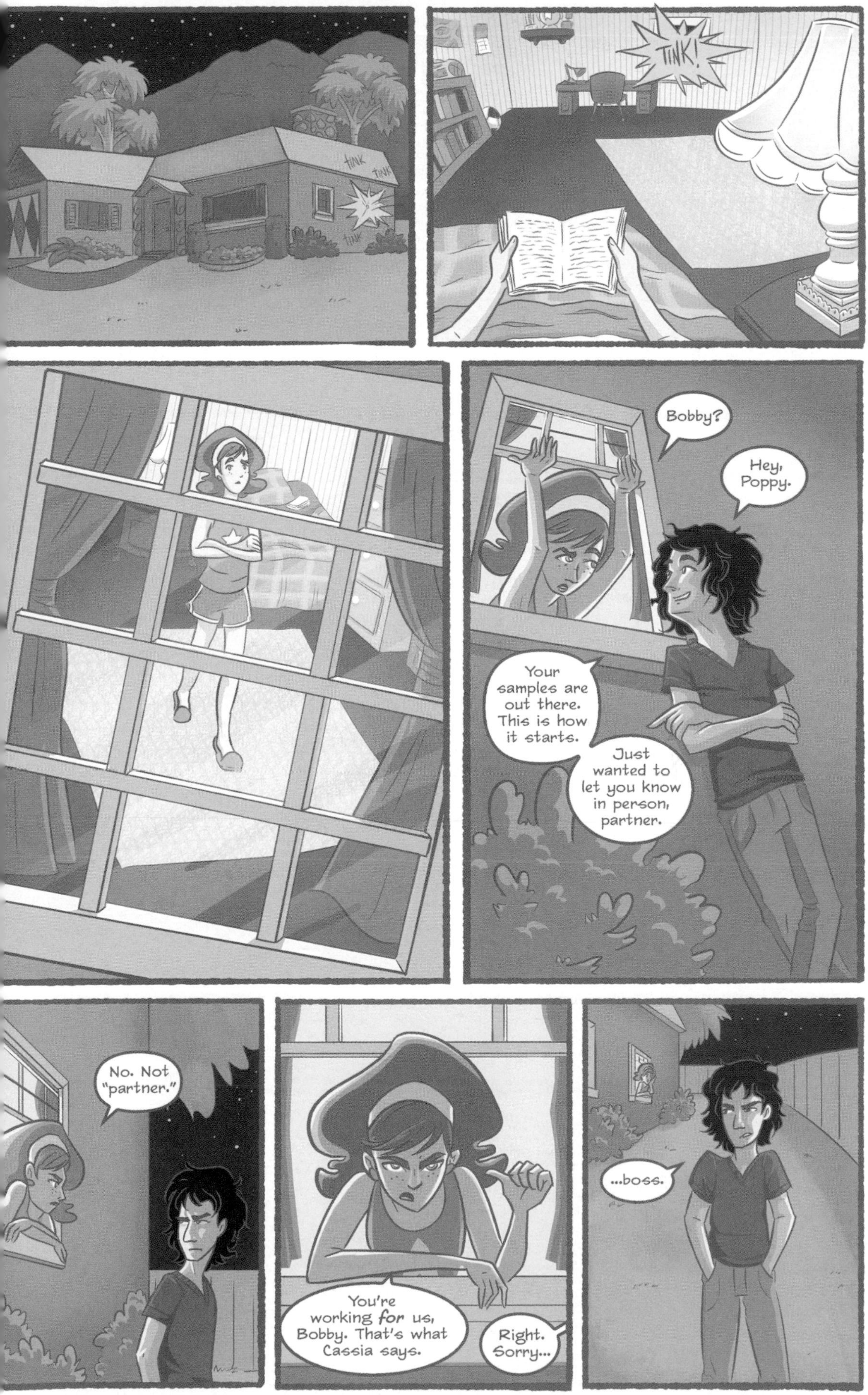
TINK
TINK
TINK
TINK!
Bobby?
Hey, Poppy.
Your samples are out there. This is how it starts.
Just wanted to let you know in person, partner.
No. Not "partner."
You're working *for* us, Bobby. That's what Cassia says.
Right. Sorry...
...boss.

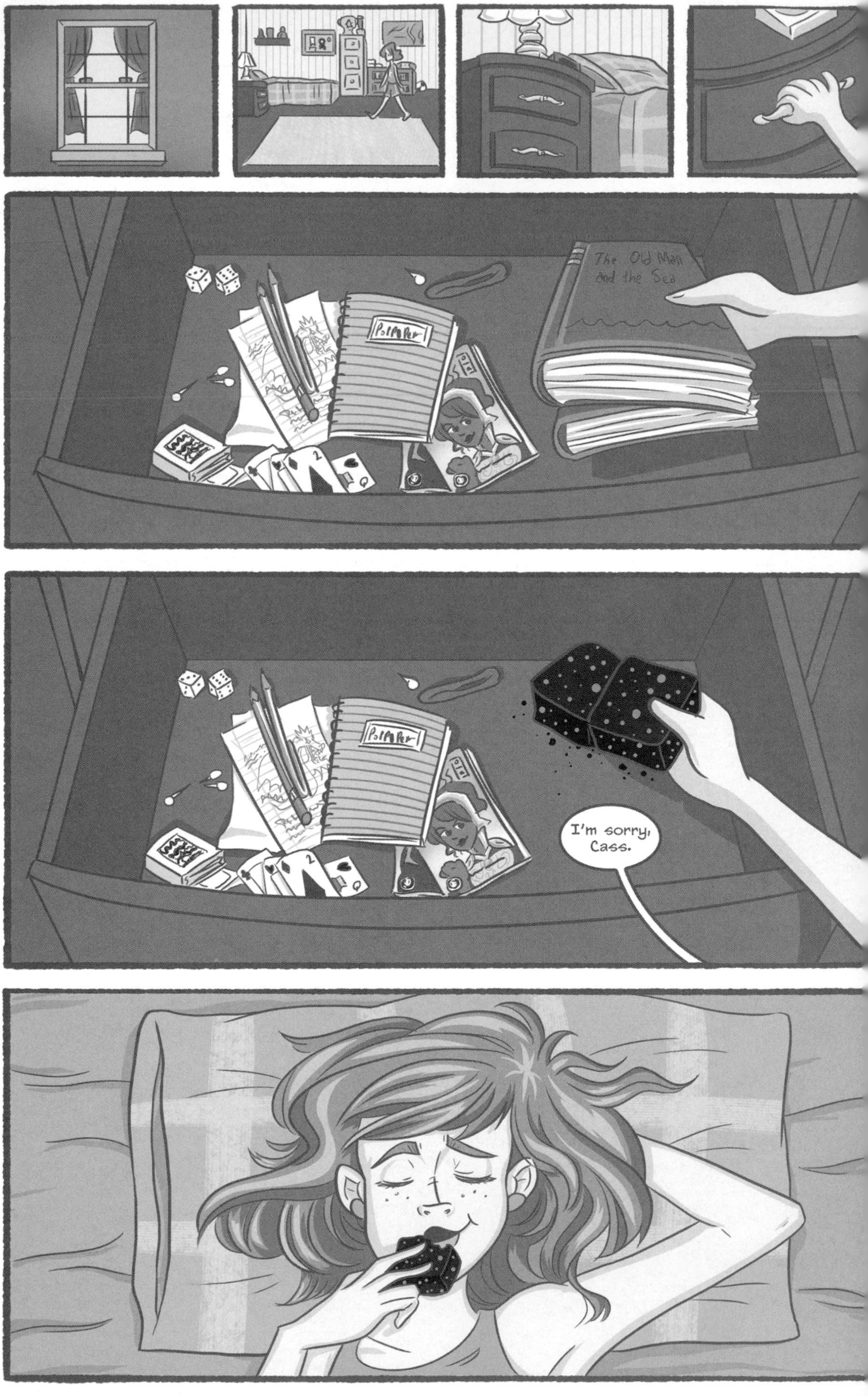
The Old Man and the Sea
I'm sorry, Cass.

# THE COOLING RACK

CONTACT: @NUTMEGCOMIC · NUTMEGCOMICS@GMAIL.COM

-ute Nutmeg readers may have noticed a new name on the cover of this issue, and that is not a typo. We incredibly fortunate to be joined on the book by our good friend—and new colorist/letterer—Josh Eckert! was a classmate of Jackie's at IUPUI, and worked with James on a few comics projects in the past, and ong other things he's currently self-publishing his all-ages series, Son of Bigfoot. In addition to his talent and e, he's also the reason Nutmeg exists, because he introduced Jackie to James after James pitched his idea a teen crime series way back in 2012. Having him on the book not only kicks things up a notch and gives kie a break, it also brings everything full circle. We only hope you like the work he's doing as much as we do!

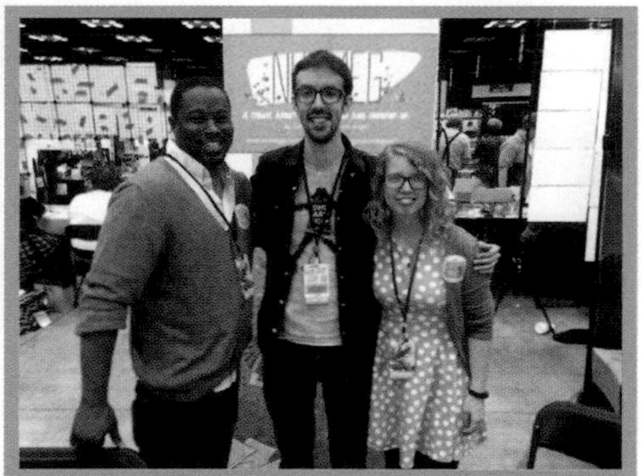

James, Josh & Jackie at Indy Pop Con 2015

**What is your comics background?**

Like so many of us, I used to draw comics as a kid, but didn't start *really* making them until about 2011 when James and I started a webcomic from a project of ours called *The Geek Zodiac* (geekzodiac.com). It was an anthology of short stories that allowed us to play in different genres (horror, action, fantasy, etc.) so not only was it a lot of fun, but I learned so many crucial things about how to make comics.

**How did you learn about Nutmeg?**

James is a geyser of great story ideas and I've been incredibly lucky to have him as a close (yet long-distance) friend who's excited to share them with me. *Nutmeg* was just another one of those amazing ideas floating around in James's head until we took notice of my friend Jackie's beautiful work and thought she would be the perfect artist to bring the story to life. She was just as excited to make it happen and, well, you need only turn the pages in this book to see how amazing that turned out.

**What made you want to work on Nutmeg?**

I know firsthand what an immense undertaking it is to draw, color and letter an entire comic, and it meant a lot to me that my friends' first published comic hit the stands without delay, so I offered to jump in and help carry the weight if needed. Now I'm so psyched to be working alongside these two and getting a front row seat to *Nutmeg*'s creation.

**Any particular books or creators in comics who've influenced you?**

Offhand I'd say Mike Mignola, Fiona Staples, and David Lapham have been influencing me a lot lately. I'm also in the middle of reading the classic 1980's manga *Lone Wolf and Cub* by Kazuo Koike and Hideki Mori. Every single issue is stunning - a master class in pacing, panel composition and dramatic storytelling.

**Aside from Nutmeg, what other comics projects are you working on?**

I'm self-publishing a comic called *Son of Bigfoot* with my buddy, Kevin Olvera. It's about a young sasquatch that runs away from his tribe to discover the truth about his legendary outlaw parents. Right now we have two issues available in print and digital at sonofbigfootcomic.com and we're working on the third issue. On top of that, I've got a crime miniseries in the works, because why not, right? Doing all this with a full-time job and a family at home isn't that crazy, is it? ...Is it?

#FIMC (Forget It, Make Comics)
Twitter: @josheck11

It's another month of Nutmeg and that means another recipe for you to try. This one is a vegan dessert and comes all the way from across the pond in Sheffield, UK courtesy of our lovely and wonderful friend John Hunter and his wife, Heather Fenoughty. Thank you both for sharing this with us!

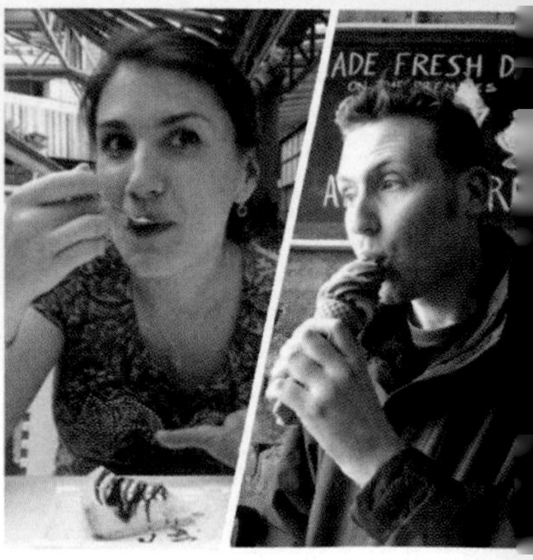

# VEGAN RAW CHOCOLATE ICE CREAM TORTE

Inspired by http://freakinhealthy.blogspot.co.uk/

## FOR THE CRUST

- 1 cup almonds
- 1/2 cup cacoa powder or cocoa nibs (everyday cocoa or carob powder may be substituted)
- 16 dried, pitted dates
- 1 teaspoon vanilla extract
- pinch of sea or pink salt

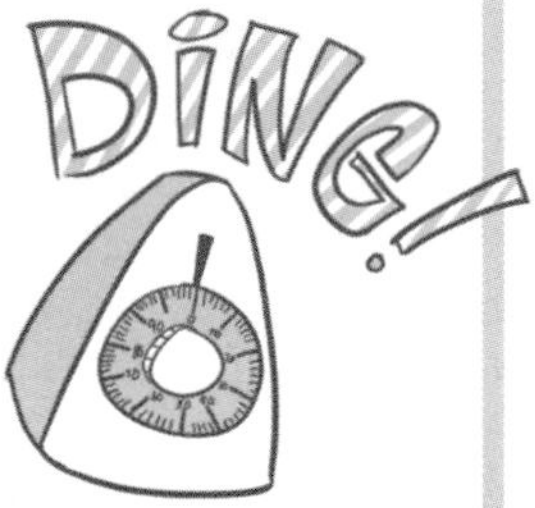
DiNG!

## FOR THE FILLING

- 2 cups cashews
- 3/4 cup cacao powder (or cocoa or 1/2 cup carob powder)
- Scant 1/2 cup unrefined cane sugar, coconut sugar, sweet freedom or agave syrup
- 1/2 cup coconut oil, melted
- 1/2 cup water
- 2 teaspoons vanilla extract
- Optional: 1 teaspoon orange extract, half teaspoon chilli powder

## INSTRUCTIONS

1. Soak cashews in cold water overnight for 8 hours, or in warm water for twenty minutes. Rinse and drain well
2. Blend all the crust ingredients in a food processor until combined; it should still be crumbly and just start to stick together. Add a teaspoon of water if it isn't coming together after 7 or 8 minutes, but do give it chance til then. You want the crust to stay as dry as possible, not too moist or chewy.
3. Press into the base of an 8- or 9- inch springform or loose-bottomed cake tin, and chill in the refrigerator
4. For the filling, melt the coconut oil if it isn't already liquid.
5. Puree the cashews, unrefined sugar or vegan sweetener of choice, vanilla extract and water until smooth, using a high-powered or immersion blender. Optionally, add the orange extract and chilli powder for a bit more oomf.
6. Add the cacao powder and coconut oil. Blend again until completely combined and completely smooth. You may need to stop and scrape down the sides of the jug or bowl every now and again.
7. Pour onto the crust in the tin and smooth over with a spatula (if you like, reserve a small amount of the mixture before adding the cocoa powder - now is the time to get creative with swirly patterns!). Sprinkle on a few cocoa nibs too, if you've any left over from the base.
8. Freeze for one hour minimum. For a proper 'ice cream' effect, freeze overnight.
9. Carefully remove from the tin and serve immediately, or for a slightly softer, more ganache effect, allow to sit at room temperature for10 minutes or so before serving.

# IN "BROAD" DAYLIGHT

by James F. Wright

illustration by Josh Eckert

By now you've probably heard about Broad City, Comedy Central's phenomenon starring real-life friends Abbi Jacobson and Ilana Glazer. As of this writing it's got two seasons under its belt, with a third guaranteed. It's the show that launched a thousand thinkpieces--or at least a hundred. So, what's one more?

I stumbled upon the show via a veritable deluge of gifs on Tumblr in 2014 and had no idea what it was about, but once I caught up I saw why it's so beloved. Though recent years have seen plenty more of it, it's still unfortunately rare to find entertainments starring or featuring women, particularly those focusing on female friendships. Rarer still are those in which these women traffic in the tropes familiar to dude/bro/stoner comedies--from Cheech & Chong to Dumb & Dumber to the multiple filmic pairings of Seth Rogen and James Franco. Broad City's Abbi and Ilana are raunchy and dumb and gross and funny and honest, often in the same scene.

The plots, such as they are, of each episode are wonderfully simplistic and sometimes misleading. In "Working Girls," Abbi misses the delivery of a package she told her neighbor she'd pick up for him. In "Last Supper," Ilana takes Abbi out to a fancy restaurant for her birthday. On paper there's not much going on, but so much of the joy of this show is how these events unfold, and how Abbi and Ilana deal with these situations. It's equal parts verbal quips, absurdist humor, and physical comedy. It's ego (Abbi) hanging out with id (Ilana), and the friendship between self-conscious Abbi and devil-may-care Ilana feels true.

In a wider sense, it also uses humor to tap into that feeling of being young in a big city and having no idea what to do with your life, yet still seeking to live on one's own terms. Abbi, an artist, makes ends meet working a dead-end job as a cleaner at a hip, swanky gym. Ilana "works" at a GroupOn-like company, but spends most of her time scheming and scamming for extra cash. And while these two are the focus of the show, the other characters they meet in their adventures—Ilana's on-again, off-again dentist boyfriend, Lincoln (Hannibal Burress); Abbi's roommate's boyfriend, Matty Bevers (John Gemberling); a host of one-off guest stars (Rachel Dratch, Amy Poehler, Seth Rogen)—are similarly trying to figure things out and how they fit in with their fellow city dwellers.

At 10 episodes, Broad City's first two seasons feel breezy enough to marathon them in a single, lazy weekend, but with enough depth to want to revisit them as soon as they're over. Abbi and Ilana are entertaining on their own, and in their own worlds, and even more so when they team up. As my friend Lisa so aptly put it when I watched it with her and her fiancé, "I want a friendship like that." We're so often shown ostensible friendships between women that are competitive or petty, yet Broad City is refreshing by showing us one built on love, support, and respect. It's not that the two leads don't fight, it's more that when it happens it's resolved quickly, and nothing's ever said that can't be taken back.

Even though Broad City is tonally, structurally, and pretty-much-every-other-way-ly different from Nutmeg, I was drawn to it because both feature interesting examinations of friendships between young women. As a guy writing a series starring an all-girl cast, I'm going to get a lot of things wrong--and I know that I already have--but seeing how Broad City approaches it with humor and aplomb has proved enlightening for me. I hope I'm able to bring some of that same verve to our book.

(Broad City airs on Comedy Central. The first season is available on DVD. It is definitely NSFW.)

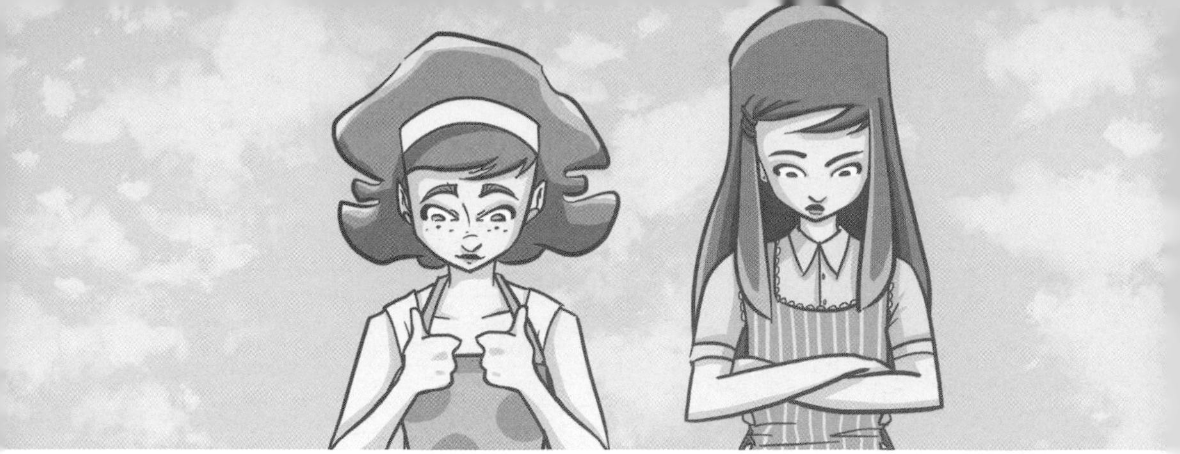

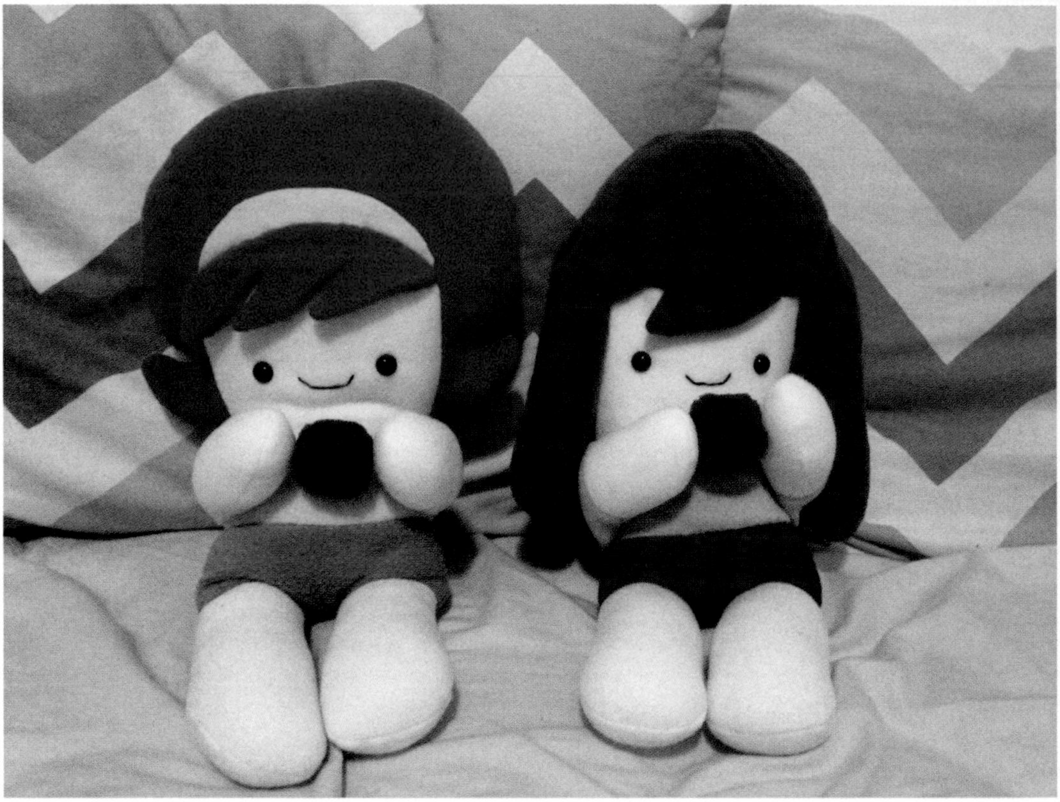

# POPPY AND CASSIA PLUSHIES

In 2014, when we started doing our first convention appearances with Nutmeg, we thought a lot about our table setup, wanting something bright and inviting but not overwhelming. Jackie did most of the heavy lifting: designing our front and standing banners, picking out the pastel color scheme of the bowls and receptacles, and even sewing our tablecloth. But something was missing.

At Emerald City Comicon this year we met @iamuhura who suggested we check out the fantastic and friendly Sushi You Can Hug on Etsy (www.etsy.com/shop/Cornstarch). Next thing we knew, we had the two plushies of resident Nutmeg criminal masterminds Poppy and Cassia, each holding a special Patty Cake brownie of her own. Not only do these add a fun element to our table, they just look and feel fantastic. We call them "the babies." You should come meet them at one of our shows!

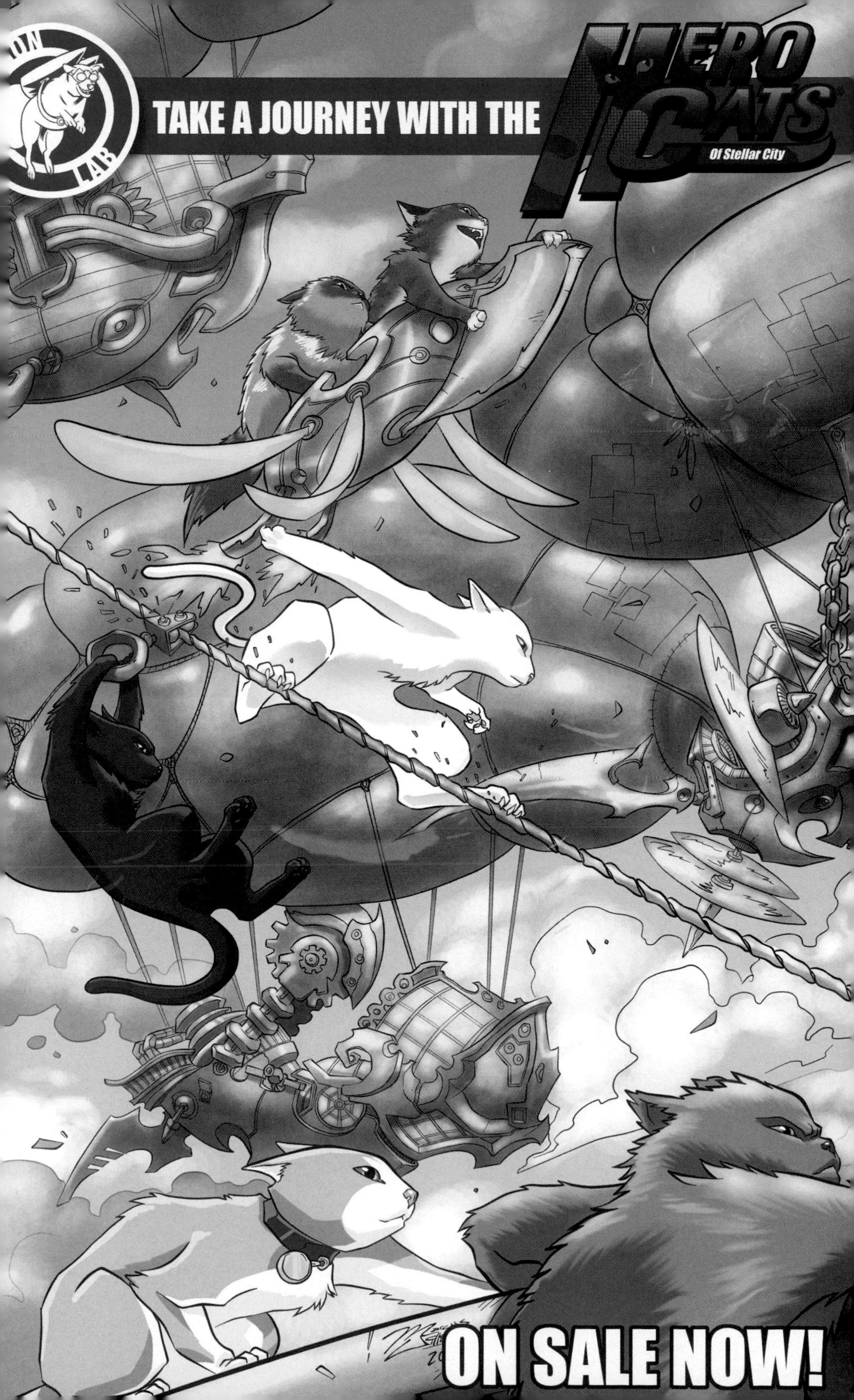

TAKE A JOURNEY WITH THE
HERO CATS
Of Stellar City
ON SALE NOW!

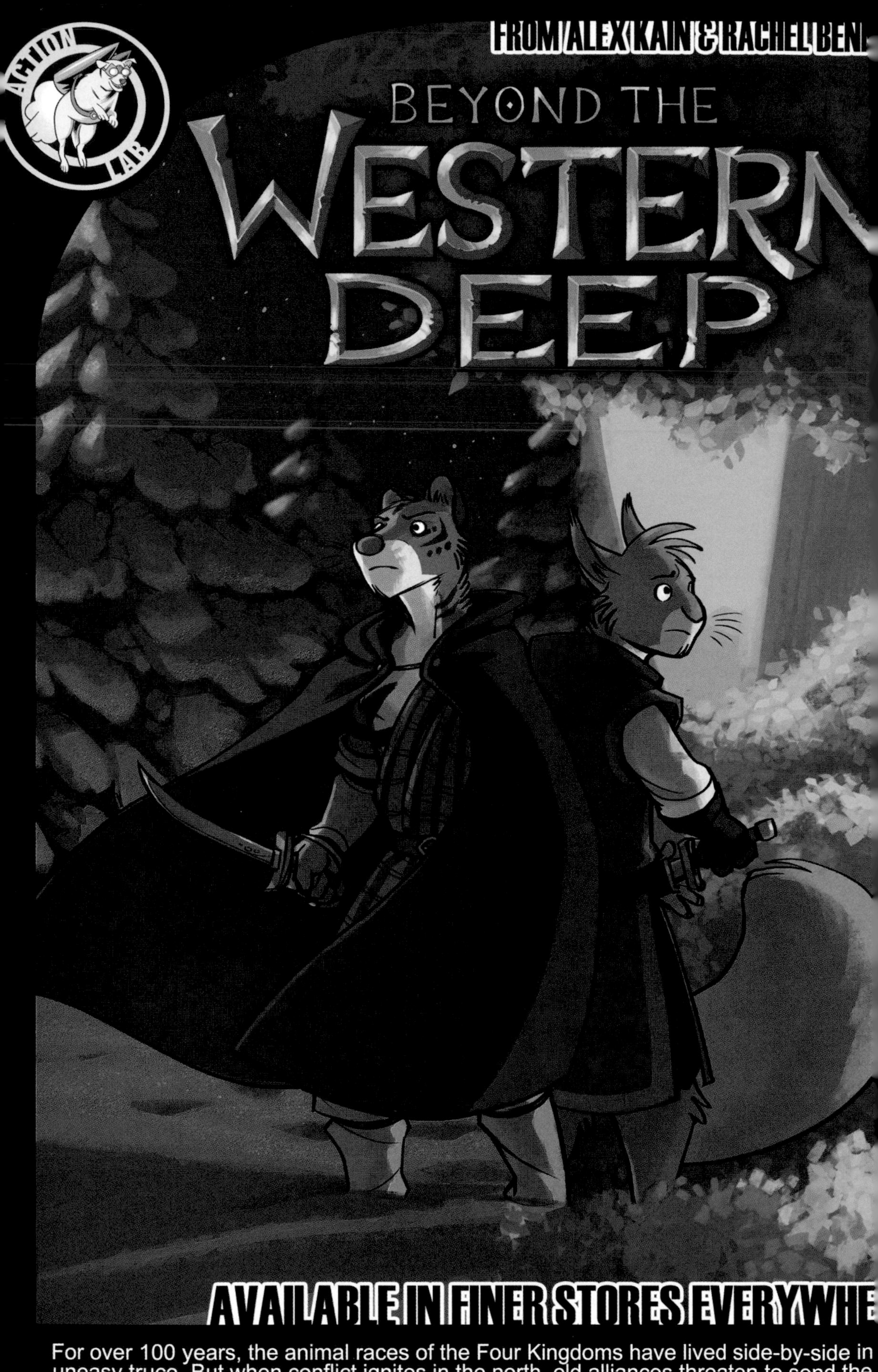

ACTION LAB
FROM ALEX KAIN & RACHEL BEN
BEYOND THE
WESTERN
DEEP
AVAILABLE IN FINER STORES EVERYWHE

Las Vegas, 1981. Gareth Thompson, a Vietnam veteran and single father, has just
accepted a security job at the new fantasy-themed "Archon Hotel and Casino." However,
he'll soon discover all the Orcs, Elves and Dragons at the Resort are not people in
costumes, but actual creatures of myth and legend.

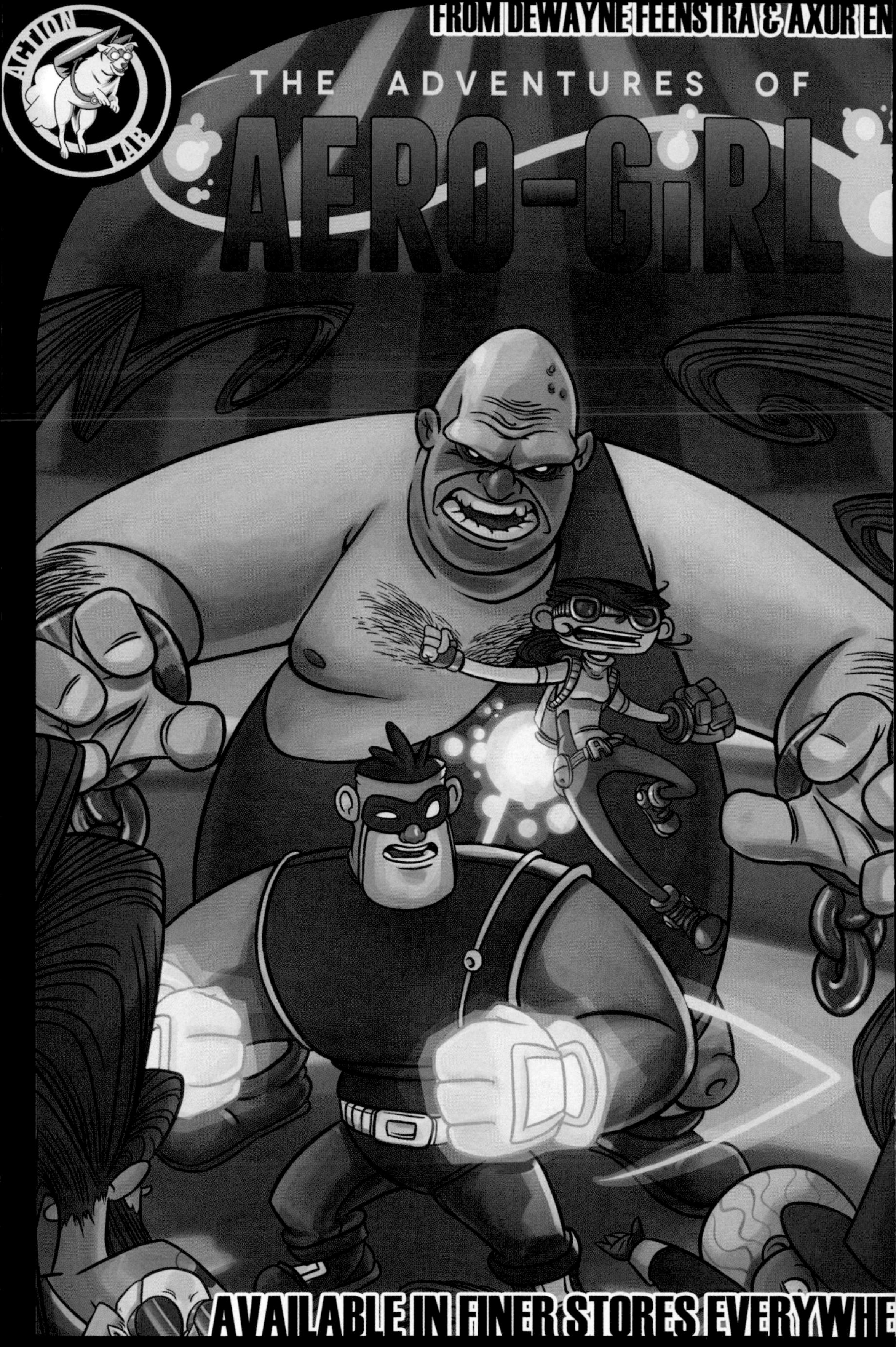
ACTION LAB
FROM DEWAYNE FEENSTRA & AXUR EN
THE ADVENTURES OF
AERO-GIRL
AVAILABLE IN FINER STORES EVERYWHE

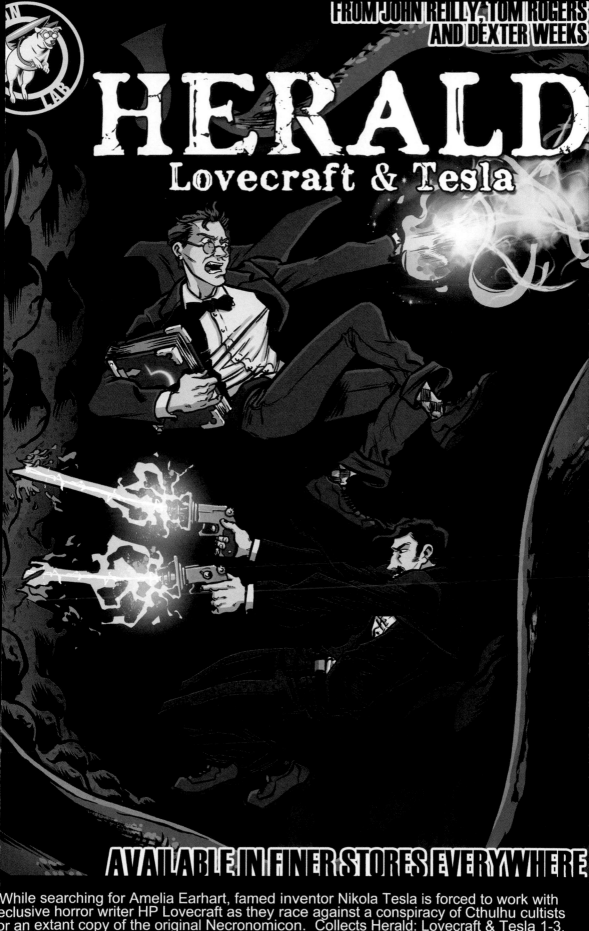

ACTION LAB

READ MORE NOW

Nutmeg - Action Lab
www.actionlabcomics.com
00511
7 02382 69089 2

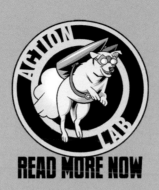

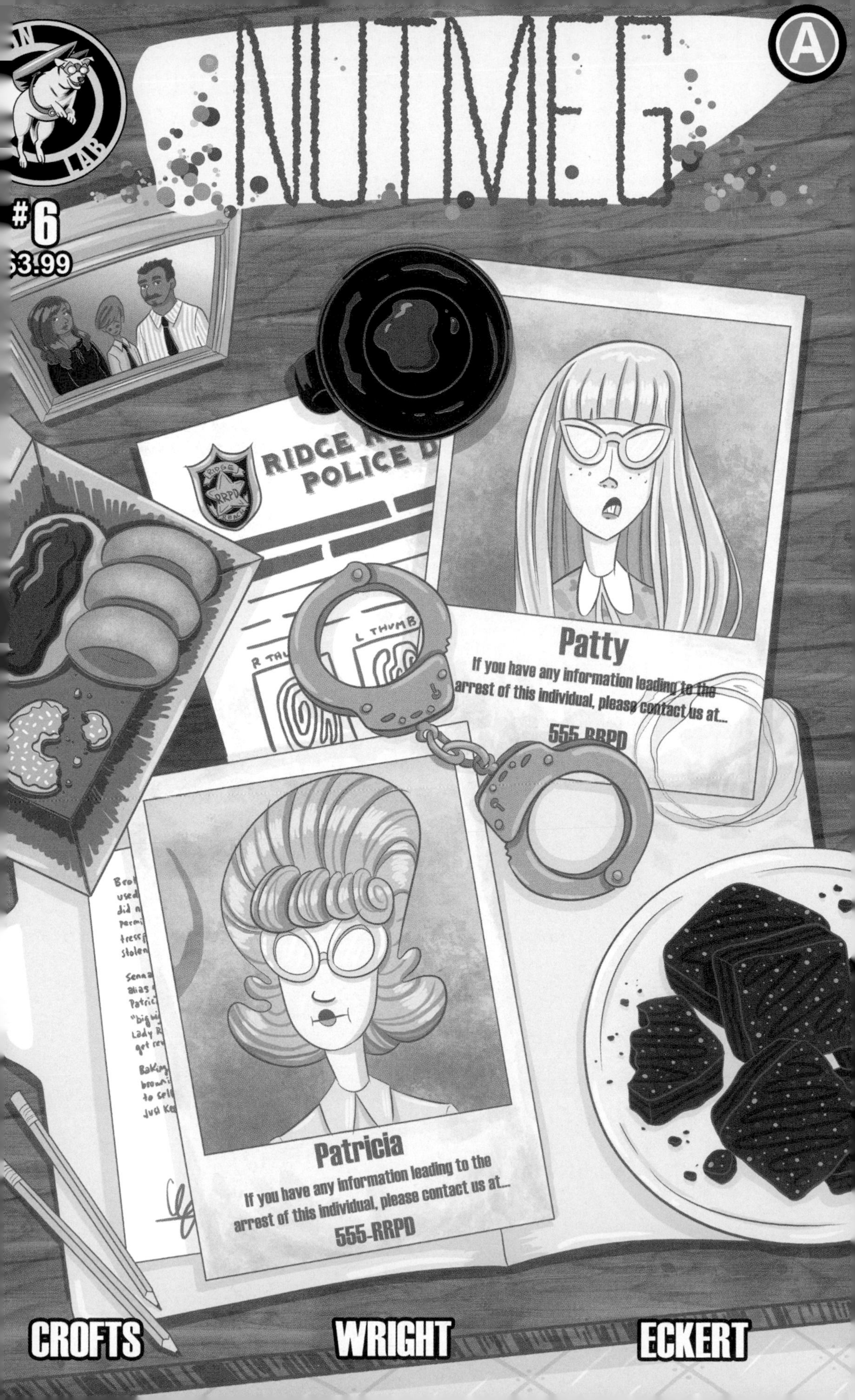
NUTMEG
A
#6
3.99
RIDGE
POLICE
L THUMB
Patty
If you have any information leading to the arrest of this individual, please contact us at...
555 RRPD
Patricia
If you have any information leading to the arrest of this individual, please contact us at...
555-RRPD
CROFTS
WRIGHT
ECKERT

# FROM ALL-AGES TO MATURE READERS
## ACTION LAB HAS YOU COVERED.

 *Appropriate for everyone.*

 *Appropriate for age 9 and up. Absent of profanity or adult content.*

 *Suggested for 12 and Up. Comics with this rating are comparable to a PG-13 movie rating. Recommended for our teen and young adult readers.*

 *Appropriate for older teens. Similar to Teen, but featuring more mature themes and/or more graphic imagery.*

 *Contains extreme viloence and some nudity. Basically the Rated-R of comics.*

 **FIND YOUR NEW FAVORITE COMICS.**

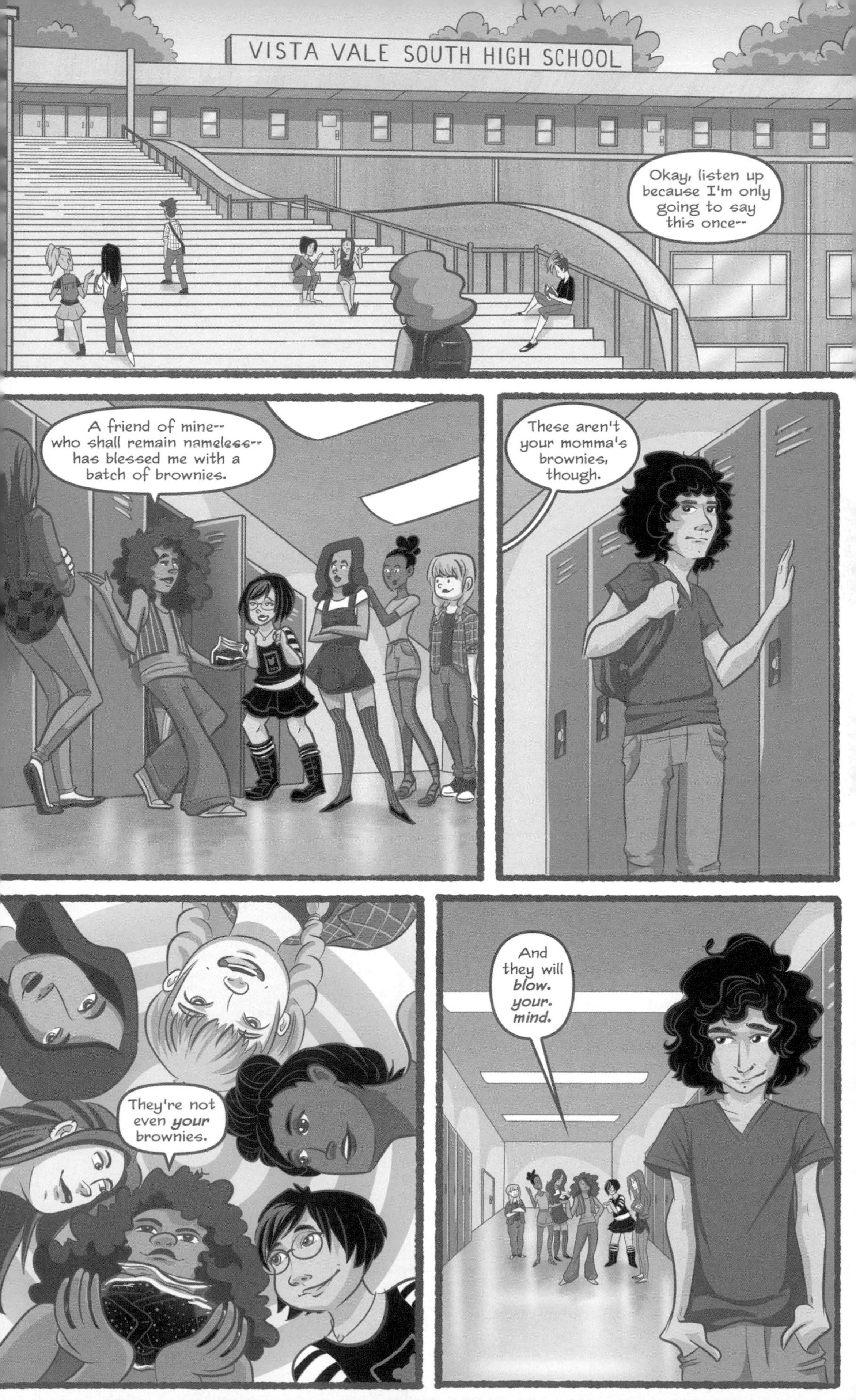
VISTA VALE SOUTH HIGH SCHOOL
Okay, listen up because I'm only going to say this once--
A friend of mine-- who shall remain nameless-- has blessed me with a batch of brownies.
These aren't your momma's brownies, though.
They're not even *your* brownies.
And they will *blow. your. mind.*

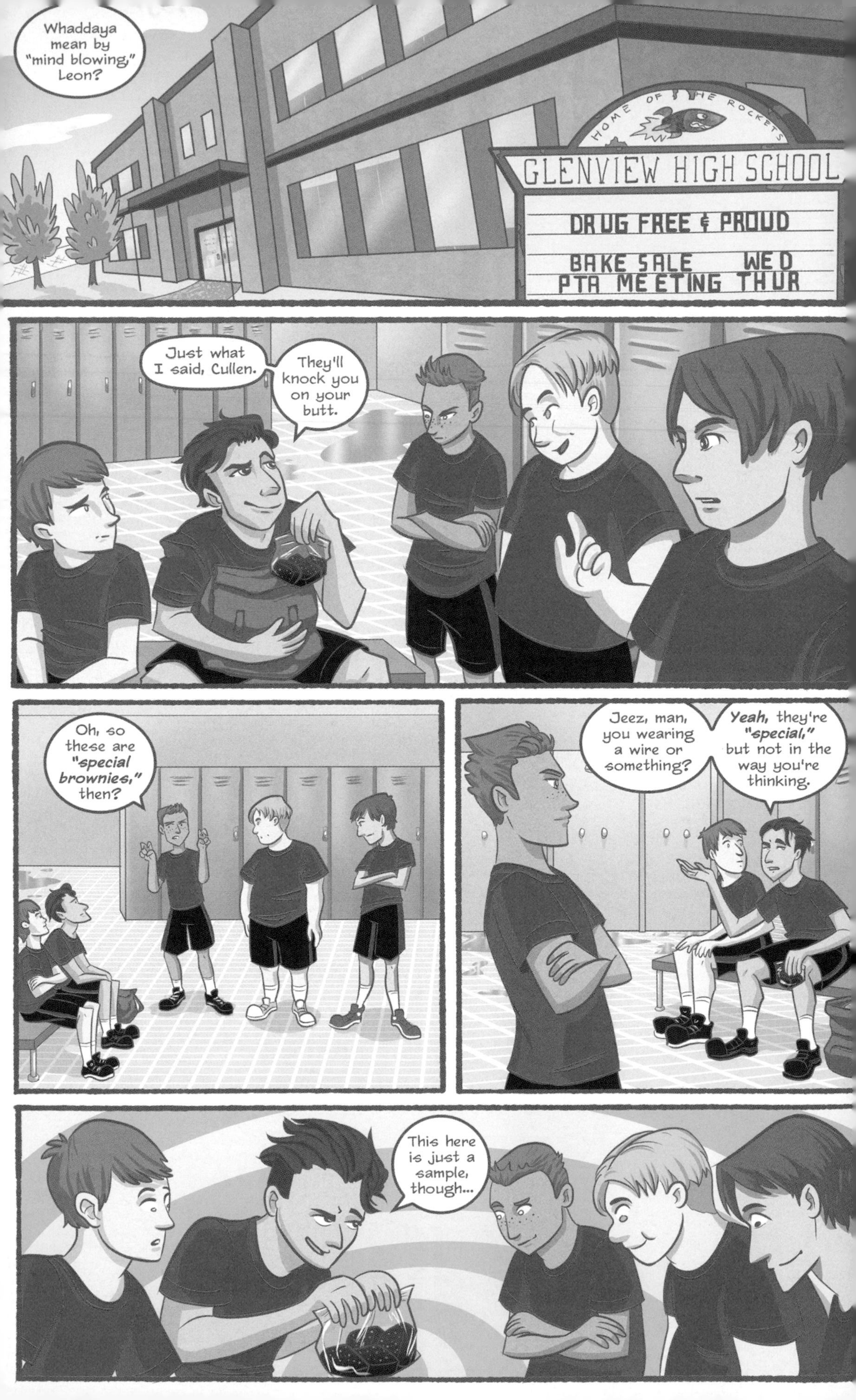
Whaddaya mean by "mind blowing," Leon?
HOME OF THE ROCKETS
GLENVIEW HIGH SCHOOL
DRUG FREE & PROUD
BAKE SALE WED
PTA MEETING THUR
Just what I said, Cullen.
They'll knock you on your butt.
Oh, so these are "special brownies," then?
Jeez, man, you wearing a wire or something?
Yeah, they're "special," but not in the way you're thinking.
This here is just a sample, though...

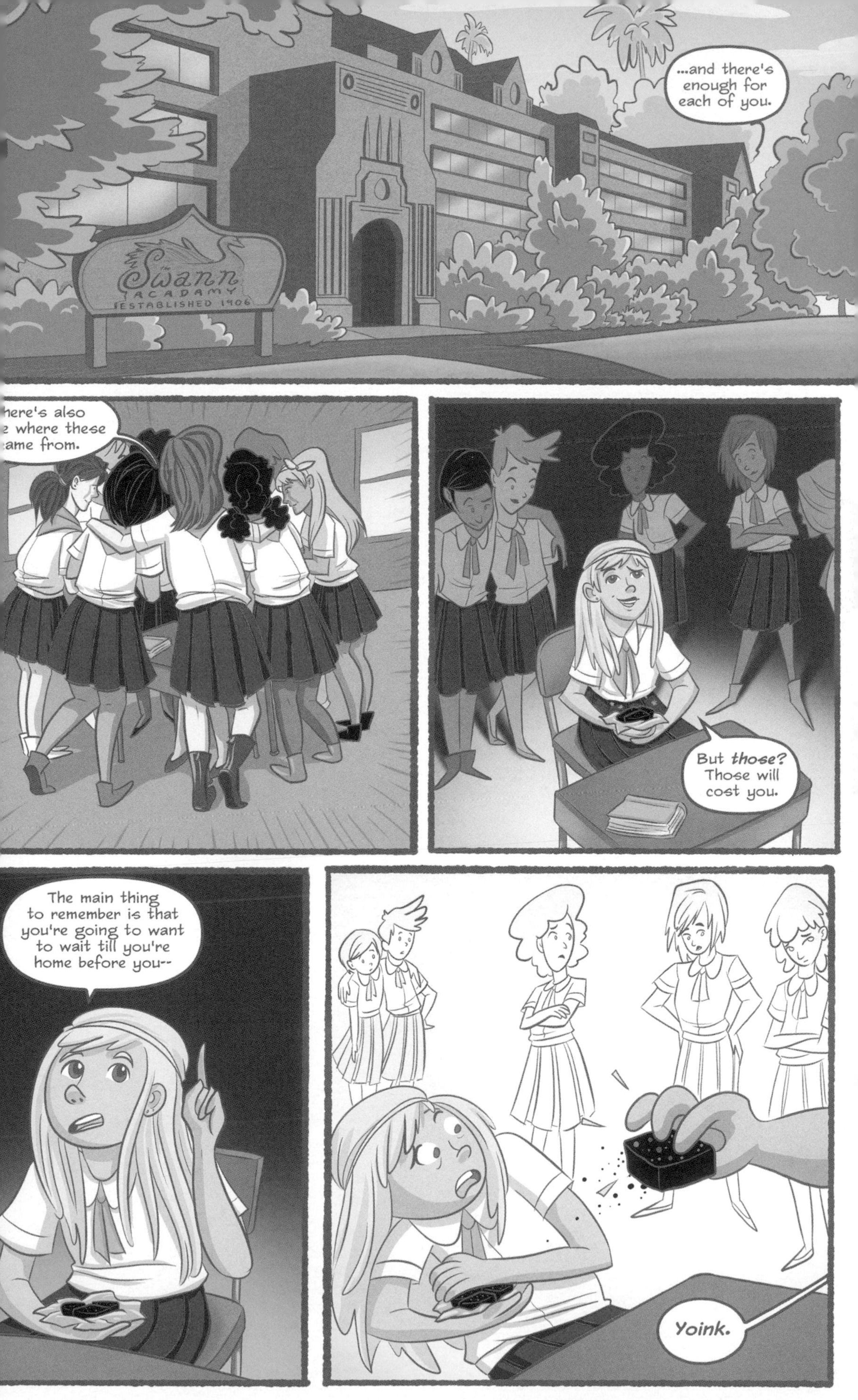
...and there's enough for each of you.
THE Swann ACADAMY ESTABLISHED 1906
here's also e where these came from.
But those? Those will cost you.
The main thing to remember is that you're going to want to wait till you're home before you--
Yoink.

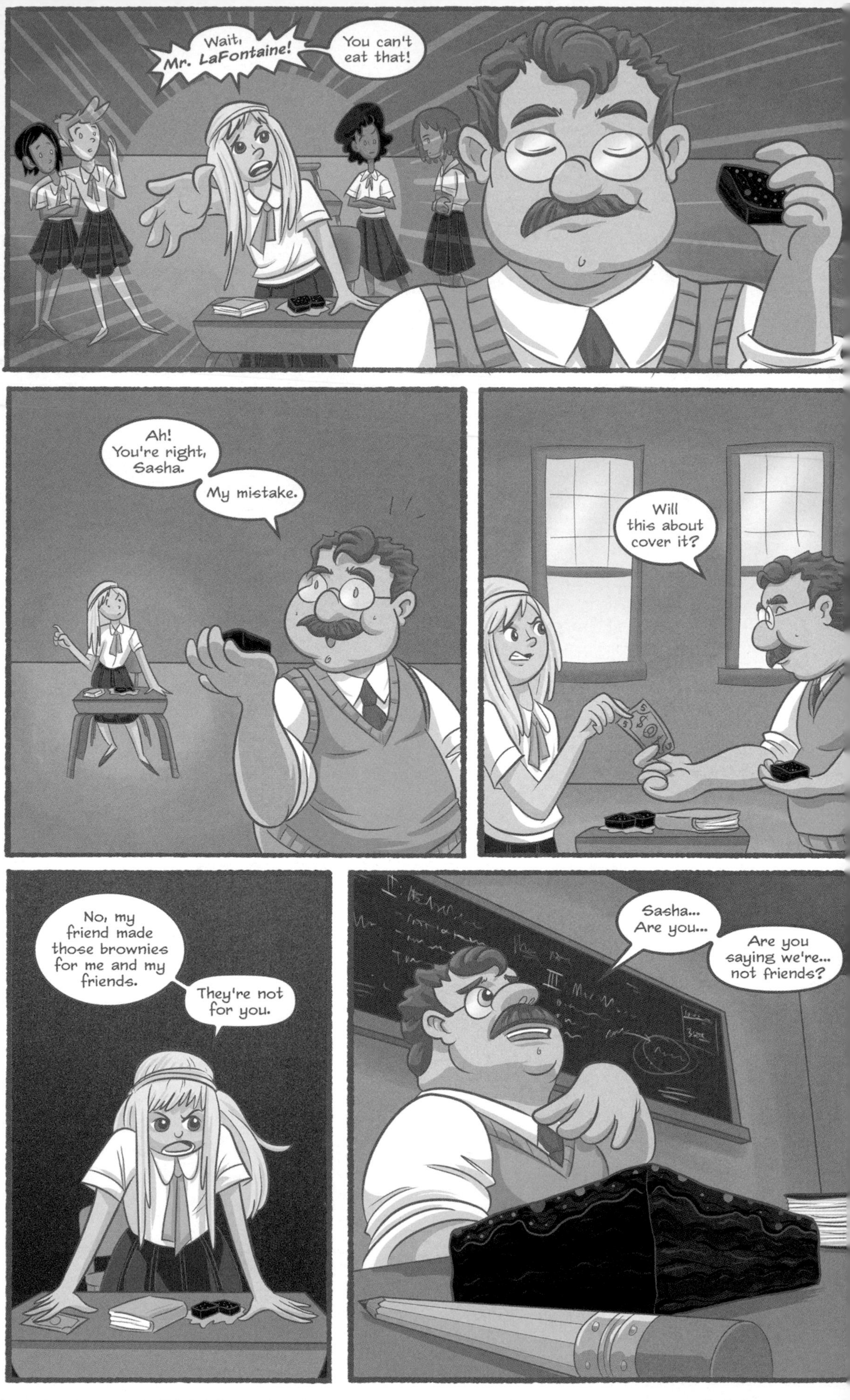
Wait, Mr. LaFontaine!
You can't eat that!
Ah! You're right, Sasha.
My mistake.
Will this about cover it?
No, my friend made those brownies for me and my friends.
They're not for you.
Sasha... Are you...
Are you saying we're... not friends?

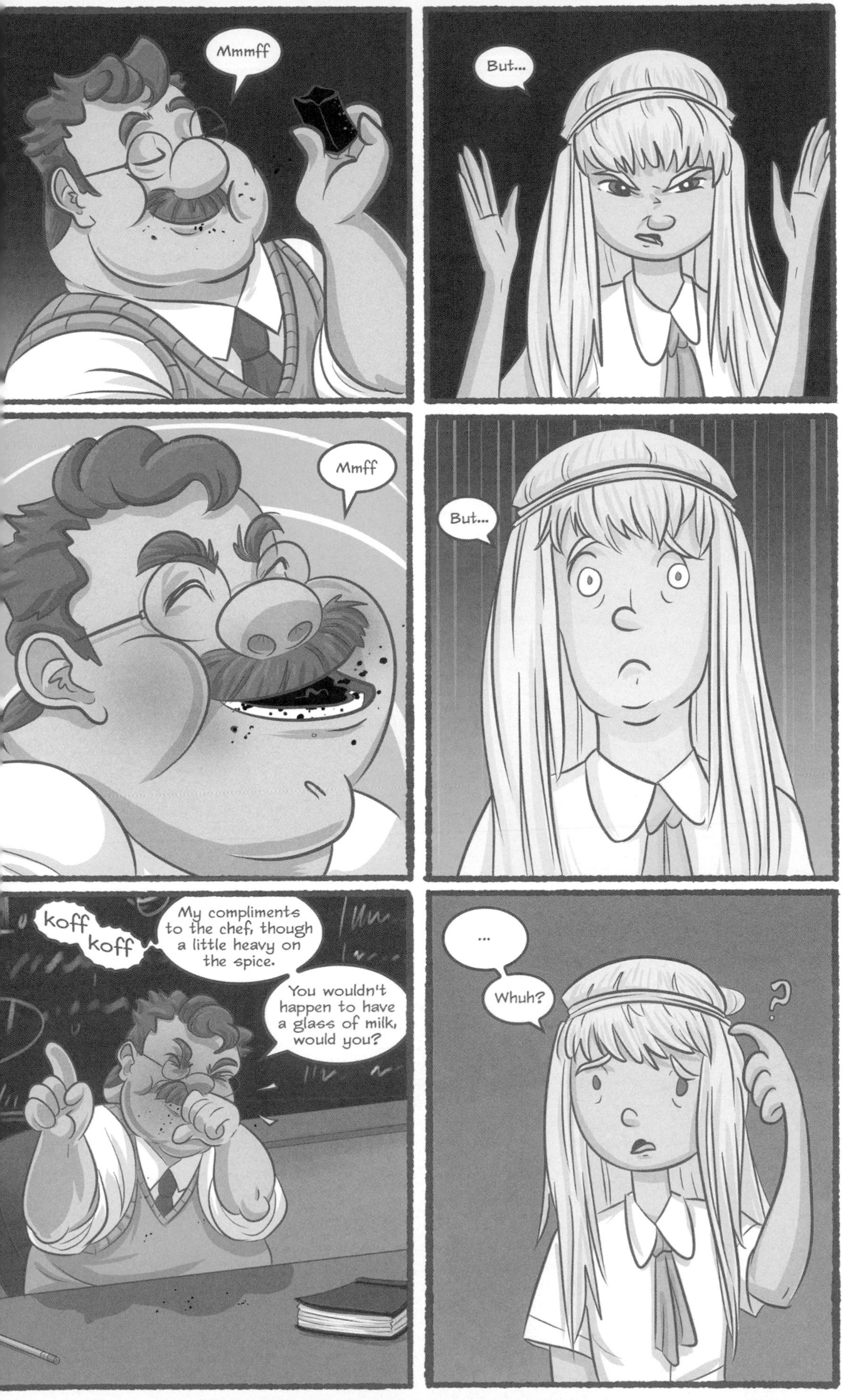
Mmmff
But...
Mmff
But...
koff koff
My compliments to the chef, though a little heavy on the spice.
You wouldn't happen to have a glass of milk, would you?
...
Whuh?
?

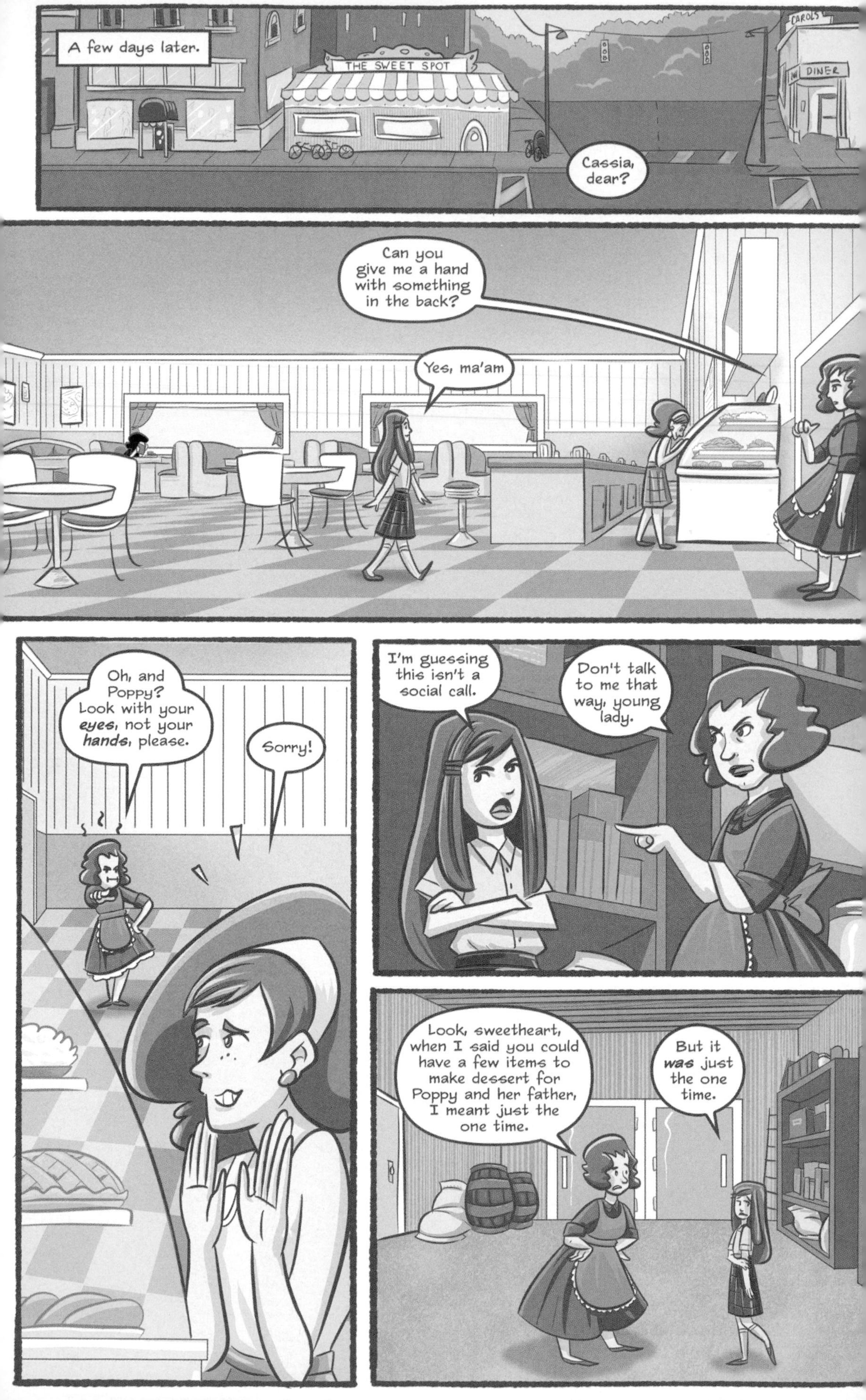
A few days later.
THE SWEET SPOT
CAROL'S
DINER
Cassia, dear?
Can you give me a hand with something in the back?
Yes, ma'am
Oh, and Poppy? Look with your *eyes*, not your *hands*, please.
Sorry!
I'm guessing this isn't a social call.
Don't talk to me that way, young lady.
Look, sweetheart, when I said you could have a few items to make dessert for Poppy and her father, I meant just the one time.
But it *was* just the one time.

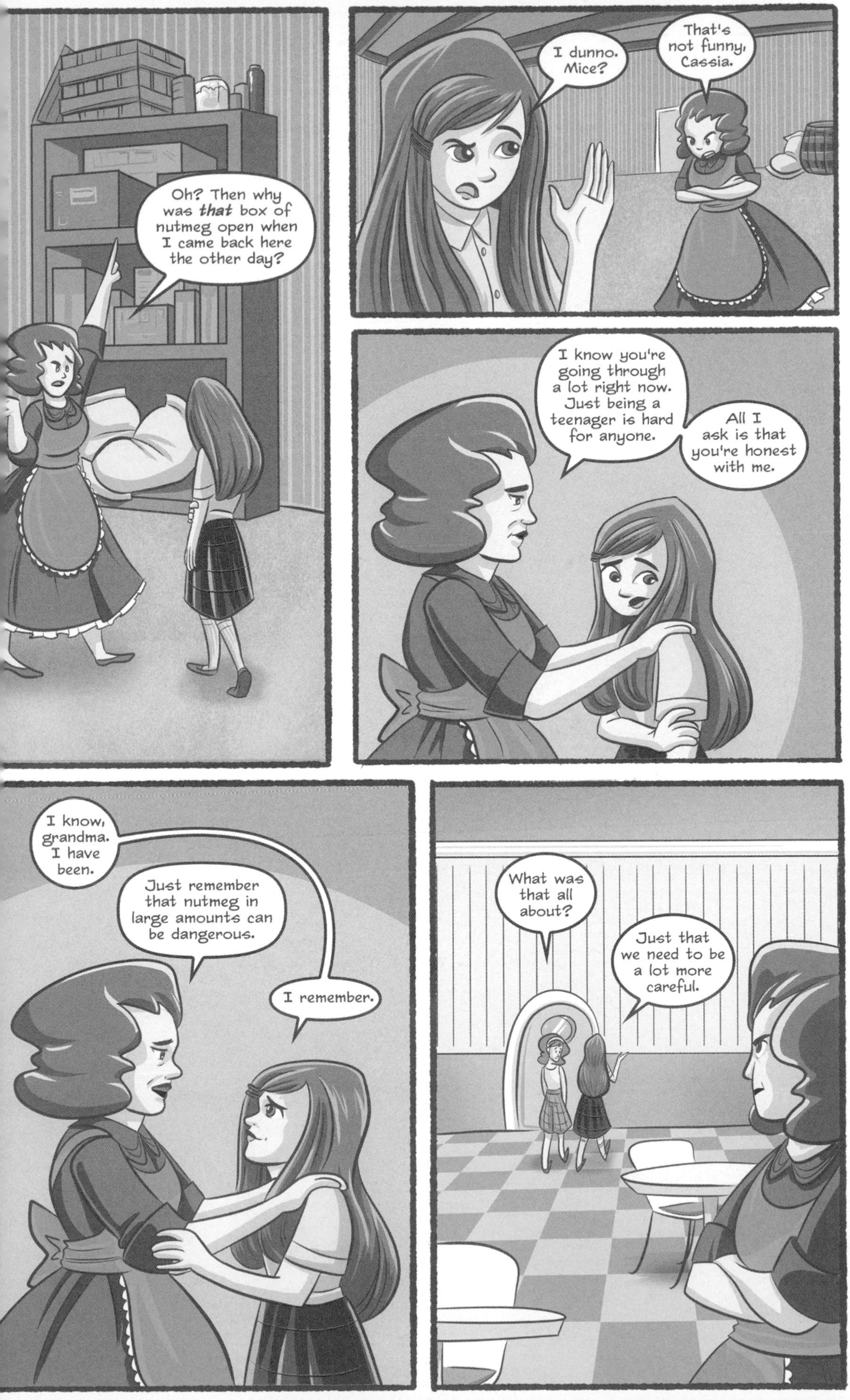

Oh? Then why was *that* box of nutmeg open when I came back here the other day?
I dunno. Mice?
That's not funny, Cassia.
I know you're going through a lot right now. Just being a teenager is hard for anyone.
All I ask is that you're honest with me.
I know, grandma. I have been.
Just remember that nutmeg in large amounts can be dangerous.
I remember.
What was that all about?
Just that we need to be a lot more careful.

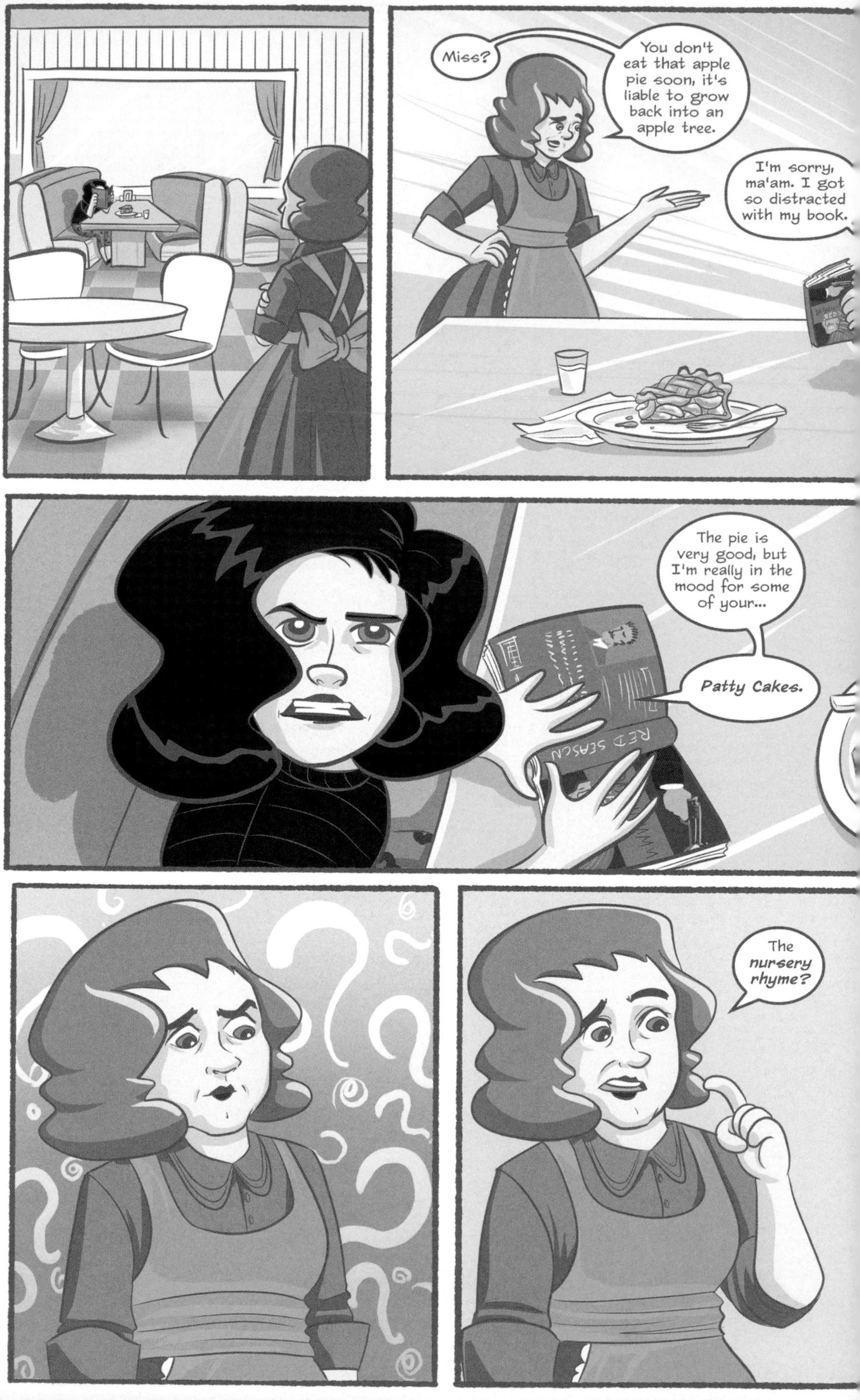
Miss?
You don't eat that apple pie soon, it's liable to grow back into an apple tree.
I'm sorry, ma'am. I got so distracted with my book.
The pie is very good, but I'm really in the mood for some of your...
Patty Cakes.
RED SEASON
The nursery rhyme?

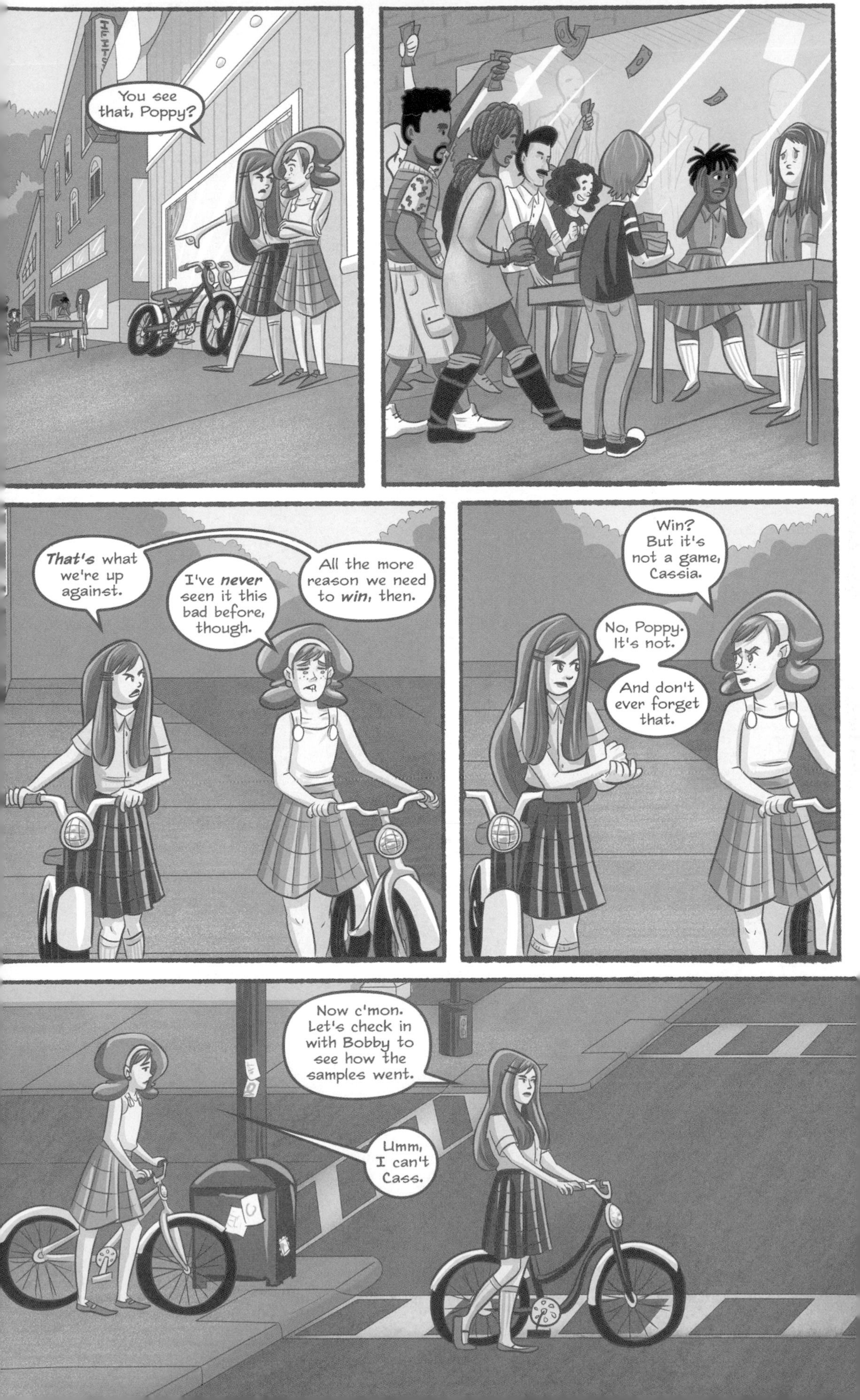
You see that, Poppy?
That's what we're up against.
I've never seen it this bad before, though.
All the more reason we need to win, then.
Win? But it's not a game, Cassia.
No, Poppy. It's not.
And don't ever forget that.
Now c'mon. Let's check in with Bobby to see how the samples went.
Umm, I can't Cass.

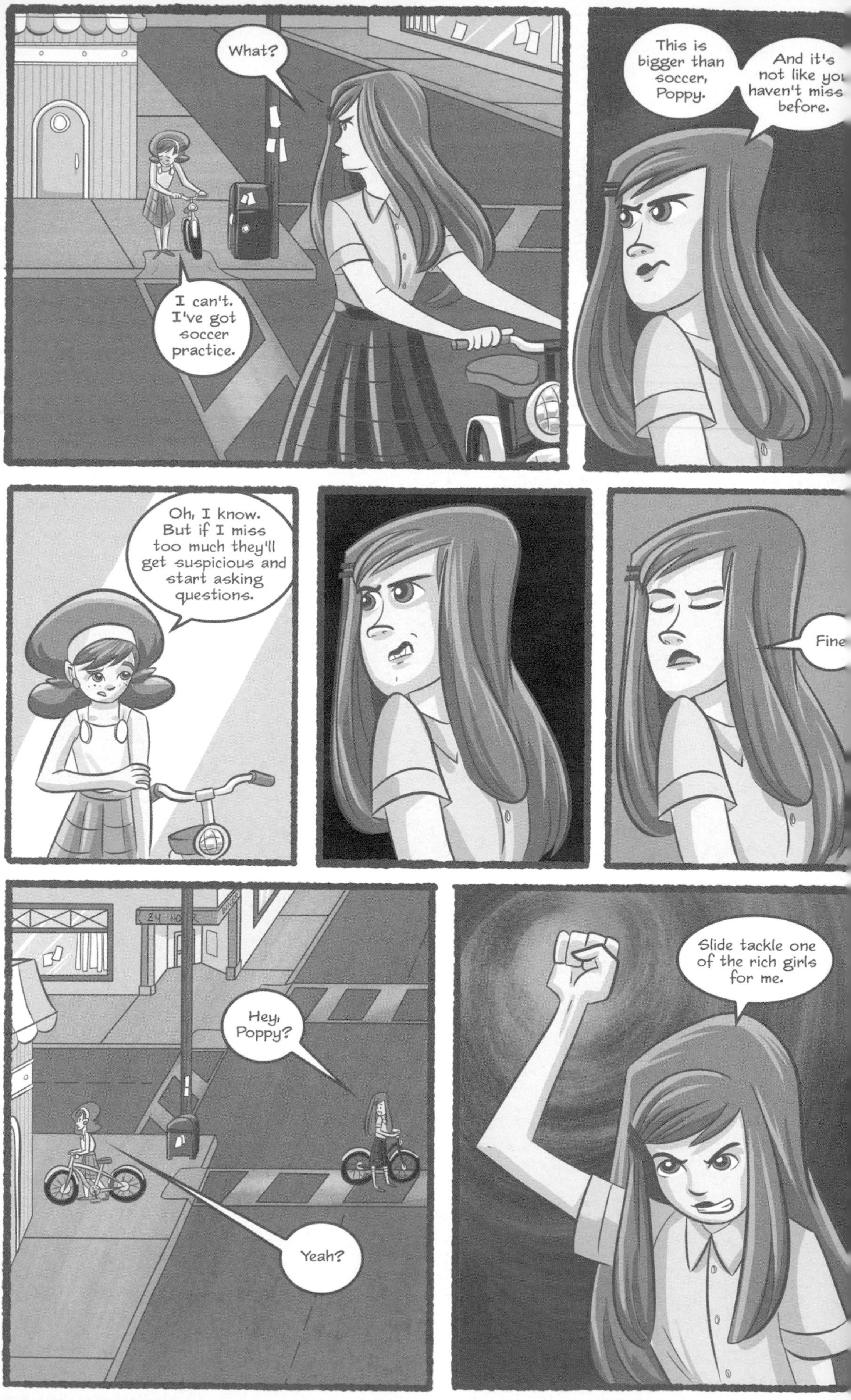
What?
I can't. I've got soccer practice.
This is bigger than soccer, Poppy.
And it's not like you haven't miss before.
Oh, I know. But if I miss too much they'll get suspicious and start asking questions.
Fine
Hey, Poppy?
Yeah?
Slide tackle one of the rich girls for me.

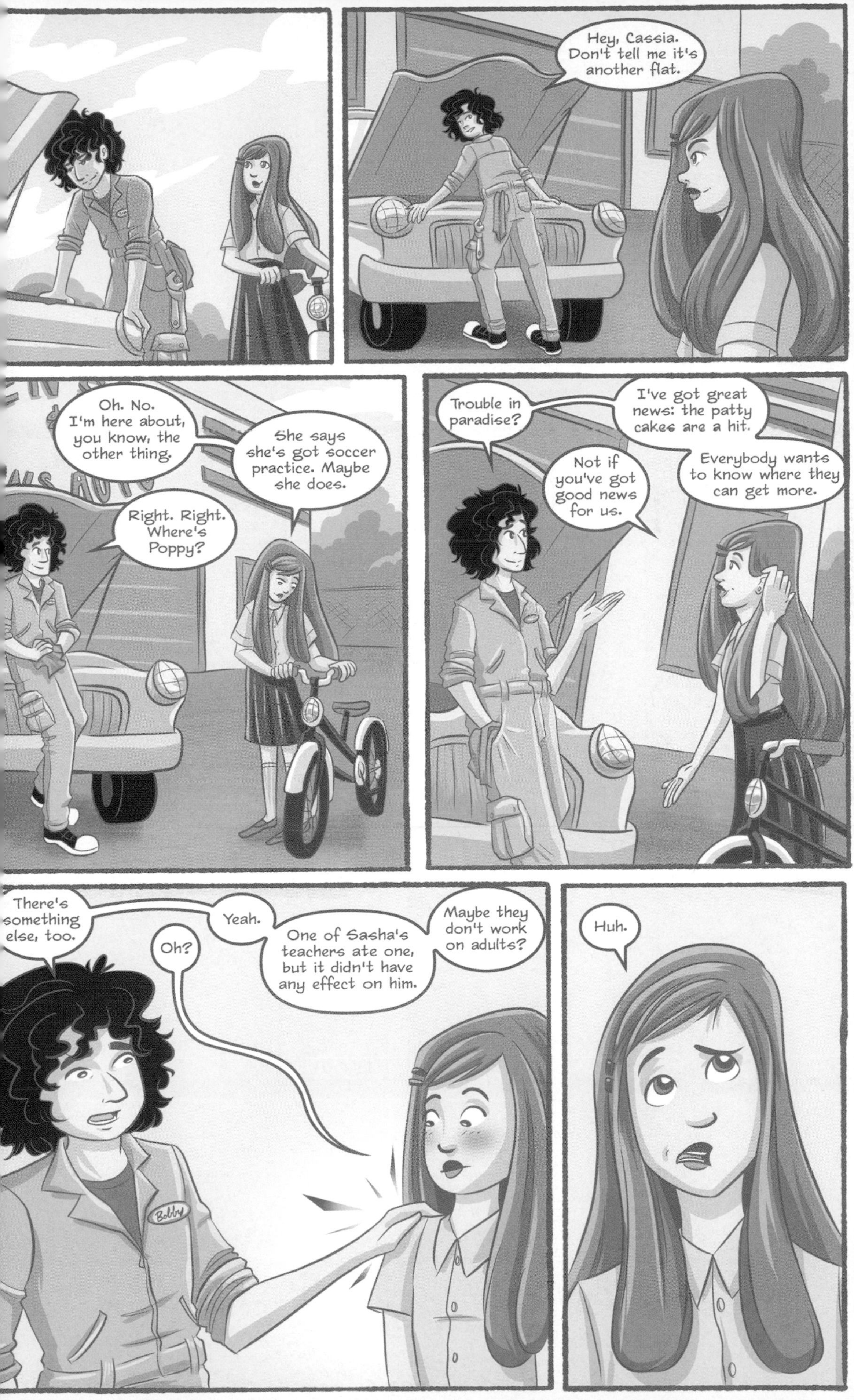
Hey, Cassia.
Don't tell me it's another flat.
Oh. No.
I'm here about, you know, the other thing.
Right. Right. Where's Poppy?
She says she's got soccer practice. Maybe she does.
Trouble in paradise?
Not if you've got good news for us.
I've got great news: the patty cakes are a hit.
Everybody wants to know where they can get more.
There's something else, too.
Oh?
Yeah.
One of Sasha's teachers ate one, but it didn't have any effect on him.
Maybe they don't work on adults?
Huh.
Bobby

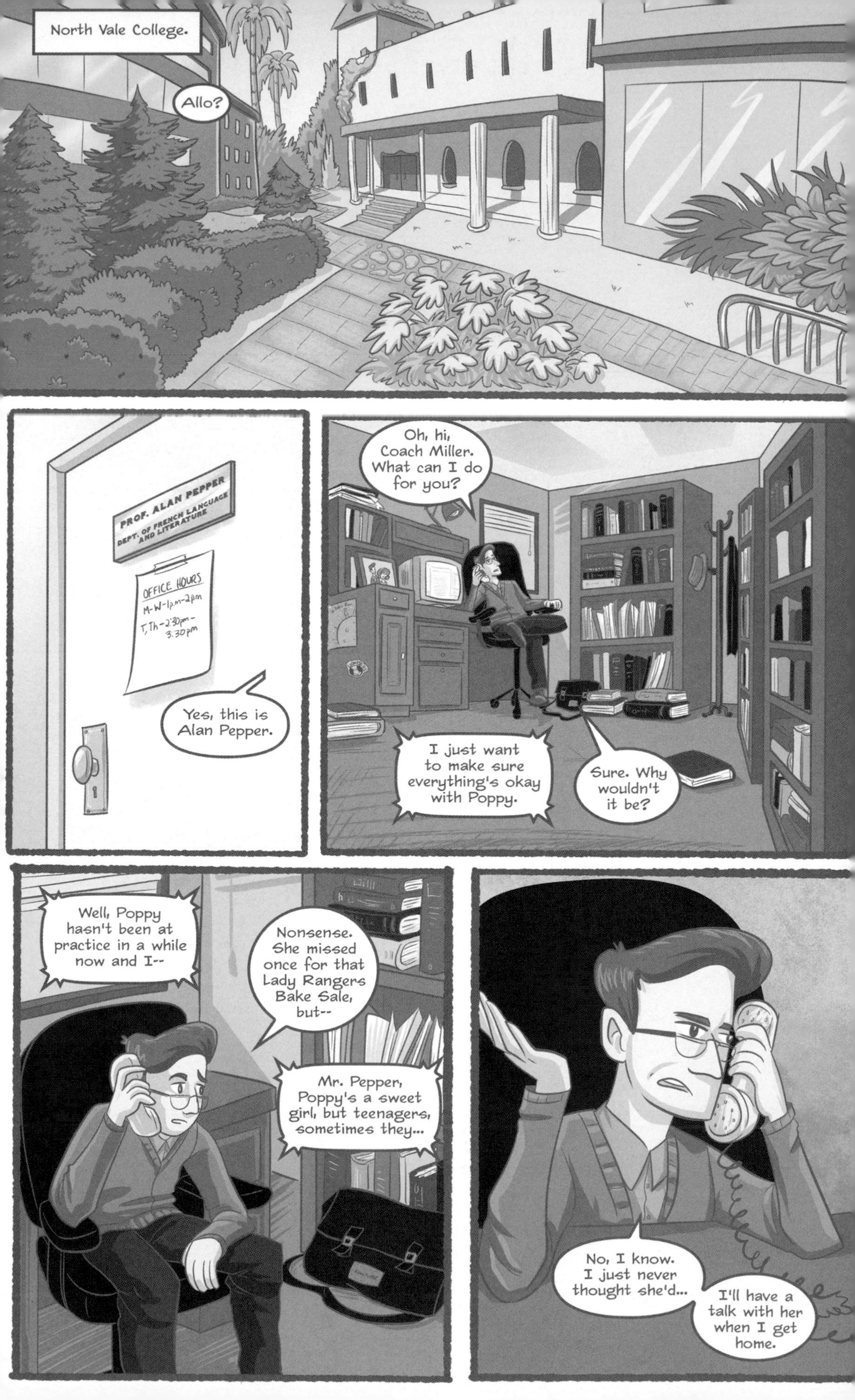
North Vale College.
Allo?
PROF. ALAN PEPPER
DEPT. OF FRENCH LANGUAGE AND LITERATURE
OFFICE HOURS
M-W-1p.m-2pm
T,Th-2:30pm-3:30pm
Yes, this is Alan Pepper.
Oh, hi, Coach Miller. What can I do for you?
I just want to make sure everything's okay with Poppy.
Sure. Why wouldn't it be?
Well, Poppy hasn't been at practice in a while now and I--
Nonsense. She missed once for that Lady Rangers Bake Sale, but--
Mr. Pepper, Poppy's a sweet girl, but teenagers, sometimes they...
No, I know. I just never thought she'd...
I'll have a talk with her when I get home.

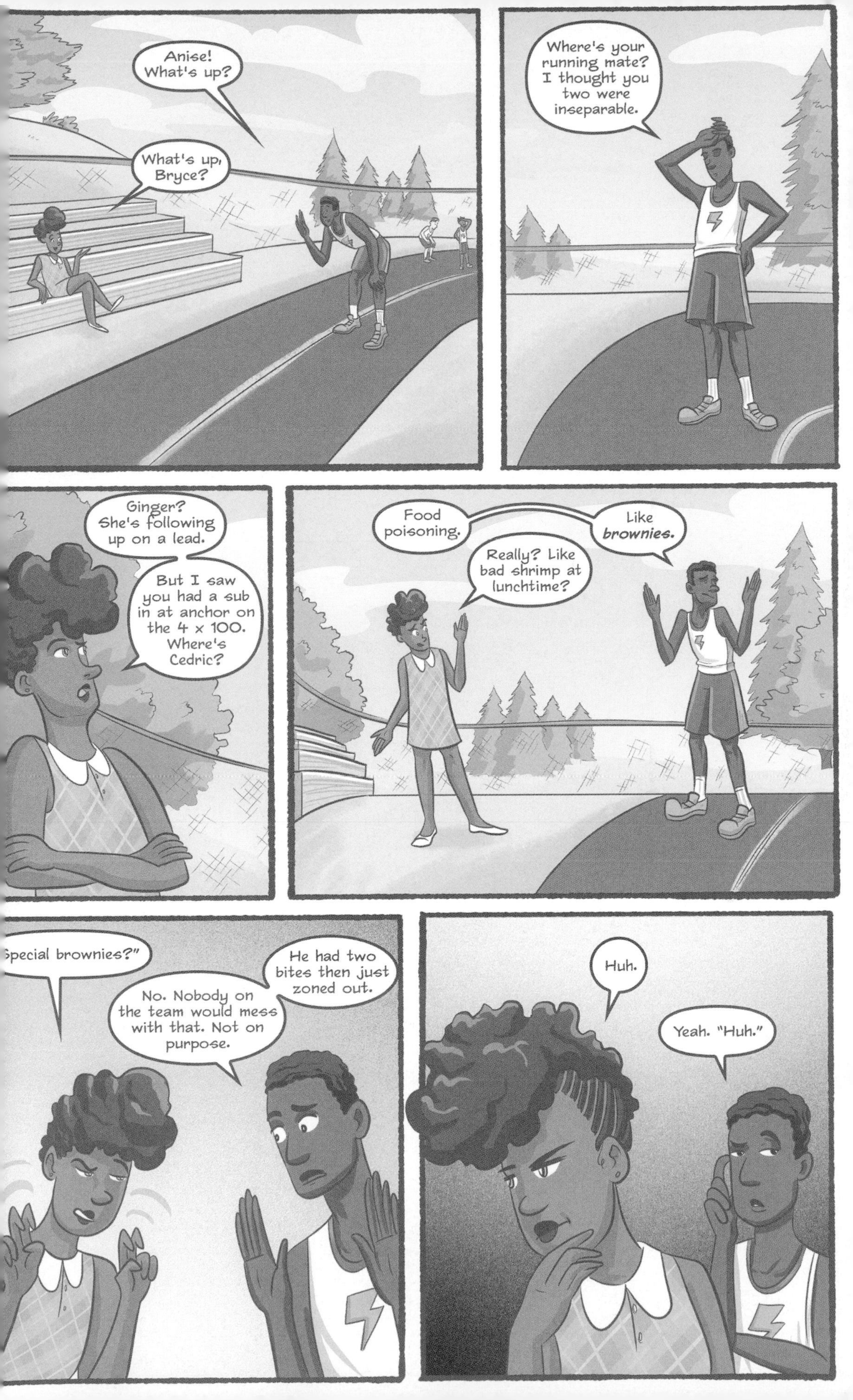
Anise! What's up?
What's up, Bryce?
Where's your running mate? I thought you two were inseparable.
Ginger? She's following up on a lead.
But I saw you had a sub in at anchor on the 4 x 100. Where's Cedric?
Food poisoning.
Like *brownies.*
Really? Like bad shrimp at lunchtime?
Special brownies?"
He had two bites then just zoned out.
No. Nobody on the team would mess with that. Not on purpose.
Huh.
Yeah. "Huh."

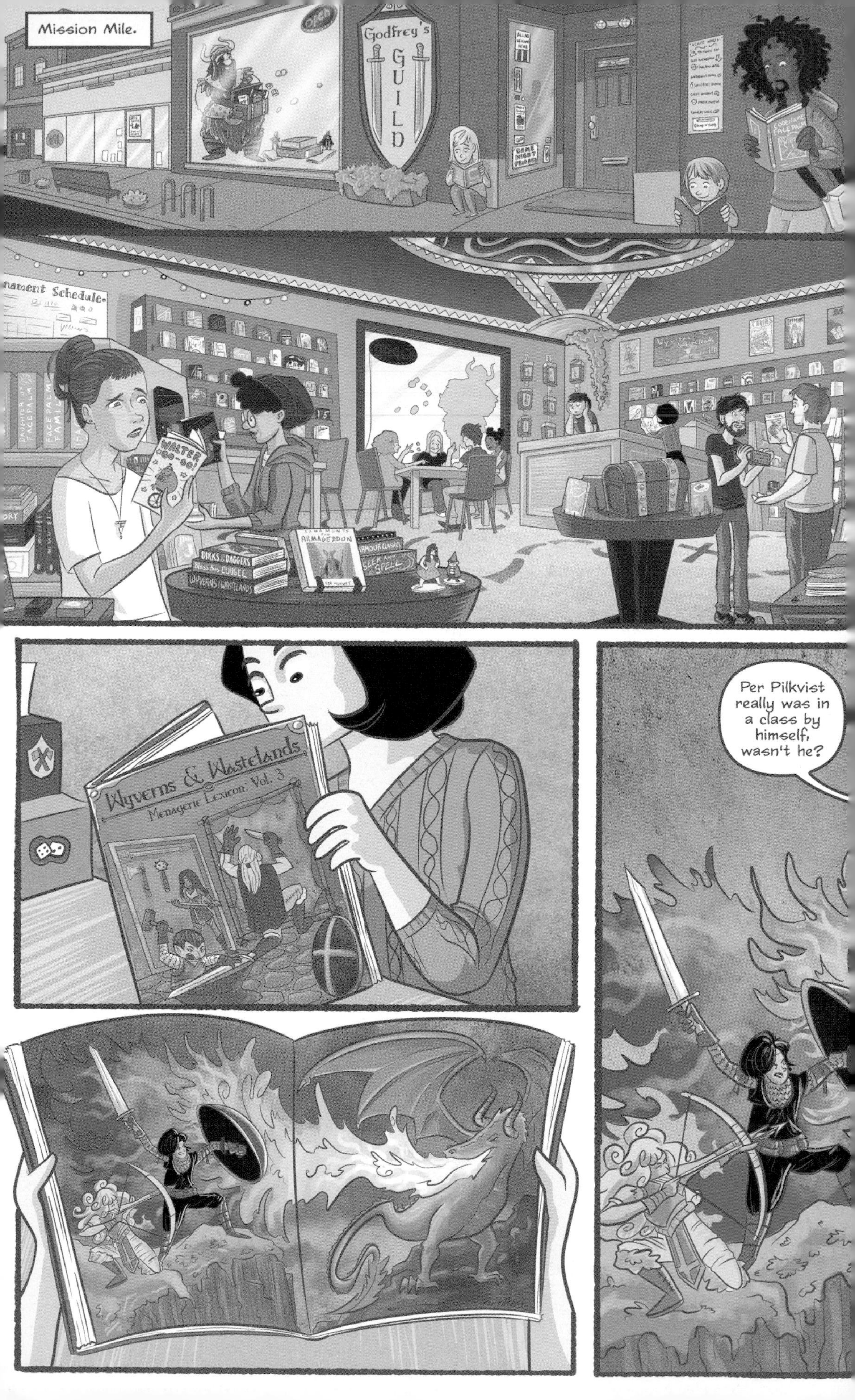
Mission Mile.
Godfrey's GUILD
nament Schedule.
WALTER GO-GO!
DIRKS & DAGGERS
Bless this CUDGEL
WYVERNS & WASTELANDS
ARMAGEDDON
SEEK AND SPELL
Wyverns & Wastelands
Menagerie Lexicon: Vol. 3
Per Pilkvist really was in a class by himself, wasn't he?

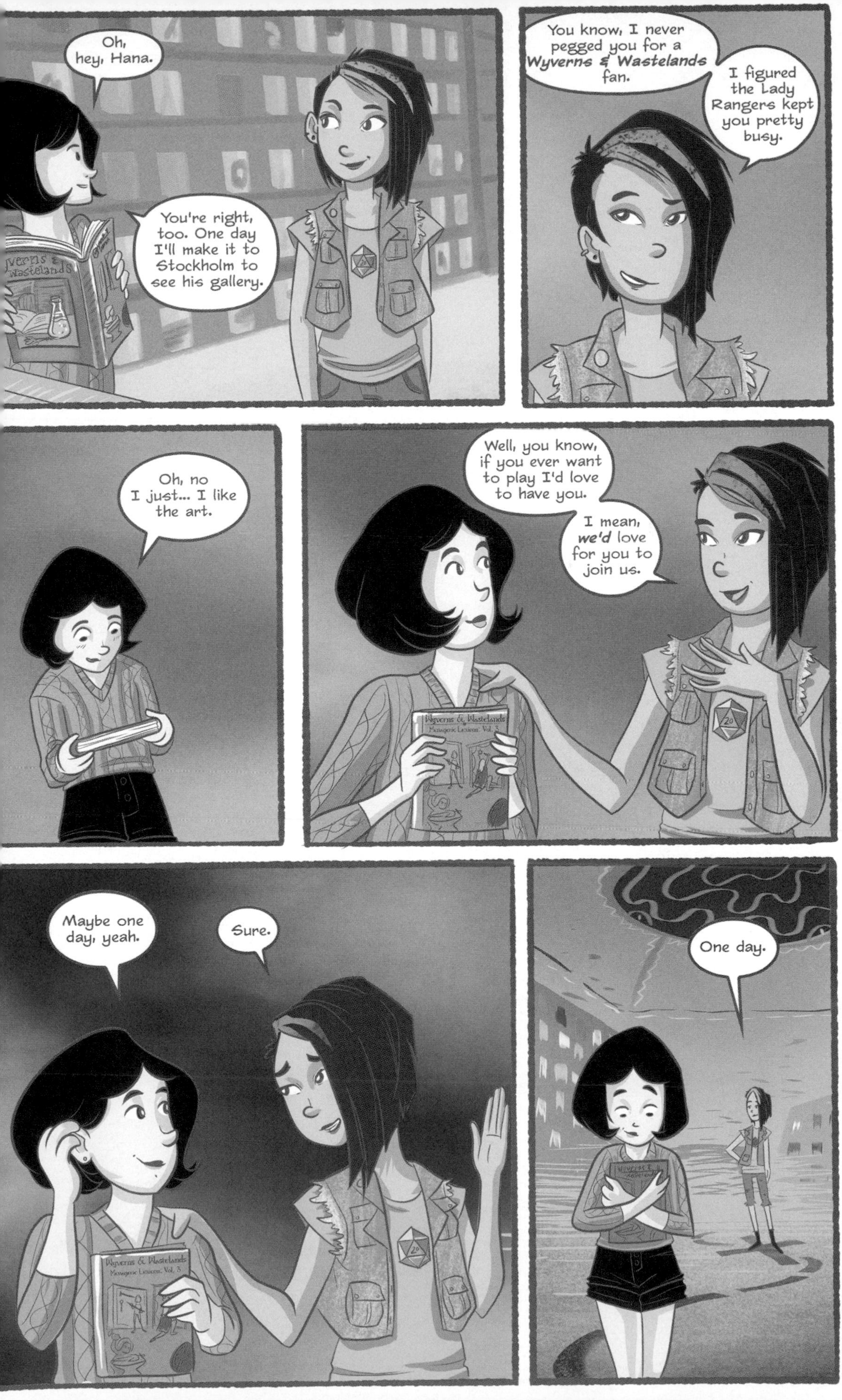
Oh, hey, Hana.
You're right, too. One day I'll make it to Stockholm to see his gallery.
Wyverns & Wastelands
You know, I never pegged you for a **Wyverns & Wastelands** fan.
I figured the Lady Rangers kept you pretty busy.
Oh, no I just... I like the art.
Well, you know, if you ever want to play I'd love to have you.
I mean, ***we'd*** love for you to join us.
Wyverns & Wastelands Menagerie Lexicon: Vol. 3
Maybe one day, yeah.
Sure.
Wyverns & Wastelands Menagerie Lexicon: Vol. 3
One day.

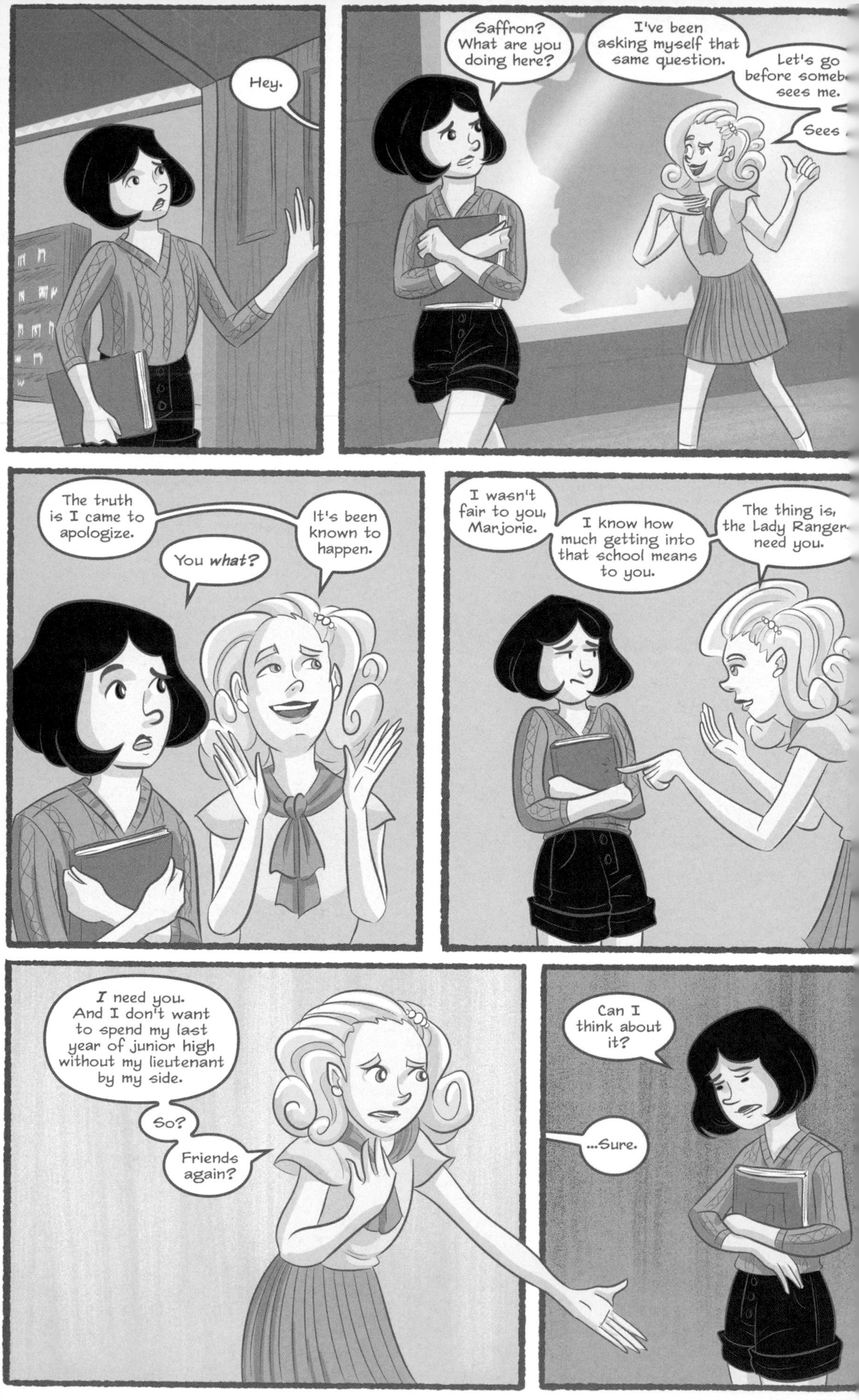
Hey.
Saffron? What are you doing here?
I've been asking myself that same question.
Let's go before someb sees me.
Sees
The truth is I came to apologize.
You *what?*
It's been known to happen.
I wasn't fair to you, Marjorie.
I know how much getting into that school means to you.
The thing is, the Lady Ranger need you.
*I* need you. And I don't want to spend my last year of junior high without my lieutenant by my side.
So?
Friends again?
Can I think about it?
...Sure.

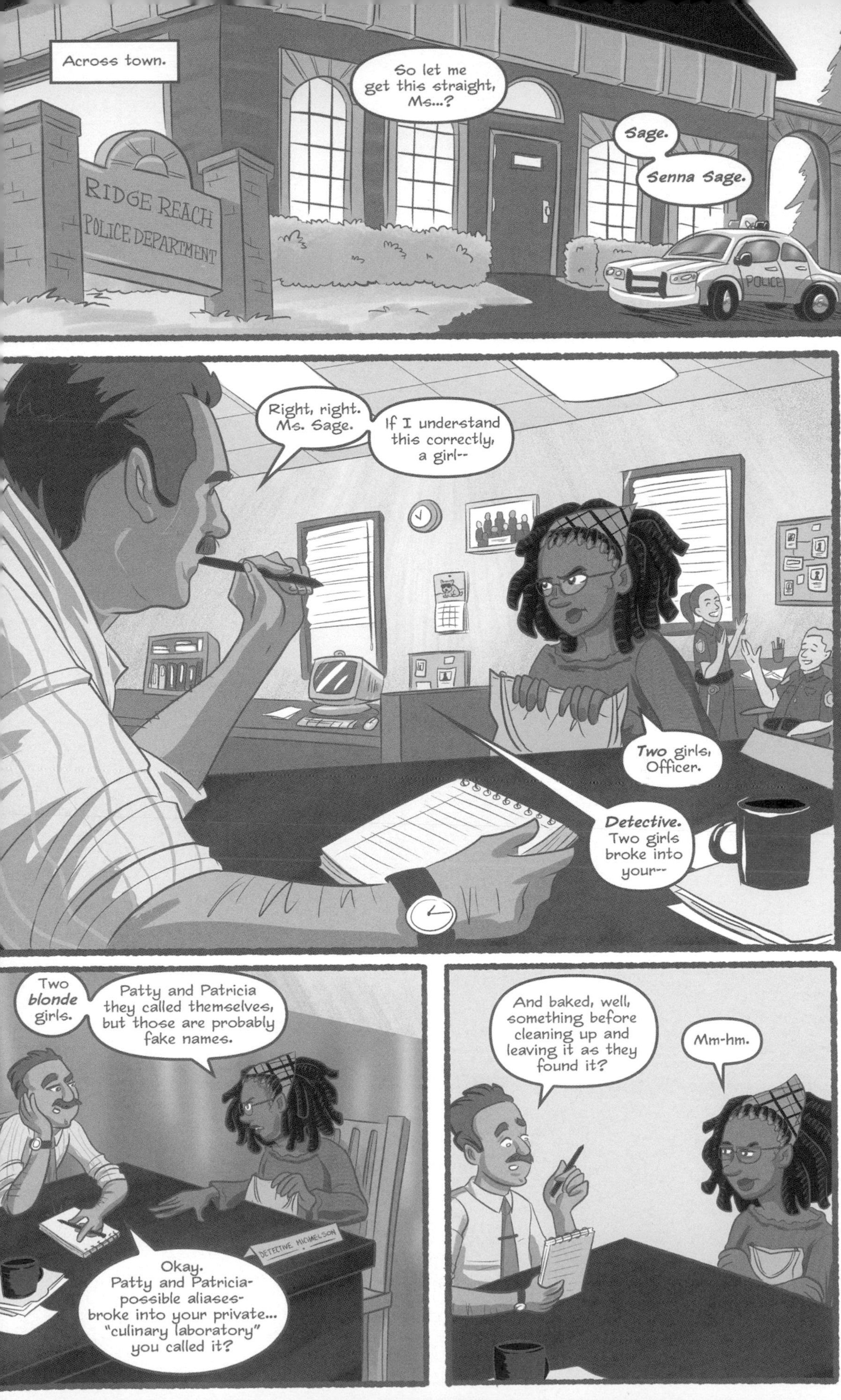
Across town.
So let me get this straight, Ms...?
Sage.
Senna Sage.
RIDGE REACH POLICE DEPARTMENT
POLICE
Right, right. Ms. Sage.
If I understand this correctly, a girl--
Two girls, Officer.
Detective. Two girls broke into your--
Two blonde girls.
Patty and Patricia they called themselves, but those are probably fake names.
DETECTIVE MICHAELSON
Okay. Patty and Patricia- possible aliases- broke into your private... "culinary laboratory" you called it?
And baked, well, something before cleaning up and leaving it as they found it?
Mm-hm.

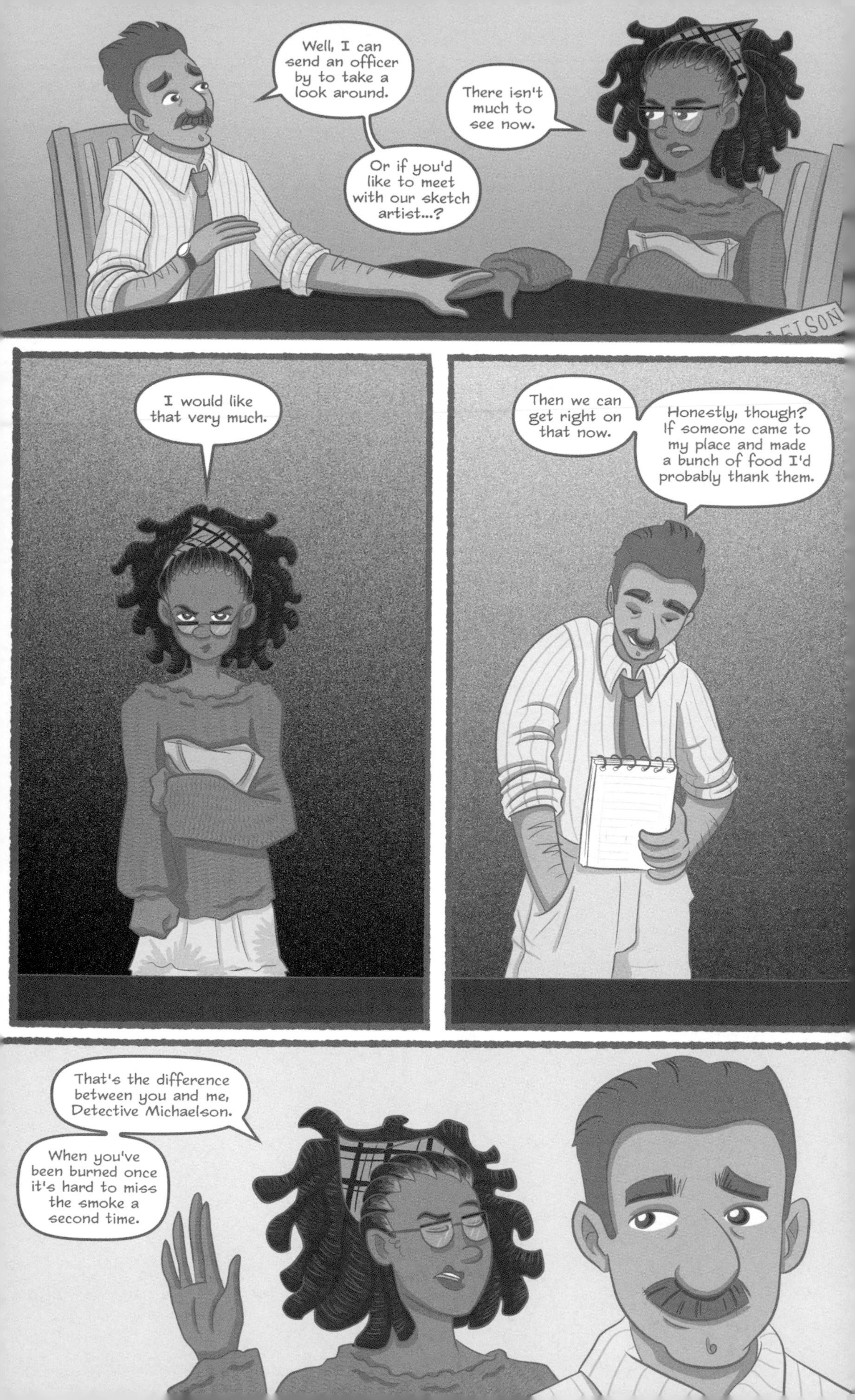

Well, I can send an officer by to take a look around.
Or if you'd like to meet with our sketch artist...?
There isn't much to see now.
I would like that very much.
Then we can get right on that now.
Honestly, though? If someone came to my place and made a bunch of food I'd probably thank them.
That's the difference between you and me, Detective Michaelson.
When you've been burned once it's hard to miss the smoke a second time.

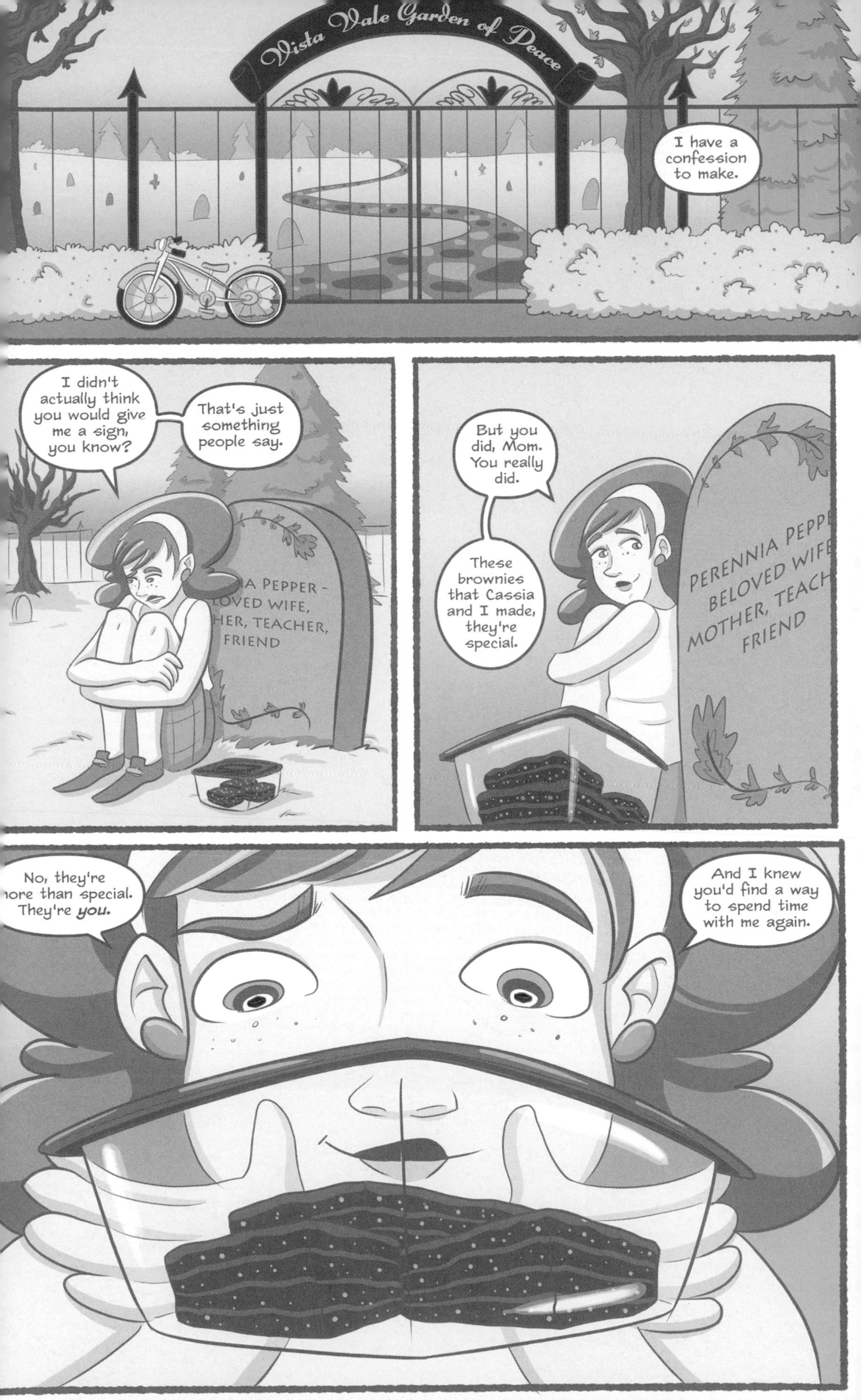

Vista Vale Garden of Peace
I have a confession to make.
I didn't actually think you would give me a sign, you know?
That's just something people say.
PEPPER - LOVED WIFE, HER, TEACHER, FRIEND
But you did, Mom. You really did.
These brownies that Cassia and I made, they're special.
PERENNIA PEPP BELOVED WIF MOTHER, TEACH FRIEND
No, they're more than special. They're ***you.***
And I knew you'd find a way to spend time with me again.

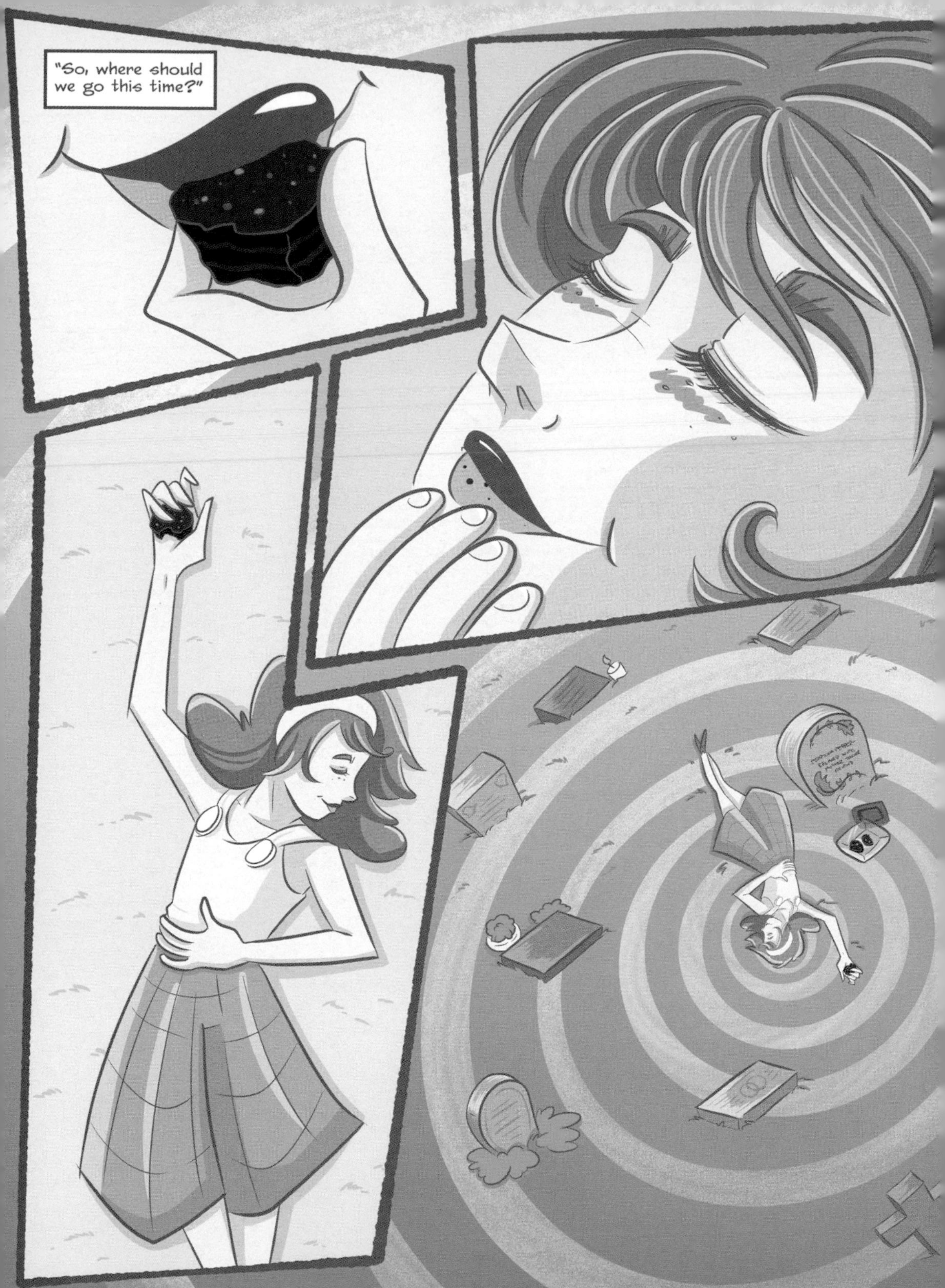
"So, where should we go this time?"

# FALL, CONCLUSION: PATTY CAKES

ART BY JACKIE CROFTS WORDS BY JAMES F. WRIGHT
COLORS & LETTERING BY JOSH ECKERT

Bryan Seaton - Publisher • Kevin Freeman - President • Dave Dwonch - Creative Director • Shawn Gabborin - Editor In Chief
Jamal Igle - Co-Directors of Marketing • Social Media Director - Jim Dietz • Chad Cicconi - ate all the brownies • Colleen Boyd - Associate

# THE COOLING RACK

**CONTACT: @NUTMEGCOMIC · NUTMEGCOMICS@GMAIL.COM**

you take a look at the header here on The Cooling Rack you'll notice that we've posted email address (nutmegcomics@gmail.com). That means that you—yes, you—can write us with questions or comments, and ifyou mark it "Okay to print" then there's a chance 'll share it here. Hey, we get lonely, too, and it's always lovely to hear from readers and ns and friends. That's what Jim did and here's the message he sent us!

I am a grown ass man! That's what I like to tell my wife when she starts jamming about something or another. I picked up your comic and embarrassingly lied to the cashier that it was for my wife knowing full well the first two pages I glanced at sold me. I usually pick up what a lot of people consider "chick" comics and for the most part they end up not being for me. But I have a real good feeling about Nutmeg. I am a grown ass man and I dig Nutmeg. I won't even lie when I put it on my pull list.

Thanks,
Jim
South Gate, CA

*Don't worry, Jim! Nutmeg was co-created—and is written—by a "grown ass man." We're happy that our book captured your interest so early. And we're very glad that you no longer have to lie to your local comic shop about it. Enjoy Nutmeg proudly, that's what we say. And stick around because Poppy and Cassia's journey is just getting warmed up.*

*- Jackles & Jambles*

u may have noticed the introduction of a series called Wyverns & Wastelands in this ue. It's a surprisingly deep and engaging role-playing game system, notable among her things for its imagery by celebrated Swedish fantasy artist, Per Pilkvist. At present e Wyverns & Wastelands library consists of the following:

The Master Guide
Menagerie Lexicon Vols. 1-3
Armaments for Armageddon: Weapons Codex
Bless This Cudgel: A Clerics' Guide
Dirks & Daggers: A Thieves' Guide
Somethings From Nothing: A Conjurers' Guide
Seek and Spell: A Sorcerers' Guide
Armour Classics: A Guide for Protection

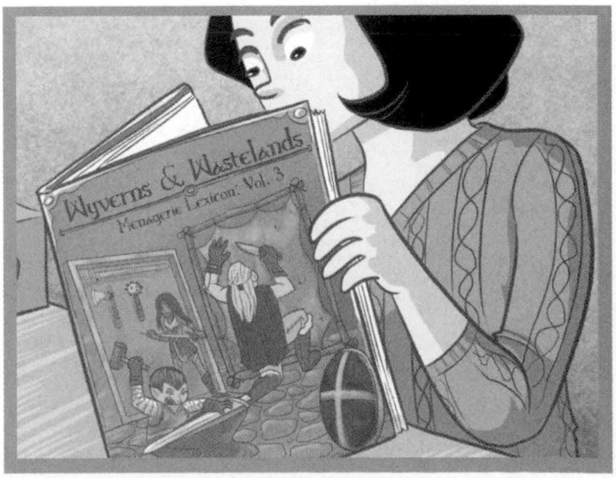
Wyverns & Wastelands
Menagerie Lexicon: Vol. 3

# TEAM NUTMEG'S 2015

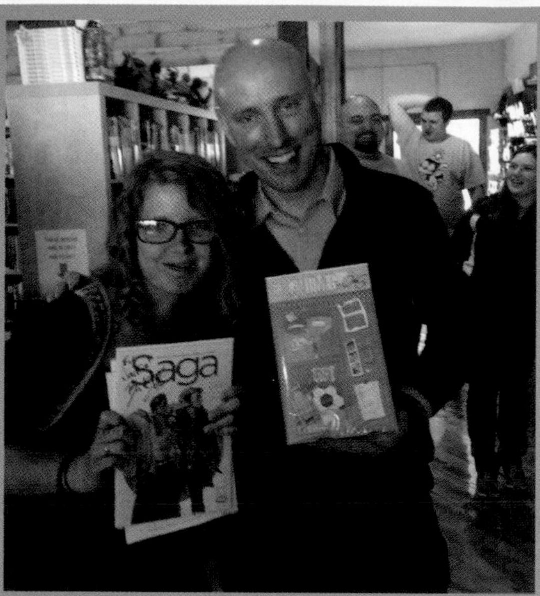
Saga

Jackie with Brian K. Vaughan at Aw Yeah Comics (IN)

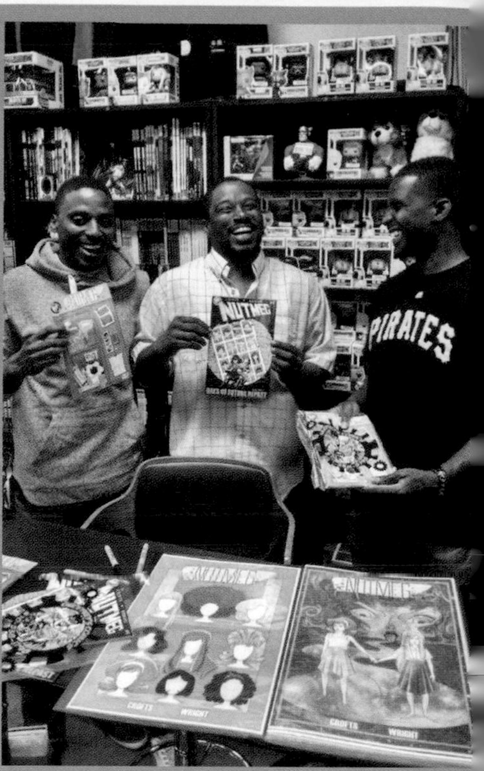
NUTMEG
PIRATES

James signing at Geoffrey's Comics in Gardena (

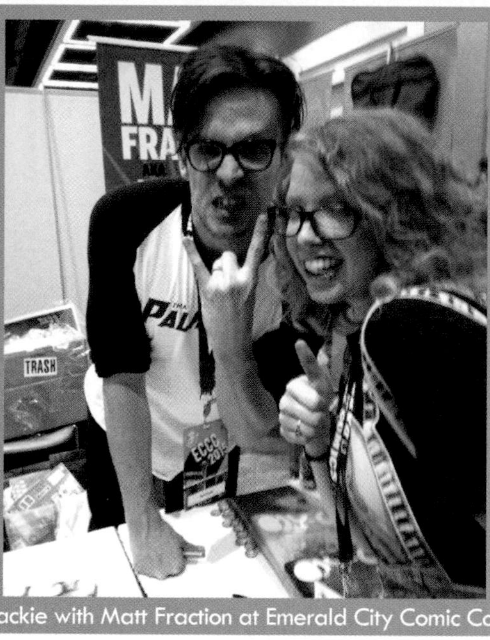
TRASH
ECCC 2015

Jackie with Matt Fraction at Emerald City Comic Con

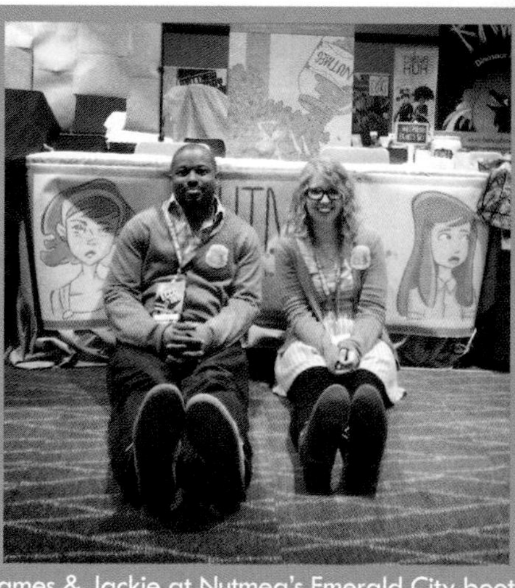

James & Jackie at Nutmeg's Emerald City booth

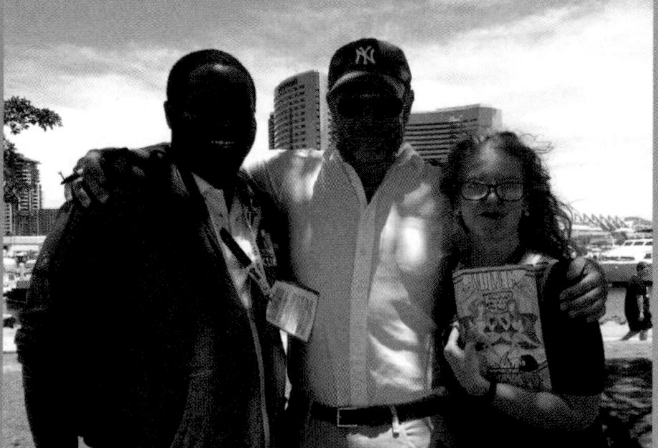

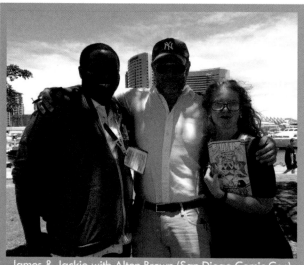

James & Jackie with Alton Brown (San Diego Comic Con)

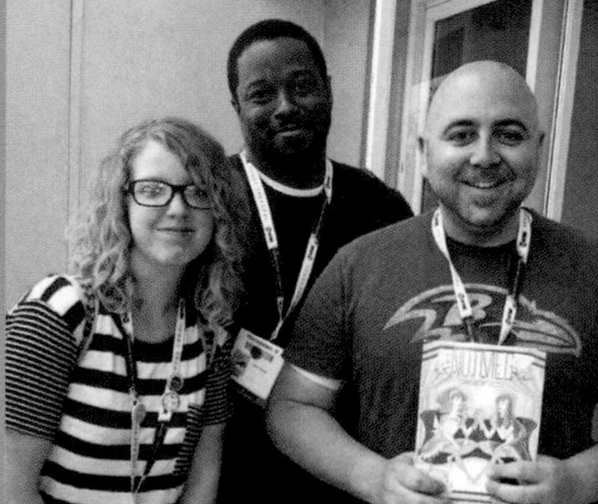

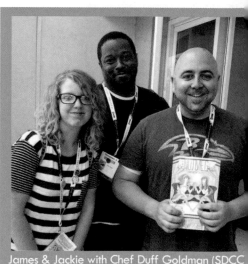

James & Jackie with Chef Duff Goldman (SDCC

ʍould be easy—and not entirely correct—to assume that we spend all of our time in ⱔ kitchen making batches of Nutmeg for all of you readers out there, but the truth is 're always devouring all kinds of comics (to say nothing of other media). Some of these ⱔgs influence Nutmeg, consciously or unconsciously, and some of them are just things 're digging right now.

On the home base front—that is, books from our publisher, Action Lab Entertainment — we'd be remiss if we didn't mention Princeless by Jeremy Whitley and a team of great artists. While it's tonally different from our book, we think a lot of our readers would get a kick out of this fun and engaging fantasy series about a young heroine and her journey to save her sisters. And there's a new spin-off series, Raven The Pirate Princess, about the exploits and adventures of, well, the titular pirate captain. Also from Action Lab is Dave Dwonch's Cyrus Perkins and the Haunted Taxi Cab, a horror/murder mystery (don't worry, it's not super scary) about a cab driver trying to unravel the mystery of a boy who died in his taxi.

On the horizon from ALE are a handful of books we've been lucky enough to get an early peek of. Josh Henaman's Bigfoot: Sword of the Earthman, a pulp-tastic, action-packed Martian adventure that sees Bigfoot on the alien planet and wielding a broadsword. And Shawn Pryor's Cash + Carrie, an all-ages book about a pair of teenage detectives working to solve the mystery of their school's kidnapped mascot. So keep your eye out for those. What's great about the Action Lab stable of books is that there really is something for everyone, across a bunch of different genres to boot!

Elsewhere, there've been a a few books that caught us by surprise these past few months. One of which is SuperMutant Magic Academy by Jillian Tamaki (published by Drawn & Quarterly). A collection of humorous, mostly single-page comics depicting the lives, trials, and tribulations of the students—some magical, some mutants, some somewhere in between—at the titular school. Unlike, say, X-Men or Harry Potter, the students' powers and abilities take a backseat to their personalities and views on the world.

Another one worth checking out is Giant Days by John Allison and Lissa Treiman (published by Boom! Studios). It's an incredibly funny and honest story of three freshman at a university in the UK. There's nothing supernatural or superpowered about it, just great characters and great observations about becoming an adult.

And, finally, there's Paper Girls by Brian K. Vaughan and Cliff Chiang (published by Image Comics), which as of this writing just debuted. The story of four girls in Cleveland in the 1980s who discover some otherworldly goings on during their post-Halloween paper route. It's a little harder-edged than Nutmeg (read: swearing, mostly) but it should appeal to some of our older readers.

What are you reading and enjoying these days?

# KRISTIN'S PEAR TART RECIPE

This month's recipe comes by way of our friend Kristin. In her words, "This recipe is fast and loose so I hope that works for you." Even better, it's versatile enough that it can be made in a vegan-friendly version as well. See? You've got options.

Enjoy and we'll see you again next time!

## INGREDIENTS

Puff Pastry (Store-bought is fine. Pepperidge Farms brand might be vegan.)

2-3 Pears

1/2 teaspoon Cinnamon (or Nutmeg!)

2 tablespoons of Honey (You can substitute Agave syrup for vegan version.)

1 teaspoon flour

## INSTRUCTIONS

Follow instructions on Puff Pastry packaging for preheating oven.

Peel and slice pears in to 1/4 inch slices. Toss in a bowl with the spices, Honey/Syrup, and Flour.

Unwrap and thaw puff pastry according to package and cut into 3" x 5" rectangles.

Arrange pear tart slices in the center of each rectangle in an attractive pattern, pressing down slightly so they stick.

Spoon a bit of extra pear juice into the center. You may need to tug the edges of the pastry up slightly to form a dish.

Bake until the puff pastry is puffy and golden and the pears are tender.

NOTE: You can also use apples or plums in place of the pears for this recipe, whatever happens to be in season.

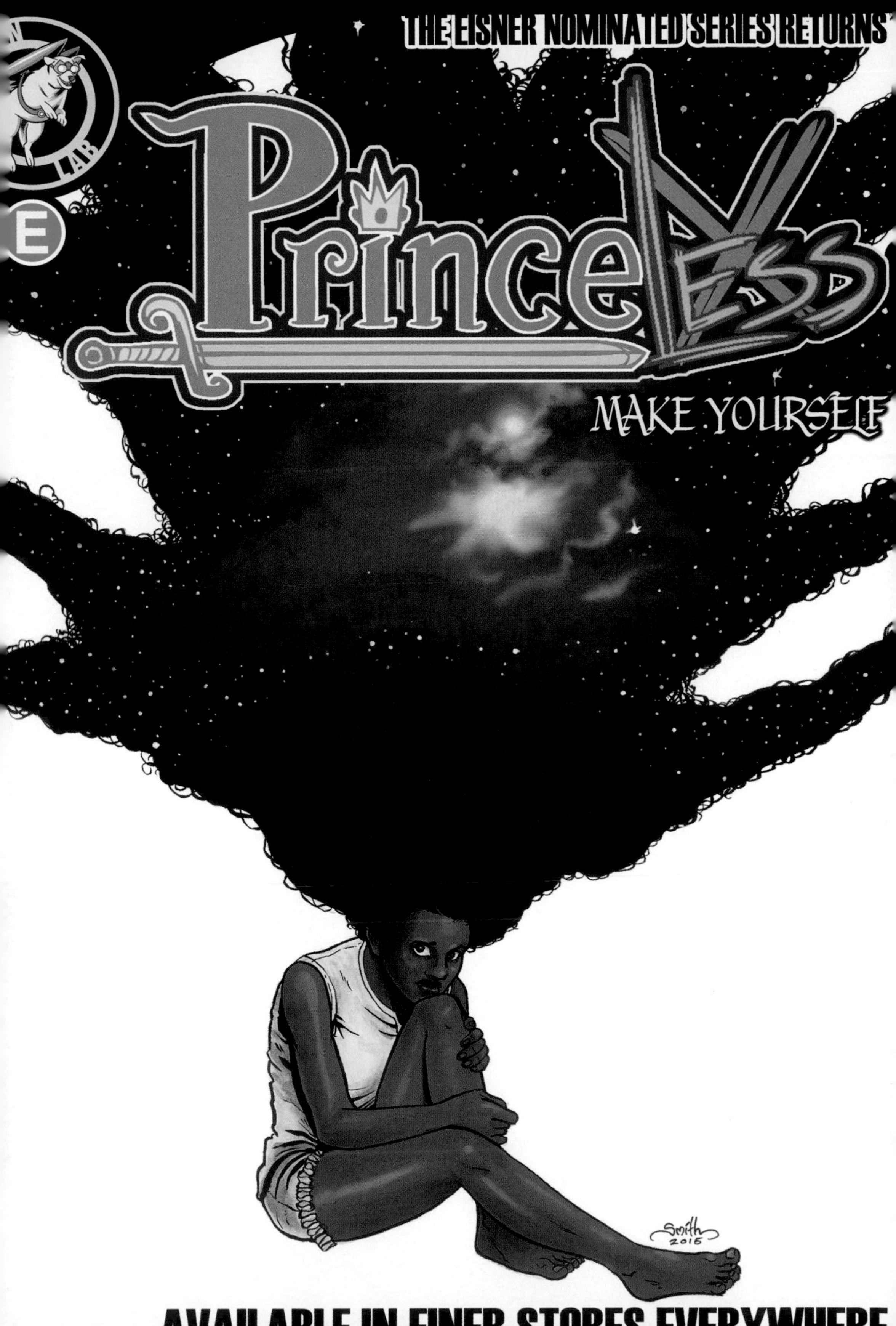
THE EISNER NOMINATED SERIES RETURNS
E
Princeless
MAKE YOURSELF
Smith 2015
AVAILABLE IN FINER STORES EVERYWHERE

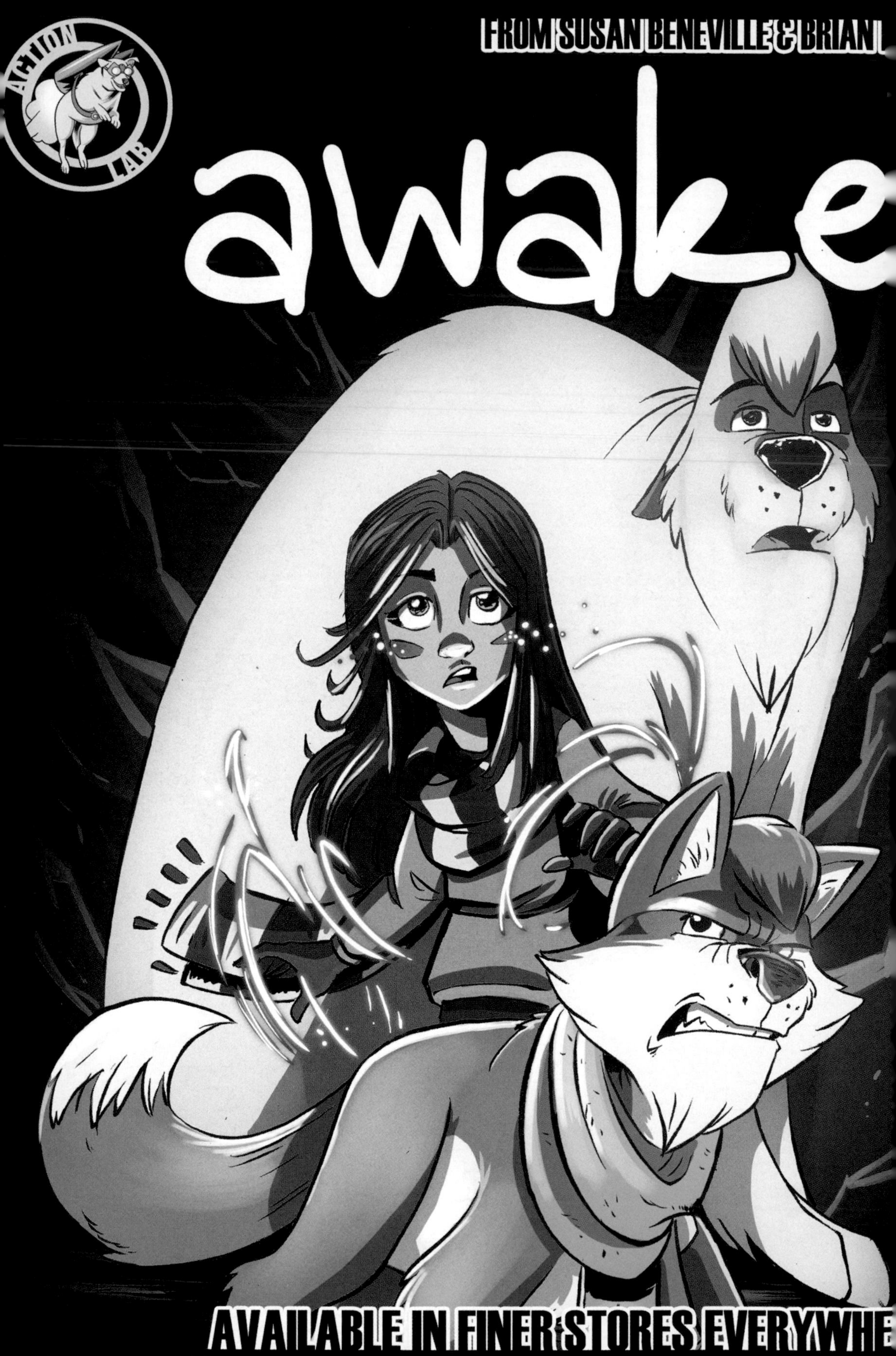
ACTION LAB
FROM SUSAN BENEVILLE & BRIAN
awake
AVAILABLE IN FINER STORES EVERYWHE

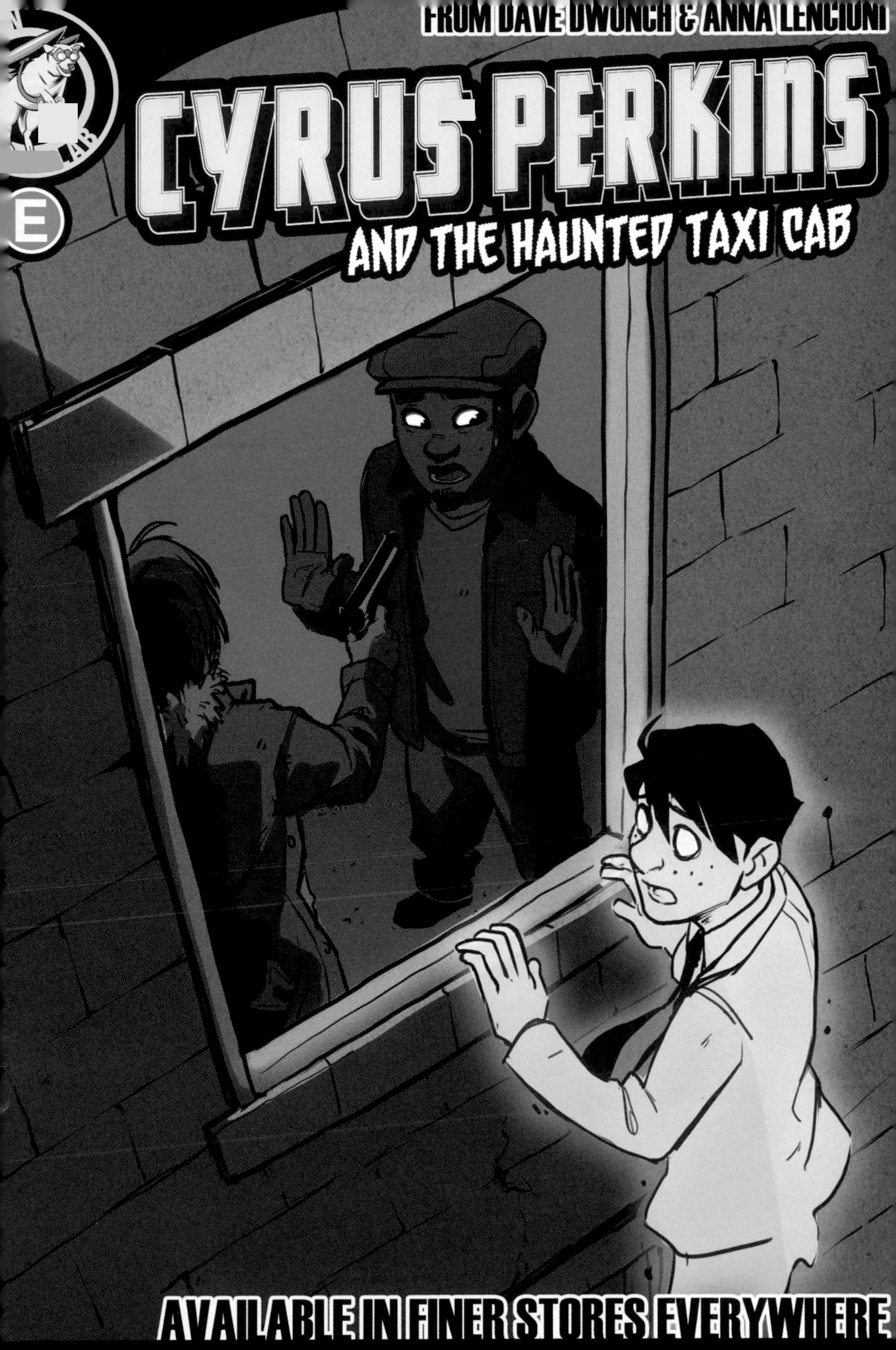
FROM DAVE DWONCH & ANNA LENCIONI
CYRUS PERKINS
AND THE HAUNTED TAXI CAB
E
AVAILABLE IN FINER STORES EVERYWHERE

In 1969 a timid teen sets out on a road trip. His goal? Find out the origins of his bizarre super human abilities. Always the follower, his trip is derailed when he befriends a group of extremist war protesters.

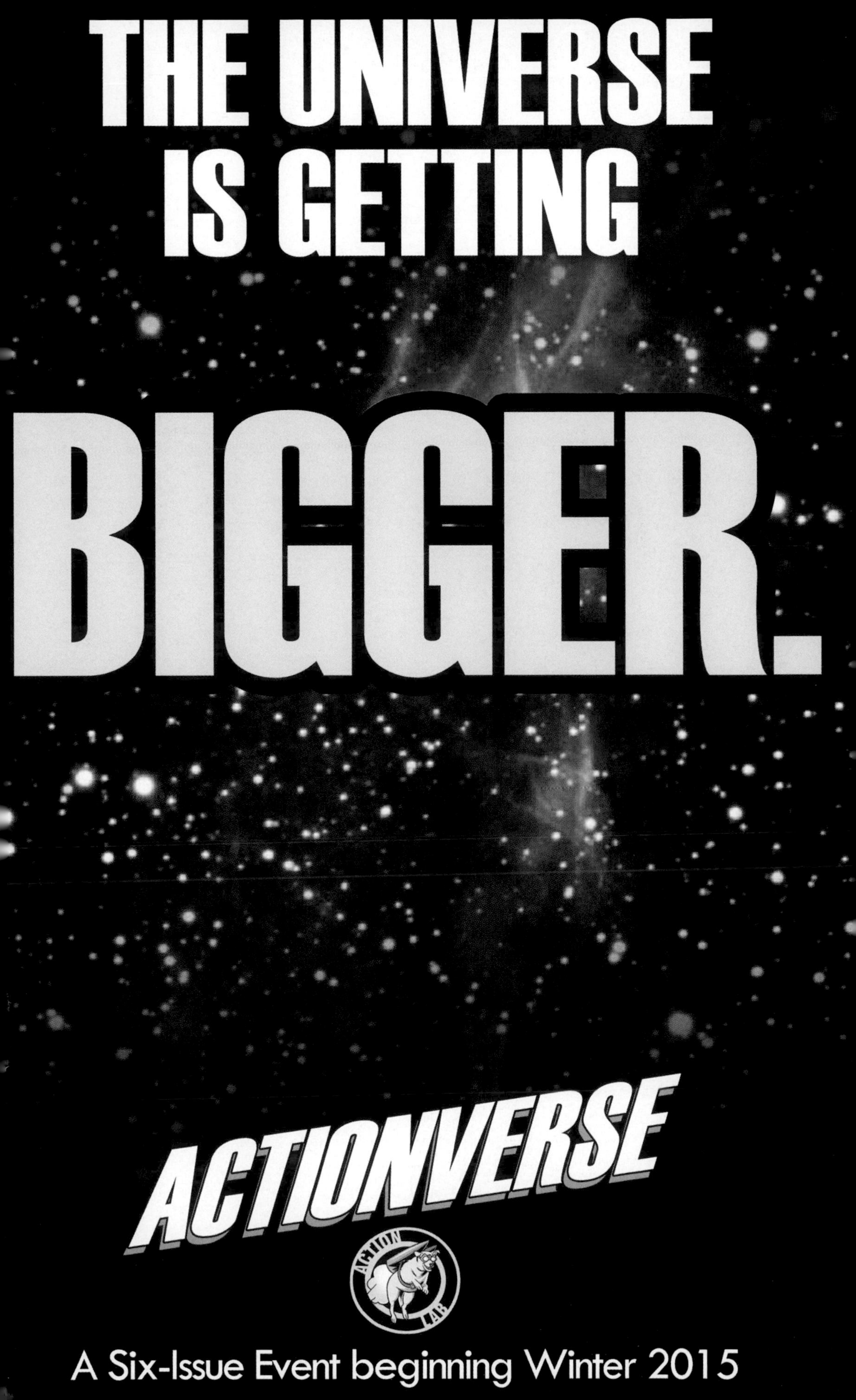
THE UNIVERSE
IS GETTING
BIGGER.
ACTIONVERSE
ACTION LAB
A Six-Issue Event beginning Winter 2015

ACTION LAB

READ MORE NOW

Nutmeg - Action Lab
www.actionlabcomics.com
00611
7 02382 69089 2

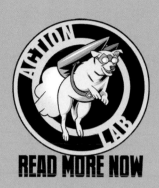

ACTIONLABCOMICS.COM